EXPUNGED

STEPHEN PIERCE

ISBN: 979-8-9997152-0-3 (paperback)
ISBN: 979-8-9997152-1-0 (e-book)

www.stephen-pierce.com

To my friends, family and readers who encouraged me along this convoluted writing journey. Your kind praise and desire to know more of the story of these characters kept me going despite the fervent attempts of my imaginary friends to resist sharing the details of their lives. I especially want to thank Dave, Jeff, Leigh and Cathy for making me think harder about what it takes to make characters come alive.

Other titles by Stephen Pierce:

Invisible Defense

 This bizarre murder case with a wacky legal defense of human spontaneous involuntary invisibility intertwines the paths of two truth peddlers—newspaper reporter Clark Solo and Pastor Dan—with a self-seeking couple plagued by intentionally forgotten characters from their shadowy pasts. As Clark covers the trial of a bizarre love affair turned murder, Justin Alexander risks everything for the woman of his dreams—and at the heart of his nightmare—to prove she is more than the sum of all her lies. Love and forgiveness, however, are not words Alicia Bauer truly understands. That is, until trapped by her own cons, she discovers their real meaning in the past—hers and Clark's. As the murder trial unfolds, Clark finds invisibility makes more than just attention-grabbing headlines—it hits home.

Prologue

"JOEY, I'M HOME."

The clank of a bulky teal-and-black suitcase punctuated her announcement. Gloria Maldoon pulled the rolling dresser through the garage entrance of her Midtown Terrace home and down the narrow hall toward her bedroom. She could see the amber glow from her son's room.

"The airport took forever at baggage claim," she explained as she neared his bedroom.

"I know you keep telling me to limit myself to just one carry-on bag, but I need too much stuff to keep these old bones looking good."

She knocked on his door. It opened slightly, emitting a slight groan.

"Aren't you going to tell your poor mother hello?"

She pushed the door open even farther.

"Joey?"

The room was empty.

She turned toward the hall bathroom. It, too, was fully lit and empty. She looked back into an impeccably clean room, which was noticeably out of character, and laughed.

"Somebody must have replaced my boy with someone else."

Gloria turned off the light and continued down the hall to unpack from her latest road trip. She stopped at the bathroom to flip that switch off as well. She hated being gone from Joey so much, and this trip was a couple of days longer than normal. Yet, the single mother knew she could rely on him. She regretted that this was the only way of life he had ever known. Gloria took comfort in believing her only child seemed to thrive on the independence her frequent three-day jaunts gave him. She was pretty sure he understood. He definitely heard her complain that businesses will not pay consultants to tell them what to do unless they visit the worksite. Despite the rant, the only way she knew how to do her job was to talk to the real people, not just the company figureheads. She needed to see the people who do the hands-on work to figure out the real *whys* behind how a company works, or more often than not, doesn't work.

She bounced up the stairs, something her formerly athletic body could still do despite flying a desk most days. One perk of her travels was access to a gym at odd hours of the night, which was essential to warding off the inevitable extra pounds that come from dining with clients. The sensible diet emanating from her kitchen at home whimpers in submission when clients take her to their cherished local eatery. The recommended dish was never waist friendly.

"Joey, are you up here?" Gloria asked as she topped the stairs.

Light poured through the wall of windows on the far side of the living room, illuminating the modest décor and framing an orange tree serving as the centerpiece of the terraced backyard garden. By San Francisco standards, she lived in a spacious two-bedroom home. She bought the house back in the 1980s, long before the unexpected happened. Their circle of friends could not understand how her so-called husband of twenty years could suddenly abandon her when her barren body surprised the career-minded couple with news of a baby boy.

"At least you are consistent?" she grumbled as she looked for her son in the well-lit kitchen.

Gloria glanced toward the front door, more accurately the floor in front of the door with the mail slot. She hoped to see nothing but found disappointment instead.

"Joseph Alan Maldoon!" she groused.

The mother of a teenage boy took a deep breath, walked over to the pile of scattered mail, and started gathering. As each piece became part of the growing bundle in her arms, she reminded herself this was not how she had trained him.

When she stood, Gloria spied more mail properly sorted into three piles on the counter. Now, this is how the efficiency expert had trained him. The smallest pile had bills and correspondence that he guessed his mom probably should read. Pile two contained the maybes. The largest pile was junk mail, but Joey did not always guess the piles correctly, so she required him to leave it for her to toss. Out in front of this collection was a single business envelope with "Mom" scrawled across the front.

"I guess this will tell me where my welcome home party is," she thought to herself.

She opened the envelope and pulled out a typed note. A few lines into the letter, it fell from her fingers.

"No!"

Chapter 1

LANA SOLO FELT her back pocket buzz as she stepped off the bus. It was Jeans Day at The Academy, a rare occasion when students did not have to wear the standard uniform. The school halls were awash in a kaleidoscope of colors instead of the typical sea of nondescript khaki pants and waves of purple, yellow, black, and green polo shirts. As a freshman, Lana typically wore a purple polo shirt.

The name on the phone shocked her. She hadn't heard from Joey Maldoon since he had disappeared from her life. He abandoned her after a couple of dates without even a courtesy lie about why he wanted to break up.

"I need to see you."

"DIKY," she texted back, as if she doubted this really was the same boy who shattered her world.

"It's me. Joey."

"You exist?"

"I deserved that."

"And more!"

"Let me explain F2F."

"IDK."

"Please!!!"

"G2G."

Lana lied, sort of. She had to get to class, but she had more than enough time to give him an answer. Time was not the problem. She did not know what to do. She did not know what to say. Her anger told her to delete the message from the boy who so callously dumped her and to forget he had ever existed. Something else told her she needed to be more gracious.

She also was not sure she wanted to deal with the inevitable drama that comes with high school romances. Since Joey's sudden departure a few months ago, Lana had experienced the drama overflow from someone else's relationships gone awry. Along with her dad and godmother, she had been held captive twice in one weekend as two men went to extremes for the love of the same woman. The first one held them hostage in a failed attempt to rescue his fiancée from another kidnapper. Barely two days later, the trio were once again staring down the barrel of a gun. This time, the fractured mind of the other kidnapper taunted them because her dad had written articles about her possible connection to several murders. The entire weekend felt like a soap opera gone wrong and made her reticent about doing anything that ruffled her quiet, boring normal. Then again, it was Joey.

"I'm begging you. Let me explain," he pleaded.

Lana placed her phone in silent mode and tucked it back into her hip pocket. Whatever Joey needed to tell her would have to wait.

Chapter 2

THE ABRUPTNESS OF HER TEXTS perplexed him. It was not what he had expected. It was not what he had hoped would happen. He was not sure why he thought he could just waltz back into town as if nothing had ever happened. He needed to recalibrate.

Joey typed, "I came back because of you" while he waited for her to respond to his last text. Nothing. He glanced at the time at the top of the phone and knew the first-period bell had already rung. She would not answer him until after lunch, if at all. He backspaced until his latest plea disappeared.

"That was probably too much, anyway. I'll just have to wait and see what happens next," he thought.

The conflicted teen looked around the BART station to get his bearings. He heaved onto his shoulder the scruffy blue-and-black duffel bag he had been sitting on. Joey followed the crowd toward the exit and emerged onto the street. The smell of dark roasted coffee greeted him. His feet followed his nose to a caramel-colored food truck snuggled against the curb. A little jolt of caffeine should help reset his mind.

Reconnecting with Lana was supposed to be his first contact. A simple prelude to the more arduous task of standing before a mother who thought her only child had suddenly abandoned her and run away. He was told that he had to prepare himself for an intense emotional reaction when she discovered her worst fears had not come true.

Random thoughts swirled through his head as Joey ambled up 24th Street toward his mother's house. He kept trying to figure out what to do next; it was making him dizzy. Despite dozens of mental dry runs, he had yet to figure out how to explain the last few months. Then an odd thought occurred to him, and it seemed just too simple of a solution. Should he even try? Would it be better to avoid that conversation? Maybe he should just say he needed to focus on reigniting the former life of Joey Maldoon.

The teen stopped at a luggage storage facility and offloaded his heavy duffel bag. Now, he sported only a more manageable red-and-gold backpack and an empty coffee cup. The caffeine concoction had failed to supply him with the answers he wanted, so he tossed it and continued his trek.

The house—his home—was now in sight. If he were lucky, his mother would be away on one of her frequent business trips, and he could delay the emotional encounter a few more days.

Chapter 3

CLARK SOLO STUDIED the spreadsheet. He did not yet understand the significance of what he was looking at, but his gut instinct told him it must mean something. Clearly, it meant something to the person who spent countless hours compiling the particulars of eighteen murders over nearly as many years.

"The connection is in the defense claims," was all the anonymous emailer wrote about this massive collection of data.

At first, the sparse insight into interpreting the data puzzled him. Past so-called news tips spent a great deal of time focused on convincing him how all their random information fit together. Maybe it was the absence of this distraction that piqued his interest. This person knew to share just enough to nudge him in the direction they wanted. Normally, Clark would have dismissed the email after a cursory read, attributing it to the hordes of conspiracy theorists who feel compelled to share their latest cogitations. Unsuspecting journalists who allow themselves to get sucked into this vortex of confusion and delusion waste countless hours and, ultimately, produce nothing. Editors don't like that. They have newspapers and airtime to fill. Reporters, who become convinced despite reality, pick up the sleuthing work on their off time. Their obsession, even if it pans out, often pushes away the rest of their real world in its pursuit. Clark did not want that. He was just getting back to having a life he could enjoy.

Yet, he felt compelled to study this list of victims and murderers. He recognized a few of the names, including his first major crime story: the murder of Sally Jean McPherson by Tory Avlah. The accused in that case claimed the victim's massive array of injuries resulted from his failed attempt to resuscitate her after she fell and hit her head on a coffee table. The jury may have bought the premise of his story: Avlah feared calling the police because of a prior run-in with the law. They might have accepted his reason for dumping her body in a local creek instead of calling the authorities. The twelve jurors could not accept, however, his confession that he considered dismembering her body and stuffing it in a trunk in the attic.

Clark knew the defense needed repentant testimony from Avlah to explain away the more devastating injuries, but his claims were too bizarre for the jury to make that leap. No jury could have made that leap, yet the defense pursued it anyway. Something about that case always bothered him. Sometimes he would convince himself that it was his inexperience. Other times, he just knew that neither the prosecution nor the defense was telling the whole story. He tried vainly back then to figure out what they were hiding.

The anonymous tipster seemed to have the defense connection correct. The defendant in the current story making headlines—Mikhail Kuzmin—also laid claim to an equally preposterous story of failed heroism. This barista slash struggling actor met up with Teri Marcos at a local meat market bar, one of those sufficiently raunchy places young urbanites go with reasonable expectations of fulfilling their lustful desires. In the early morning hours back at his apartment, police responded to several complaints from neighbors about loud noises and screams. When Kuzmin opened the door, he was covered in blood. The police described him as unusually distraught and mumbling. It took the police several seconds to understand his repeated message of, "I was trying to save her. I was trying to save her."

On the living room floor beside a black grand piano, the police found an unconscious and badly beaten Marcos. She died from her injuries a couple of hours later at the hospital.

Clark noticed in police photos that a toppled bust of the Greek god Dionysos lay on the floor beside Marcos. Clark had to stifle a laugh.

"Gee, I wonder why the police report didn't mention that the statue was of a character from Greek mythology known for bringing madness to his friends and enemies," he thought.

As he continued to examine the photos, some items seemed strange given the obvious signs Marcos had put up a struggle. Undisturbed on the piano were a candelabra filled with white candles that dripped red wax and a vase of flowers with a prominent message card in it. The card was smoky red with wavy gold lines.

Clark noted another common link between these two bizarre cases: defense attorney Greg Vernier. He checked a few more of the murder cases, and the flamboyant defense attorney's name popped up a few more times.

"Hmmm," Clark thought. He recalled joking about the defense in those other cases but laughed it off as Vernier just being Vernier. Clark never imagined there could actually be a connection between those cases.

Chapter 4

ORANGE WAS NOT HER COLOR. Alicia Bauer could tolerate a splash of the vibrant fruit here and there, but never an entire ensemble. The faded orange sneakers of her jailhouse attire, she secretly confessed, were her style. She could see herself wearing them with a pair of olive skinny jeans and a drapey navy blue blouse. The perfect handbag would be the soft brown leather clutch she picked up with Justin during one of their Carmel excursions.

Alicia knew those nostalgic days were over, at least the way they once were with her impetuous fiancé. After all, she was in jail. Justin kept reassuring her about his marriage proposal, but she was not so sure. Something nagging at her conscience told her that a white, or more like off-white, wedding dress was not in her immediate future. No, for now, she would have to settle for wearing orange T-shirts and baggy orange sweats, both of which hung on her like a painter's drop cloth.

Thanks to the high-priced lawyer Justin insisted upon, her time in jail may end soon. He had a plea deal on the table that traded some of the financial freedom she had built up for physical freedom. The lawyer made it sound so easy.

"All you have to do is turn over your unsubstantiated art commissions," he told her.

"All? Or just what they know about?"

Her rebuttal question, apparently, suggested she had committed more crimes. The fact that she had several offshore bank accounts alluded to that as well. The lawyer responded with a deadpan look over his reading glasses that seemed to stare into Alicia's soul. Then, like lawyers do, he dropped the proverbial other shoe.

"You will also have to provide details on who bought the art and antiquities you redirected without documented permission."

Alicia could tell the lawyer thought he was so clever. His legalese sounded so much better than stolen. He explained that the prosecution lacked any witnesses who could prove the owners had not given her oral consent to sell the art.

"Conveniently, your fully crazed half-brother created that minor obstacle for the district attorney," the lawyer had smugly pointed out.

Alicia knew what he meant. Rudy Johnson had killed them. The revelation to the world that her onetime high school boyfriend had murdered four men with whom she had been involved flooded the headlines. Some spoke of the disgraced elite of the local art scene with pity; others used the fact that Johnson was her half-brother to pile on their indignation. Ironically, those men might still be alive if the father of that small-town boy hadn't used a confession of an affair with her mom to scare Annie Zimmerman away from Rudy. The same affair that pushed away the man she had always thought was her father.

That was but one of many twists of fate that unraveled her life when she got involved with Justin. The uniquely contrived life she manufactured for the target of her criminal intentions dissolved. The person she had become, with and because of him, was an actual person with honest feelings, even feelings as scary as love. Her hates changed as well. The man she had spent a lifetime hating for being a deadbeat father who abandoned her as a child ultimately saved Justin from a murderous fate. Admittedly, it was not Frankie Zimmerman's purpose at the time, but she was still grateful. Maybe not enough to keep his name, though. Not that she wanted her biological father's name, either. She mentioned to her fancy lawyer that she was thinking about officially changing her name to Alicia Bauer.

"Annie Zimmerman no longer exists," she told him.

"Maybe not, but let's see how things play out before you go making plans based on your past relationship with Mr. Alexander," he cautioned.

Once again, she knew what his polite words meant. There was no guarantee of Justin Alexander in her life. His continued presence was already a mystery to her, and, apparently, to her lawyer as well. Justin could have justifiably walked away from the carefully constructed persona she created for him. He had no way of knowing if the person he fell in love with even existed or could again. Sometimes, she was not sure either. She—the consummate con artist, as one newspaper reported—spent so much time pretending to be a certain image for him she was not sure what part of this Alicia Bauer character she contrived to manipulate him and what part was her true identity.

Forced captivity, however, once again gave her plenty of time to contemplate the absurdities of her life. Some things she knew for sure, or at least she hoped for some sense of confidence in her knowing. Her days as a con artist were over. No more peddling lies and her physical attributes to manipulate self-absorbed men to part with a chunk of their fortunes. She longed for genuine relationships. Not just her romance with Justin, but other friendships her improvised characters enjoyed. As the weeks passed by, she discovered Alicia Bauer was probably more like the real thing, at least the person she wanted to be, than any other identity she had used.

"Like that means anything," she thought. "Alicia Bauer is the most honest lie I've ever told."

Chapter 5

"CLASS, I UNDERSTAND from Mrs. Gates that some of you just finished studying the philosophers Thomas Hobbes and Jean-Jacques Rousseau. That's good news. You will have a leg up in this unit. We will examine how philosophical trends influenced literature. For the rest of you, you will want to pay attention to the supplemental reading list. It will make our discussions more interesting, and stuff from there will find its way into my exams."

Emily Geoffrey smiled at her fourth-period literature class as they groaned. She ignored the predictable response and pressed on.

"Who can tell me the difference between these two notable thinkers—Hobbes and Rousseau?"

Blank stares responded to her question. She often wished students were more like dogs and cocked their heads when they did not understand something. Instead, she had to *decode* whether their non-response was ignorance or peer intimidation. With this group of students, she felt confident it was the latter.

"Mrs. Gates said you all did well on her exams, so I know one of you must have an answer."

A timid hand floated up from the back of the class. Emily nodded for her to proceed.

"Hobbes said man is inherently bad and needs society and rules to reign in his behavior, while Rousseau said man is basically good and becomes corrupted by his circumstances and environment."

"That's a fair enough synopsis to get us started. I knew you guys could remember it. Do you have any idea how this notion has played out in literature?"

This time, the blank stares were more like puppies.

"I guess that means I need to do some teaching now, huh?"

Emily laughed at her own humor. A couple of students smiled politely, but the stoic blank stares remained.

"It will all become clear as mud over the next few weeks as we compare and contrast several literature examples. On one side, we are going to read excerpts from William Golding's *Lord of the Flies*. I think most of you will enjoy this book, which was written shortly after World War II. Golding explores the darker side of humanity and stresses the importance of reason when combating man's capacity for evil. At the other end of the perspective, we will explore William Blake's *Songs of Innocence and Experience*. In this collection of poems from the late 1700s, Blake expresses the notion that reason itself, stemming from the experiences of life, is what corrupts us from innocence."

"Old poems again?" a mumbled grumble erupted from the center of the classroom, which clearly came out louder than the less-than-literary teen intended.

"Yes, Tommy, torturous poems again. And yes, you will still have to summarize your papers with a haiku."

A chorus of groans responded.

"So, let's turn to page 144."

* * *

Lana struggled to listen to Ms. Geoffrey. Her mind kept slipping over to the text from Joey, arguing whether he was an innate bad person for his abrupt disappearance or were there some external factors in play. The texts seemed sincere, to the degree such context can be read into a series of short blurbs. Finally, the bell rang.

"Remember, your assignment is to write three hundred words on how today's reading reflects some aspect of the human condition. I look forward to hearing your haikus tomorrow," Emily belted out as the room quickly emptied for lunch. Lana lingered in her seat.

"Auntie Em?" Lana's use of the family nickname for her godmother meant her question was not about the pending assignment.

"Yes, sweetie," she said from her perch on the front of her desk.

"Remember me telling you about a boy named Joey?"

"Yeah, I think so."

Lana stood there silently. Emily waited for her to muster the courage to speak about the boy who had been at the center of the drama that reignited her relationship with Lana and her father. She could see words bubbling up to her mouth, but they did not have the courage to leave her lips.

"Has something happened?" Emily asked, trying not to insert too much concern into her tone.

"Yeah."

"Do you want to tell me about it?"

"I need to talk to somebody about it."

"Well, thank you for thinking you can come to me."

Emily scooted herself off her big desk, walked over to Lana, and sat sideways in the student desk in front of her.

"Tell me what's up?" she said in full Auntie Em mode.

Lana handed her phone to Emily with her own plea.

"What do I do?"

After a few moments of staring at the screen, Emily thumbed out a few characters, pushed send, and handed the phone back to her goddaughter.

"This," she said.

Chapter 6

THE SUN POURED through the tall Victorian windows, casting a patch of sunshine beside her on the couch. Gloria ran her hand over the mustardy brown leather; its warmth felt cozy. She looked back at her friend and smiled.

"It was like this, you know, that day."

Her words stumbled across her lips as she held back the heartbreak behind them.

"I remember," Gayle Maddox said, nodding her head slowly in agreement.

Today was the three-month anniversary of Joey's disappearance. She wanted to comfort Gloria, but knew words were of little use to a grieving mother. So, she did what she knew best: warmed her friend's cup of coffee and nudged a plate of scones that she had picked up from the bakery around the corner.

"No, thanks. Two's my limit. I shouldn't haven't eaten the third one."
A muffled laugh accompanied Gloria's confession.

"Like it would make a difference," Gayle playfully chided. "You are just as skinny as the day I met you. I am too, but that's a totally different story."

This time, hearty laughter filled the room. Unlike the low rumble of Gloria's laugh, Gayle cackled. Her generous rolls quaked in sync with the intensity of her robust laugh, the spectacle of which spiraled her laughter even more out of control. She did not know whether to grab her aching sides or wipe the tears from her face. Gloria handed her a napkin.

"Thank you," Gloria told her friend. "I needed a good laugh today."

"I wish I could do more."

Gloria opened her purse, pulled out a white envelope, and set it on the table. After a few seconds, she pushed it toward her friend.

"Read it. Read it aloud, please."

"Are you sure? Do you really want to go through that again?"

"Let's be real. I'm going to go through it, regardless of whether I want to or not."

Gayle wanted to cry. What else could she do? She could not utter the words, "We think of Joey as our son, too, and my heart is as broken as yours." Maybe not exactly the same, but she still mourned the loss of Joey. Gloria never seemed to understand how much she and Bobby fulfilled their desires to be parents through Joey. A missing father figure made it easy for Bobby to step into that role. Frequent business trips made Gayle practically Joey's other mom.

Gayle nodded in concession and picked up the envelope with "Mom" scrawled across the front. She pulled out a crinkled piece of paper. Tears had smeared some of the ink. Gayle took a deep sigh and began reading. "Dear Mom," her somber voice replacing the gaiety of moments earlier.

> *By the time you read this letter, I will be long gone. I know you, Mom, and the first thing you are going to do is blame yourself somehow. Then, you will spend countless hours trying to figure out what you could have done*

differently. Please don't. Under the circumstances, I couldn't have asked for a better mother. You did everything you could for me; maybe even more than you should have. I wish I could explain why I can't stay. It would only make things worse. There are just some problems that are not fixable, at least not without hurting someone more by your presence. I know my leaving might hurt you (it hurts me, too), but not as much as the hurt that would happen if I let what occurred in the past come to light. I promise I will come back someday, when none of this will put you at risk. Until then, know that I love you more than you can ever know.

Joey

Gayle looked up from the letter, and an unexpectedly stern face glared back at her. She expected tears, a welling up of emotion, but not a cold and analytical stare.

"I've read this note at least a thousand times, and I still don't understand it. There is nothing in his past. He has always been a good boy. I don't know who wrote this, but it doesn't sound like my Joey," Gloria said.

"I get it, but the police didn't seem to think much of it."

She knew the words weren't comforting; however, allowing her friend to get all worked up over this note again would not help much, either.

"They didn't do much thinking at all," Gloria admonished.

Chapter 7

CLARK ADMIRED THE DÉCOR of the small conference room in Greg Vernier's downtown law office. His eyes kept being drawn to a sleek wooden mask, sitting atop a glass column that made it appear that the mask floated in mid-air. The sharp angular features of the black-and-cream caricature, as well as the symbol on its forehead, conveyed a much larger presence than Clark could describe. He thought the overall office design—a blend of traditional African art with a crisp modern edge—said a lot about the career journey of this lawyer. His maiden office in private practice, back in the foothills of the Sierra Nevada where they first met, reflected more poverty than posh.

"You like that one?" Vernier asked as he entered the room fifteen minutes after Clark.

"I do. It's both disconcerting and captivating," Clark said, with his eyes still on the mask.

"I picked it up on one of my excursions through West Africa."

"What does that symbol mean?"

"Those diagonal slashes and curved lines on the forehead are Adinkra symbols for Gye Nyame, which speaks to the supremacy of God."

"Well, that explains a lot," Clark said with a dismissive snort, as he turned to greet the defense attorney. The rolled-up sleeves and no-jacket look reminded Clark of the early days of Vernier's practice, a sharp contrast to the current highly tailored presentation for the courtroom.

"Yes, it does," Vernier said, ignoring Clark's sound effects. "Now that we have that easy mystery solved, please have a seat and fill me in on this other mystery you have encountered."

"It certainly has me baffled. As I mentioned to you earlier on the phone, I received an email with some detailed documentation and a bold claim linking all eighteen murders. Normally, I would have dismissed it as conspiracy nonsense, but my gut tells me there is something here. I recognized a few of the names as cases you've represented, including the Kuzmin case and the first case I covered of yours back in the day."

Clark handed Vernier a copy of the email and the detailed spreadsheet documenting all the cases.

"Tory Avlah?"

"That's the one."

"Are you saying that there's a connection between a case from fifteen years ago and the case I'm currently working on?"

"More like seventeen years ago, and, yes, this mystery person says the connection is in the defense claims. I checked it out, and one thread stands out. All the defendants claim they were trying to save the victim at the time of the murder."

"I'm assuming they were all convicted."

"Yeah. Why?"

"I recognized the names of my other clients on that list. The truth didn't work for them."

"Truth?"

"Yes, truth. I recall that being something of importance to you. I know you kept looking into that murder case after Tory's conviction."

Clark chuckled to himself. Apparently, his efforts back then to be a stealthy investigative reporter were not as good as he thought. Hopefully, he had improved.

"Something just didn't seem right. Not sure what exactly. Maybe it was the softball second-degree charges. Maybe it was the insane defense. Nothing about the case seemed to gel like other trials. I kind of got the impression that you and the district attorney were holding back something. I couldn't find enough information to substantiate my gut feeling. I finally dropped the matter when I came to San Francisco."

"Your instincts were right."

The defense attorney paused and eyed the reporter he had worked with for a good part of the last two decades. Clark could read his facial expression.

"You are wondering if you can trust me, right?" Clark asked.

"The thought occurred to me."

"Even more so, you are concerned about how this story will affect your current case."

"That, too, is a consideration."

"My record speaks for itself, so I will not try to justify why you can trust me. If this story pans out, it is a boon for your client. If it doesn't, nobody will be the wiser."

"Seems like you have this all figured out."

"Enough, anyway. So why do you say my instincts were correct?"

"When they found Tory, he was a babbling mess. Much like Mikhail. Tory kept asking for somebody, but nobody could make out a name. By the time he was coherent, Tory was rather fuzzy on the details and claimed he had no idea what man he had been talking about."

"Mikhail talked about a mystery man?"

"Yes, but not in a way for us to figure out a name. After a couple of days, both of them were back to a so-called normal. Remorse over what had occurred consumed them, but they adamantly insisted they were only trying to save their victims."

"Same storyline for your other clients?" Clark hoped just a little for a different answer than he knew he was going to hear.

"Basically."

"Any theories?"

Vernier shook his head.

"Not really. If there is somebody behind these murders, he / she / they have been smart enough to stay under the police radar. Look at the location and frequency. They seem spread just far enough apart to keep the dots unconnected."

"Smart, as in police-trained? You think the mastermind behind these murders might be a cop?" The same thought had occurred to Clark.

"It is not for me to think; it's your story. If it were me, I would explore the possibility. Too many jurisdictions for a local coverup, though. Federal maybe?"

"Anything else stand out? Anything in the cases you didn't handle?"

"Nothing you probably hadn't noticed already. Most of the accused are unattached men with names that sound Arabic or eastern European."

"Yeah, I caught that. Don't suppose you have contact info on the handful of fellas you represented."

"If we do, I'll be glad to share," Vernier said as he tapped the intercom button. "Nora, could you come in here, please?"

"Yes, Mr. Vernier."

"Well, you haven't unraveled any great mysteries here, but at least we seem to be seeing the same things. That's something, I guess."

Nora opened the door and stood quietly, waiting for instructions.

"Nora, please give Mr. Solo the information to contact some of our former clients."

"Will do."

"Clark, please keep me informed."

"I will, as is appropriate."

Clark stepped toward the door to leave the conference room and stopped. He turned back to Vernier.

"It just occurred to me I should ask if I can trust you."

"Why?"

"You clearly had suspicions already that your cases on this list had connections, yet you never mentioned this at trial."

23

"Touché, my friend. I shouldn't have to remind you that knowing there are similarities among some cases does not mean I knew there was a connection, certainly not one that a judge would let me use in court. Nor did I share when I discovered these details about the cases."

Clark gestured an expression of concession to the lawyer. He knew Vernier had just side-stepped the question, but Clark decided to give him a pass for now. He offered a compliment instead.

"Nice digs. Quite an upgrade from that first place. I'm assuming this office isn't still on wheels."

"Not wheels, rollers. Got to keep everyone safe in case of an earthquake."

Chapter 8

AFTER NEARLY AN HOUR of walking, Joey's legs ached from the infamous San Francisco incline. His time away had been on flatter ground, and long hikes weren't necessary at the compound. The temperature, a few degrees higher than normal, added to his discomfort. Tired and thirsty, he was glad to spot his mother's gray and charcoal house, even if he dreaded the inevitable encounter inside.

Joey approached the front door with the key in his hand but changed his mind. Gloria Maldoon was a country girl at heart, who pulled out her pistol before asking questions of unexpected noises in her house. Joey pressed the doorbell, discovering his mom had yet to get it fixed. He knocked. Nobody answered. He knocked again, this time not so gently. Still no answer. He inserted the key and gradually opened the heavy steel-and-glass door.

"Mom?" His tentative voice conveyed hope that he was alone.

No answer.

He went up the stairs to the main living area of the two-story home and meandered around the room as if it was his first time in the house. Everything seemed to be in the right place, exactly where he had committed it to memory. Joey ran his fingers across the photos adorning the fireplace mantel. He stopped at a small photo of an older woman who seemed out of character for the nostalgic setting. She was making an apple pie. Something about the woman in the picture made him think Sally Jean McPherson would have been more at home in a biker bar. Joey had never met Nana, and Gloria rarely spoke about her mother.

On the shelves flanking the gray leather couch, he picked up his only sports trophy—a soccer participation trophy. A handful of science fair ribbons streaming from the shiny plastic boy kicking a ball served as a reminder Joey was not the athlete in the house. He stopped at the kitchen window overlooking the patio and admired the hillside garden. He stuck his head in the refrigerator and frowned. Nothing looked appealing.

Joey finally made his way downstairs to the bedrooms. He glanced at the master and could see it was empty. He went into the other bedroom, tossed the backpack on the desk, kicked off his shoes, and plopped on the bed. The bright room and comfortable bed differed vastly from the humble surroundings he had endured recently. The smell was better, too. As he lay there, his mind drifted to that place and how glad he was to be out of there.

Like so many runaways he met there, the teen had become jaded by the reality of a world much harsher than he expected. From the protective bubble his mom created, leaving seemed like a simple solution to his big problem. Then, he envisioned running away like a long sleepover at a friend's house. Now, he knows it is a complete break from a familiar world and a plunge into a place where unfathomable choices become rationalized options. If he had thought things through a bit more, he probably would not have bolted so quickly. He certainly hadn't thought enough about money. Sure, he had gathered all his meager savings, but it did not last long on the streets. He had no way to replace that money—that is until he landed at Charlie's mansion.

Technically, it was not a mansion, but that's what everybody called it. The abandoned building had seen better days. More than half a century ago, it was part of a massive shipbuilding complex on the northern tip of the San Francisco Bay. In the aftermath of military base closures, it was just another abandoned building with a leaky roof. The only heat came from bits of daylight that poked their way through paint-covered windows. Still, it was not all bad. Charlie ensured that at least your bed, an old metal cot with an even older thin mattress, was dry. He laughed at that phrase as if it were some sort of holy barometer of legitimacy. He might as well of said, "At least he made the trains run on time."

Charlie made other things work around that place. The gangs left them alone, for the most part, and no one went hungry for long. He made sure everyone who stayed there felt like family, his family. These luxuries, however, came at a price that Charlie knew how to extract. Even with him more than an hour away by ferry, Joey could feel Charlie's hold over him. He could not think about that now.

Joey pushed himself off the bed and fumbled through his backpack. He pulled out a well-worn blue spiral notebook and browsed through the familiar journal entries.

The strangest thing happened today at the library. I was busy texting Lana about how great I thought our second date had been when this guy sat at my table. He just stared at me for a while, saying nothing. I was too shocked at first to respond, probably because the red tattoo dripping from his right ear distracted me. When I returned to my text, he blurted out in a loud whisper that I was not who I thought I was.

A buzz interrupted his reading. It was Lana.

"Ok YAC @ 4:30 Don't be late!"

"Interesting," he thought. "The Youth Activities Center at her church."

He replied with a thumbs-up.

Chapter 9

"ZIMMERMAN, you have a visitor," the guard bellowed at Alicia's round cement table on the edge of Cell Block Seven-Alpha's dayroom.

Alicia's heart skipped a beat. She looked forward to these temporary glimpses into the outside world, especially when they involved Justin. The visits with him started out awkwardly at first. All the questions and, worse yet, the answers. The long stretches of silence. The inability to touch. It certainly was not the way to rekindle a relationship harmed by life's quirky little smacks of humility.

"Is it Justin?" Teenage excitement tinged her voice, earning her heckling coos from the other inmates at the table.

The guard's stern demeanor faded to let the hint of a smile emerge beneath her twinkling green eyes. She stepped back so Alicia could stand and position herself for the parade to the videoconference room. In-person visits were reserved for legal counsel only.

"Officer Andrade?" Alicia asked as the cell block door closed behind them. The echoing clank of the electronic lock made the silence that followed seem even more eerie. They waited for the next door to open.

"Yes, Alicia."

"Will I ever get used to that sound?"

"I hope not. That means you've been here too long."

The door opened, but she would not move until Andrade gave her the go-ahead. Alicia understood the purpose of this well-choreographed procedure, but it still felt demeaning. A few guards took advantage of this time to entertain themselves by flaunting their authority over the inmates. One even went so far as to make clicking sounds. It made her bristle. She wanted to show him what this filly looks like when she goes all bronco on his inflated ego. She also wanted to get out of this place as soon as possible. She kept telling herself that they weren't worth it.

"Let's go see Justin," Andrade commanded.

Alicia smiled. Andrade was not one of those renegade guards.

"Yes, ma'am."

She stepped forward into the carpeted corridor, turned left and walked past six solid doors on the right, and stopped.

"Go ahead."

Alicia took one step forward and turned toward the caged room. If she let her imagination run wild, it looked like a bank of French doors minus the glass and class. Inside was a wall of small partitions with un-comfortable-looking chairs parked in front of utilitarian boxes on the wall that housed small screens.

"I've got one to trade," Andrade told the officer inside the cage. He nodded in acknowledgment and looked beyond Alicia toward the guard behind a glass wall. He raised his right hand and made a circular motion with his index finger. The wall of bars rolled away until a door-size opening appeared.

"You are in four," he barked.

Alicia stepped forward, turned left, and strolled to her seat. She sat down and waited. After a few minutes, the image of Justin appeared on the screen. She picked up the telephone receiver.

Chapter 10

GLORIA FELT SILLY and unproductive. She spent the morning with a long-time friend bemoaning the fact that her son had disappeared. Technically, the note left behind meant he had run away. She was not so sure. It did not matter. All her tears and lamentations changed nothing. He was still gone, and she was still coming home to an empty house. The irony of her behavior did not escape her notice. The process improvement specialist had made a career out of telling other people how to be more productive, which included shedding activities that do not produce desirable results. Today had undesirable results, but today she was just a mom.

She pressed the button on the visor to lift the garage door. The heavy plywood door lumbered its way up to its almost horizontal position, wobbling more precariously on the left side than on the right. Once again, Gloria told herself she needed to call somebody to get that fixed.

She had told herself this same fleeting instruction dozens of times over the last year. Today, she was going to get something productive accomplished.

She pulled out her smartphone while still sitting behind the wheel of her marina blue sports car, a little self-indulgence to compensate herself for the frequent road trips, and summoned its assistance.

"How can I help you?" the automated voice responded.

"Telephone number of a garage door repair company."

"One option I see is a garage door repair company on Sacramento Street. Is that the one you want?"

"Yes."

Gloria sat in her car while her phone servant placed the call.

* * *

Joey heard the rickety sound of a garage door lifting and panicked. Despite rehearsing the scene that was about to happen at least six times this morning alone, he felt unprepared. He felt scared. He needed to postpone seeing his mother for a little while longer.

"You need to stick to the plan," his inner voice screamed.

This command set the teen into action. He jumped out of bed and brushed the wrinkles out of the bedspread. His eyes looked around to see what else he had disturbed. In one quick motion, he grabbed his shoes and backpack and slipped up the stairs. He stood in front of the door, listening as he slipped on his shoes.

"What is taking her so long?" he thought, resisting the urge to peek out the window. He could feel perspiration soaking his body. He wiped his hands on his jeans and waited.

Finally, he heard the familiar sound of the downstairs door opening from the garage. That was his cue. Joey opened the front door and stepped out onto the stoop. He waited to hear the garage door slap back into its down position before he made his way to the sidewalk and toward the center of town.

A couple of houses down, he stopped and turned back toward the gray house. He resisted the urge to run back home. He desperately wanted to hug his mom, tell her he was back, and start the journey back to normalcy. The plan said he needed to meet with Lana first, and Charlie would be very upset if he did not follow the plan.

"See you later, Mom," he whispered.

* * *

"Thank you. I look forward to seeing somebody next Tuesday," Gloria told the garage door repair company as she entered the house.

As was her routine, mostly because her coats hung in her bedroom closet, she proceeded down the hallway toward her room. A light gleamed from her son's room.

"Who's there?" she called out as she instinctively reached into her purse. She seamlessly put her cell phone in her back pocket, her purse on the floor and her pistol in the cradle of her right hand. A few more steps forward and Gloria tapped on the door with her foot. It slowly opened to reveal an empty room. Nothing looked out of place, but somehow the room felt different.

"Is anyone here?" she called as she stepped back out into the hallway.

In her mind, music reminiscent of every scary movie she had ever seen played so loud she was sure the intruder could hear it. She took small steps forward as her eyes darted back and forth in search of anything out of place. She saw light at the top of the stairs. The music became even more intense with each step she took. At the top of the stairs, she turned and saw a silhouette beyond the sheers in the front window.

As she stepped toward the silhouette, she felt a tapping. She screamed, instantly regretting not just swinging around. Then, she felt the tapping again. It was a special heartbeat shake on her cell phone that told her it was her dear friend.

"Gayle, you scared the peewaddle out of me!" Gloria hollered.

"How?"

"You just did," Gloria snapped. Her focus was beyond the sheers. The silhouette had moved on.

"Sorry. I thought I'd call just to make sure you got home okay. I didn't mean to scare you."

"I know, sweetie." Gloria returned to her normal, more congenial self. "Thank you for checking up on me and being a sympathetic ear this morning. I just got spooked when I came home and saw a light on in Joey's room."

"Did you call the police?"

"No."

"Don't tell me you went into the house by yourself."

"Okay, I won't tell you."

"That's not funny."

"Doesn't matter. Nobody was there. I must have left the light on."

"It was still stupid of you to go in alone."

"I know. I know," Gloria acquiesced to her friend's concerns. "I guess something in me was just hoping it would be Joey. I guess I should stop doing that."

She opted not to mention that she was certain she could smell Joey's cologne. She did not need Gayle to think she was completely losing it.

"You can't give up hope."

"Yes, you can."

Chapter 11

CLARK KNEW there was something tangible to this story that had mysteriously landed in his email two days ago. Vernier just confirmed his gut. It was not really the words he said, but the rather cagey way in which he responded. It was more than a lawyer being selective with his words. Vernier was intentionally vague and wanted Clark to know it. Those actions spoke volumes to Clark, and he knew it was his job to figure out what they were saying. On a more basic level for Clark, this little meeting confirmed that he should trust his reporter's instincts. Vernier said he should have trusted them back then with Tory Avlah, and hinted, with so much more at stake, he should trust them now. Those instincts were telling him that this defense attorney was holding back something, if not outright lying.

"Knowing and proving are two completely different things. If you can't prove it, then it doesn't really matter what you know," Bill Buckley pointed out in the ungracious way that seems to befit most old-school newspaper editors. Clark always thought that his tussle of white hair and swollen red nose made him look like an inebriated Santa Claus. He hid his opinion on a story about as well as he hid the small flask of whisky that he had stashed in his top left-hand drawer.

"I know. I know. That's why I am asking if you are okay with me putting the time into this conspiracy theory," Clark said.

"Well, I can't say that a lawyer lying is enough probable cause to justify the time it would take to develop this into a legitimate story. We don't have the staff for you to go dark."

"Yeah, I get it. But this is different. Why would a defense lawyer, especially this one, lie when given an opportunity to use the press to manufacture an escape clause for his client? That just doesn't make sense. There's classic Vernier shadow-of-a-doubt theatrics written all over this story. Yet, he's holding back. Why?"

"That is curious. What are you hoping to find?"

"To be honest, that this is all just a bizarre set of coincidences. Otherwise, this all points to a really smart psychopath. Worse yet, a psychopath working with some type of law enforcement agency that can cover up a ton of murders."

"At least a psychopath makes for an interesting story," Bill joked without giving up his serious tone. "You realize we are dealing with multiple local police jurisdictions that are not known for playing well with each other. If this is legit, you are most likely looking at something federal."

"That's what Vernier was thinking, too."

"Any ideas about what you need to do next to unravel this?"

"I'll start with the basic groundwork. Track down Vernier's clients. Check in with the other defense attorneys to see if there are similar backstories. I know three of them; the other five I'll have to track down. Then police reports and more interviews with the rest of the convicted defendants, assuming they are even findable."

"I can have one of the editorial assistants pull any coverage we had on these characters," Bill offered, then stared intently at Clark for a few moments. You could see a question churning inside of him, wrestling with himself about whether he should give it a voice.

"Before I give you the go-ahead, I have to ask if you are absolutely sure you want to tackle this story?" he finally asked. "If this story pans out like you think, you could be putting yourself in some serious danger, maybe even putting your family at risk. If you tell me you want to hand this off, forget this entire conversation ever happened, nobody could blame you one bit."

The weight of those words fell heavily on Clark. He knew his friend was genuinely concerned. Only a few months ago, Clark stared down the muzzle of a crazed psychopath bent on killing him and his family for writing a story about a series of bizarre murders and their possible connection to Alicia Bauer. At the time, Clark did not know about the obsession this murderer had with Bauer.

"My reporter ethics tell me I shouldn't worry about those things. It's the story that's important. But the father in me says I should take some time to think about it. I'm not sure I could handle somebody putting a gun on Lana again for something I had written."

"Take your time."

"Thanks. I'll let you know tomorrow."

Clark started to leave the office but stopped and turned back toward Bill. "You know, I think there was one upside from all of that kidnapping mess."

"Yeah?"

"My relationship with Lana's godmother is changing."

"And?" Bill coaxed, with his hand turning like a waterwheel under his chin.

"We are kind of dating. It seems weird in one way, her being the childhood best friend of my deceased wife. But it seems to be working out okay."

"Well, that's good."

"I hope so. She's kind of churchy like Lois, but we made it work."

"She can't use her to replace Lois. You have to want her for her."

"Yeah, I know."

Chapter 12

"HEY SWEETIE!"

The sound of such syrupy greetings still sounded foreign to Alicia. Not that she hadn't used them before, but they had always been just part of the script she concocted to convince her *clients* to part with some of their fortunes. How polite that sounded. Part with their fortunes. Clients. Alicia spent most of her life trading the privilege of a youthful, innocent appearance for an advantage in some con. A few years after the teen ran away from home, the cons became quite elaborate. In her masterpiece scheme, she convinced wealthy men to buy expensive art. Alicia, or the particular character she played, would sell the originals on the black market and replace the art with forgeries. They never suspected that they were her careful recreations on their walls. They were more concerned about themselves and how she dolled up their arms in public and their bedchambers in private.

Alicia recoiled at her past. She no longer wanted to be that hustler anymore. She no longer wanted to exploit narcissistic men. She no longer wanted her *business* to define her relationships. Alicia wanted something real.

Justin returned her greeting with a smile and an awkward stare. The slight time-delay in the jail's inmate video visiting system took the spontaneity out of the conversation. He never quite figured out where he should look, and the orange-clad image of his girlfriend on a computer screen did not feel like his fiancée. He tried imagining Alicia sitting in the room with him. It did not work. It did not feel real. If she were really there, he could hold her in his arms, and she could nestle her head into his shoulder. He would be able to smell her alluring fragrance. He would let their words fade until her gentle snoring woke him.

Unfortunately, that part of their relationship ended when his fiancée confessed her scandalous past. That morning was still a fog to him. In his mental replay, he can see himself sitting on the sofa, motionless, as the woman he had just days before asked to marry him revealed her original intentions. He had a sordid past as well, but it was just that—in the past. Alicia could not say that. She was still working her con with Robert Keagan while she feigned a relationship with Justin. The morning crescendo came when Alicia answered his ultimatum question: "Did you ever love me?"

A tearful Alicia exclaimed, "Yes, I love you! I love you very much."

Justin knew her quick response was not enough. He pressed her further, even though he was not truly sure he wanted to know the answer.

"But when?"

He could see her shame. Alicia could not look at Justin.

"Are you asking when I started to love you, or when I figured out that what I felt was love?"

"The one that looks most like the truth."

Then smack. Her honesty hit him like the proverbial ton of bricks.

"A couple of hours after you asked me to marry you."

What happened over the next few weeks, Justin doesn't remember clearly. Days, nights, events all seem to blur together. The fog even clouded out the chaos of that night in the restaurant when somebody shot and killed Keagan. The fog did not lift when the police arrested him for the murder. It was still in place when the trial began. Clarity did not return until he realized somebody had kidnapped Alicia. His purpose in life seemed to return. He had to admit that it was rather exhilarating to lead a clandestine team on a rescue of his damsel in distress. The results, however, did not bring his lost fiancée back into his arms. Her kidnapper was one step ahead of Justin and left clues behind that would unveil to the police Alicia's criminal past.

"Are you going to say anything?" Alicia interrupted his silence.

"I'm sorry. I miss waking up beside you."

"Me too."

After another silent exchange, Alicia perked up.

"The lawyer gave me good news. He said everything was in place for the judge to accept the plea deal. They get all my money, and I get probation. I should be out of here sometime next week, maybe sooner."

"That is good news. I can't wait."

"He also said my dad set me up with a job at a little art gallery downtown and secured me a spot at the Art Institute."

"That sounds like him. Using his money to make up for lost time. Don't think that will earn him any father of the year awards."

"No, but at least he's trying."

"Yeah, he's trying all right."

Alicia smiled.

"Your so-called daddy reached out to me a few days ago, too. His lawyer said Frankie wanted to talk, but I told him to take a hike. Today, I received a certified letter from him."

"What did he have to say?"

"Don't know. I haven't opened it. Not sure I want to. Let's not forget, the scumbag tried to pin a little murder wrap on me."

Alicia sat in silence. She could not blame Justin for his anger, but it still hurt her a little. She was not sure why. Her father's reinsertion into her life was totally by accident, a mere byproduct of a juvenile retaliation gone wrong by her father toward Justin. Wait! Alicia stopped her mental pity party. Why is my brain calling Frankie my father? That was pretty much a lie, too.

"You know, I don't have a place to stay yet. Kind of lost the lease on the old apartment," Alicia offered Justin, shifting the conversation to an even riskier subject for their relationship.

"I think I can take care of that."

"A place of my own, where I pay all my own bills."

"Not exactly what I had in mind."

"I know. I've been thinking a lot in here because, well, there isn't much else that I can do. I want us to start over. I want to fall in love with you all over again. I want to do it right this time."

"And what if you don't, don't fall in love with me again?"

"That is not going to happen, but ..."

"I hate buts," Justin interrupted.

"But, if we somehow don't fall back in love again, then it will hurt a lot, but less than if we rush back into something built on lies."

Justin knew she was right. Yet, the thought of going through the courtship process all over again scared him. Not so much that she would not fall in love with him, but that he would find the real Alicia less appealing than the fake one.

"Does that mean I have to buy another engagement ring?" Justin dodged his feelings with a joke.

"No."

Alicia giggled as she looked at her left hand and rubbed where the engagement ring Justin gave her once graced her hand.

"Just to let you know. I'm not going to ask your father for permission to marry you."

"That's okay. I don't think he'll be out of prison in time to walk me down the aisle."

Chapter 13

JOEY LEANED AGAINST the stone wall, which ran along the edge of the lookout point at Twin Peaks Park. He could absorb the entire city view from here. It made him feel quite substantial to see the little people scurry about and yet very insignificant at the same time. It felt comforting to return to his place of refuge, his place to puzzle out the issues of the day. Although he lived only a fifteen-minute walk away, he did not find this place on his own. It took an outing with the youth group at church for him to discover his oasis. He recalled how Pastor Dan did one of his famous life lessons that day because the fog had rolled in and obscured much of the cityscape vista.

"This fog is so thick," he recalled Pastor Dan said.

"How thick is it?" chanted the teen wannabes familiar with the youth pastor's comedy schtick.

"The fog is so thick I tried to grab it, but I mist."

Then came the inevitable groans and his apology.

"Sorry. Sorry. I know that one was a real groaner, but it does remind me of a story, though," Pastor Dan said, making his patented switch from lame humor to a deep life lesson that sunk in far better than the youth admitted.

"Is it better than that one, or will it be another mist opportunity?" asked one kid.

"How would he know? He doesn't have the foggiest idea about how to be funny," blasted another.

"Such grace, such grace you all have," Pastor Dan said. "No, my little story today is about an elderly man caught in a terrible fog, even worse than what you are seeing here today. To be honest, the old man was not the best of drivers on a good day, and his vision wasn't what it used to be. He gripped the steering wheel tightly, as if a white-knuckle grip would somehow give him more control over the difficult road conditions. His wife pointed out that the vehicle ahead of him seemed to know where it was going and was having no problem navigating the pea-soup fog. She latched on to that solution and demanded that her husband follow the truck's lead, but the old man resisted. 'How is he going to know where we are going?' he told her. 'As if you know where you are going,' she rebuffed. After a little more badgering, he relented and started following the truck. The truck went straight for a while, then made a series of left and right turns, until it finally came to a stop in the middle of the road. The couple waited for a few minutes before the wife angrily asked, 'Why is this guy stopped in the middle of the road?' Right then, the fog miraculously lifted, and the old man could see clearly again. Then he glared at his wife. 'He stopped because he is in his driveway.'"

The group remained mute.

"Don't you get it?" Pastor Dan asked.

"Get what? That wasn't funny."

"I wasn't trying to be funny. What does this story tell us about what we should do in our lives?"

"Not to follow random vehicles in the fog."

"Yes, but what is the bigger message?"

"That you tell confusing stories," Joey offered.

"Possibly," laughed the pastor. "However, I like to think of them more like modern-day parables, and if you are having problems understanding them, well, it doesn't offend me at all. That just puts me in good company. You know, many people in Jesus's day did not understand his parables either. He said it was because they did not have ears to hear."

"They had no ears? Wouldn't that make it hard to wear shades?" joked a teen.

"Aside from the fact that nobody will invent sunglasses for about another thousand years, Jesus was not saying that they didn't have physical ears. He meant they could not understand what they were hearing because they were spiritually deaf, much in the same way that a tone-deaf person can't tell if a note is out of tune."

"Then why didn't he explain it better?" This time, the jokester's comment seemed much more serious.

"It isn't a matter of how well he explained, but how persistent they were in their unbelief. He could have gotten out the big crayons and drawn pretty pictures, but they still would have failed to grasp the truths he was sharing. There's a lot more to this discussion, but we'll have to save that question for a conversation on another day. We need to get back to my little parable of the old man in the fog. What truths am I trying to reveal?"

"Maybe that we shouldn't just follow anybody?" Lana asked.

This was the first time Joey had noticed Lana. Technically, he had seen her around school and at youth group, but she always seemed to blend into the background. Not today. Something made her stand out. Something made him see things differently, like how her long black hair framed her sparkling green eyes.

"Yes, Lana. That's right. But why is that a bad thing? In this story, the guy in the truck seemed to know where he was going."

"But isn't that subjective?" Joey asked as he walked over and sat on the lookout wall facing Lana. She was even prettier up close.

"Oh my, that's a pretty big word. Do you even know what it means?" Lana rebutted, unaware that this boy was taking notice of her.

"Yes. It means something is more about opinion than facts. As for the guy in the truck, he was going where it was good for him. Turns out it wasn't so good for the old man."

Joey smiled as he made this cocky expression with his left eyebrow.

"The old man was just confused by the fog," Lana said, trying to dismiss his logic. "His wife nagging him didn't help either. What was the poor guy supposed to do?"

Lana returned the smile. Her new braces sparkled.

"GPS would have been more objective." Joey said with such confidence.

"Wow, another big word. Don't you have to tell the GPS what your destination is?"

Pastor Dan interrupted the intellectual foreplay.

"You two clearly have ears to hear. Yes, Joey, the old man needed to use his GPS—that's God's Positioning System."

The crowd chuckled.

"And you are right that we need an objective standard if we want any hope of successfully navigating our way through the fog of life. But unlike the man-made global positioning satellite systems, God's Positioning System already knows where home is. And if we have ears to listen, we, too, can know where home is supposed to be."

There was more to Pastor Dan's lesson that day, but Joey could not recall. He no longer had eyes to see or ears to hear, at least not to what Pastor Dan was saying. Lana had absorbed all of the 12-year-old's attention, and she was starting to know it. Joey knew. Her blushing face gave her away. So did her friend Maggie. She kept prodding Lana to turn her attention away from the youth pastor. His persistence would eventually pay off.

Chapter 14

GREG VERNIER FELT exposed. In the courtroom, he understood his role. Sitting in his car staring at a disposable cellphone, he felt unsure. In the courtroom, he could predict what the other characters might do. Even when they went off script, he could guess their next step. The law only afforded them a limited number of legal options. He could count on everyone to play by the same rules, more or less, because the system required trust on so many levels to operate. Not just to run efficiently, but even to operate at all. One of those trusts was that all the players would stay in their own guarded lanes.

Vernier was not staying in his lane. He could not. Somebody else was not following the rules. They were violating the trust of the system and forcing him to reciprocate. He had to protect his clients, even the ones he knew were guilty. They deserved justice from the system just as much as the victims. The criminal defense attorney had some experience in bending the rules enough to ensure justice. This time, however, he feared he might have to cover his ears so he could not hear them break. This reality gnawed at his conscience, but not as much as the cancer he needed to expose.

The defense attorney could not follow the traditional route with what he had discovered; or more accurately, with what had discovered him. He could dramatically reveal this bombshell and sway the jury toward a verdict of not guilty for Mikhail Kuzmin. That would not be enough. He still needed to bring justice to the other names on that list. Vernier knew the system would not heal itself. The players would not take the trial evidence seriously. They would only roll their judgmental eyes and dismiss his accusations as "just another one of that lawyer's wacky defenses."

He also could not just hand what he had learned over to law enforcement and expect them to police themselves. Vernier's discovery convinced him that this was where the predatory cancer lived or at least found shelter. It was not like Vernier thought evil corruption permeated the vast law enforcement system. He was not one of those kinds of lawyers. He just understood that their rigid system of hierarchy can work against them when exposing this kind of truth. In the rules of their pond, little fish cannot eat bigger fish, and this predator had to be a really big fish. Of that, Vernier was confident. The bigger fish, however, can eat the little fish when they stray into big fish hunting grounds. But they weren't dealing with just another bigger fish somewhere up the food chain. A shark, maybe even a shiver of them, was in their midst. Chumming damning evidence into shark-infested waters made little sense. Vernier needed an outsider to expose the truth, someone who the system could not cast away easily.

Vernier continued to stare at his phone. He tried to contemplate the consequences of his next step. He considered calling his deception off, but that option was not available anymore. Not now. Once he directed his source to share that spreadsheet with Clark Solo, he sealed a fate for the newspaper reporter that Vernier could not peel back. He considered being more direct with Clark, but that could have made the story about him. That would not work. The newspaper coverage needed to be about the cancer, and the cancer alone.

He hated being so evasive with Clark today, but it worked. He could tell the longtime reporter saw through his cryptic answers. Vernier so carefully mulled over the simplest of answers, Clark could not help but figure out that the lawyer he had known for nearly twenty years was holding something back. His deception piqued the reporter's interest better than one of those fancy lures his pappy used to snag walleye. Part of Vernier wished he had looked the other way and ignored the plea for help. He toyed with the possibility of disappearing to the family fishing spot back in Minnesota. He could use a place where the cares of the world fade amongst the trees and the gentle swaying of the lake. Where the choice of which lure to use was life's biggest struggle. The nostalgia was very appealing, but he could not go there. It was too late for him, too.

"Bait delivered. May have a buddy for our fishing trip," he texted.

Chapter 15

JOEY CHECKED his vibrating phone. Seeing the name float across the screen overwhelmed him with dread. He returned the phone to his pocket and his gaze to the cityscape below. He wanted to ignore the text, but the hushed whispers he heard at the Mansion told him he could not just ignore Charlie. The reach of his patriarch of sorts permeated too deep. His control over people stretched beyond a ragtag collection of wayward teens. Somehow, Charlie could skirt the law with amazing impunity.

A chill ran through Joey. He wanted to attribute the sensation to a strong bay breeze, but the air was unusually still. He knew it was Charlie, and it made him want to run away from being a runaway. The absurdity of the thought made Joey laugh. No matter how noble he thought of it back then, running away did not work out all that well. The claims made by the lackey with a red tattoo did not become untrue when Joey suddenly left town. At best, running away—a desperate attempt at nobility—only delayed the inevitable. At worst, it introduced him to the whims of Charlie. The serendipity of how these two seemingly random events intersected initially gave Joey hope. Now, only second thoughts. He was not sure he could do what Charlie asked, not even with the promise of erasing a blemish from his mother's past.

Based on the overheard whispers, he was confident the two events were not random. But he could not have known that back then, back when the stranger with the dripping red tattoo got in his face at the library. Odd-looking people saying random off-the-wall stuff was not exactly a surprise in the city. Joey tried to do what most seasoned urbanites do—get away as quickly as possible and forget that the encounter ever occurred. Joey could not do it this time.

It was more than garish clothing—a mix of purple plaids, pool table green and splashes of licorice red that made him look like a court jester. It was more than his raspy voice and the eerie message of Joey not being who he thought he was. Everywhere the teenager went, he saw the character with the vivid, blood red tattoo. He would stare at Joey, point with his exceptionally long, skinny index finger, and wag his head back and forth. Each time, Joey would look away and try to shake off the experience. After a few days, he could not take the stalking any longer.

"Why are you following me?" Joey bellowed at the jester from his taunting post across the street.

The odd little character walked toward Joey, stopping a few feet away. The top of his head barely came to the top of the Academy logo on Joey's purple polo shirt. Then he lowered his left shoulder, cocked his head, and locked eyes with the teen. Joey took one step back, trying to hide how these antics intimidated him, and confronted the stranger again.

"Who are you, and what do you want?"

"They call me Candle," he said as he rubbed his red tattoo.

"Is that supposed to be candle wax?"

"Could be. Could be blood. You decide."

The punctuated rhythm of Candle's raspy voice added to his oddity.

"Ooookaaaay," Joey said, elongating the word as he took another step backwards. "What do you want with me?"

"Me want? Nothing. Somebody else? Something."

"What does that mean?"

Candle loped around Joey, making a rapid sucking sound through his tea-colored teeth. Joey kept his eyes looking forward. Passersby on the sidewalk averted their eyes and pushed briskly past this odd scene.

"Are you going to say something?" Joey asked after Candle's third orbit around the high school freshman.

"You not who they say. You not who you think," Candle said in a singsong fashion as he continued his meandering stroll around Joey.

"You've said that already."

"They lied. They lied. They lied."

"Yeah. Probably happens a dozen times a day. Most likely happening right now."

"Mommy, mommy. She's the liar, liar."

"About what?"

"Not what. Who?"

"What does that mean?"

"Ask your brother."

"I don't have a brother."

"Ding, ding, ding. Somebody lied. Somebody lied."

"How can I have a brother? My father abandoned us after he knocked up my mom."

"How do they lie to thee? Let me count the ways."

"Then why don't you just tell me what the truth is?"

"Truth?"

"Yes, truth. You can't know something is a lie unless you know the truth."

"Check the eyes. Check the beholder."

"How weirdly philosophical of you. Might you tell me your version of the lies I've been told?"

"I'm not the beholder."

"Then who is?" Joey's voice boomed with frustration.

"Your brother."

"And how do I find this brother?"

"You don't. He finds you."

"Then why are you here?"

"I am to prepare the way."

"The way to what?"

"Ask your brother," Joey said in unison with Candle.

The strange man, maybe a few years older than Joey, stopped his circling and eyed the teen. He made a final sucking sound and abruptly walked away.

"Mister," a child's voice and a tug on his hand brought Joey out of his reminiscent thoughts. "Can you take our picture?"

"Samuel!" admonished his mother. "I'm sorry, sir. I told him not to bother you."

"Oh, it's no bother, ma'am. Where do you want your picture?"

She handed him her phone, hoisted Samuel into her arms, and nestled the two of them against the wall.

"How about here? Is the bridge in the background?" she asked.

"A little bit."

"Okay."

"Say cheese."

"Cheese."

"Here you go," Joey said, giving her back the phone.

"Thank you so much." Then, the mother turned to her son and asked. "Samuel, what do we say?"

"Thank you, mister."

"You're welcome."

Joey pulled his cellphone out and read the dreaded text from Charlie. "Have you assimilated?"

Joey took a deep breath and replied, "Not yet. First contact tonight."

He stared at the screen, waiting for the reply.

"Don't delay. Your candle is already burning."

"No. I said I'll do it."

"Now I know you will."

Chapter 16

CLARK CALLED the second defendant on the list of clients Vernier represented. The secretary made no promises about the quality of information and admitted clients sometimes lie about their contact information. The reporter already knew the first defendant, Tory Avlah, had died a few years ago when a drug addict shot him and a young doctor. After the fifth ring, the phone acted as if it had been answered, but there was only silence.

"Hello?" Clark asked.

No answer. He hung on to his desk phone while pulling out his cellphone and texted the number. Another abyss. Clark hung up both phones and googled the number. The search showed the number was still registered to Stefan Majewski. More internet sleuthing revealed that Majewski had met his demise in a construction accident. Apparently, he had been working alone and after hours when a steel beam fell on him.

Similar results came back for defendants three and four, except their fates were suicide and a car crash. All three phone numbers were still listed as assigned to the defendants. This new oddity concerned Clark. Three numbers passed the fluke stage, passed the coincidence stage, and leaped into something probably intentional. But why? Clark called his contact at the credit bureau.

"Cindy, I need a favor."

"You always need a favor."

"I'm not asking for a credit report on the sly. I just need to know if these accounts are still active."

"What do you mean?"

"I am doing some research on a few past murder cases. I've come across three phone numbers so far that belong to dead people, but it appears the phone numbers are still current. Is there a way for you to check to see if there is still activity?"

Cindy did not answer, but Clark could hear her fingernails clicking on the keyboard.

"Names?"

"Stefan Majewski, Samuel Boskowitz and Lukas Havel."

"Seriously?"

"What? You don't know the common spellings of those names?" Clark laughed and slowly spelled the names and provided the phone numbers and the last known addresses.

"You have a reason to think something is up," Cindy said. "There are still hits on the credit report. No loans or major purchases, just a history of on-time payments."

"Is that normal for people who've been dead a few years to still show a current history?"

"Maybe in the case of couples, you might see this. There is no history of any kind of joint accounts."

"So, you think there is something hinky going on?" Clark asked.

"Hinky enough that I'm asking you for a favor. Can you send me your proof that these people are dead?"

"Will do. Thanks for helping me out?"

"Yeah, thanks for giving me some extra work to do."

"Glad to be of service."

* * *

A ping on his computer told him somebody had tripped one of his web trackers. The lawyer unlocked the bottom left drawer of his desk and removed the basket of assorted office supplies. While leaning over the now-empty drawer, he stared at the little camera hole. An audible click let him know the retina scanner had given him access to the false bottom of the drawer. He pulled out the laptop and reviewed the notice. A few more clicks on the laptop and he knew the violator.

"So, who is this Clark Solo?" he pondered out loud.

The man did his own internet sleuthing. The only name that popped up was a reporter in San Francisco who writes about criminal trials. His discovery also revealed that Clark's wife passed about three years ago from cancer, and he has a daughter. He cross-referenced this new name with his list of people he was in charge of monitoring. Another connection. Clark covered the trial of Tory Avlah.

"Why is he searching for information on people who happen to be on my list?" he pondered out loud again.

Another ping sounded. This time it alerted him to activity at a credit reporting bureau. Someone just flagged the files for Stefan Majewski, Samuel Boskowitz and Lukas Havel. This had passed the coincidence stage; this was an intentional act. He pulled out a disposable phone from the special drawer and called his client.

"Somebody is doing internet searches on people you wanted me to monitor."

"I'm assuming you believe this is more than random."

"Correct, sir. This person is searching for the names in the order they appear on your list. He seems to know their phone numbers and addresses, too."

"Well, isn't that interesting. So, who is this more-than-random person?"

"Clark Solo, a newspaper reporter."

"That name sounds familiar. Didn't he just get caught up in that big brouhaha over a call girl who hustled rich guys? She had a wacko brother/boyfriend who killed all of them except some investment guy, who ironically was on trial for their murders."

"Yes, that's the reporter."

"Sounds like a fascinating guy. Not very lucky, but interesting. I look forward to meeting him."

"Any instructions for me?"

"No. Just keep monitoring," the client directed. "By the way, the list of names. Who knows about it?"

"Only you, me and Doctor Callahan."

"That's interesting, too."

Chapter 17

EMILY COULD SEE remnants of the building's many former lives when she pulled her little sports car into the parking lot of the church. In an earlier incarnation of the building, she recalled it was one of those large computer stores that, ironically, failed to adapt to the digital marketplace. Her church extensively remodeled half of the massive warehouse's square footage to create a sanctuary, several classrooms and an activity center that serves as a before-and-after-school spot for neighborhood youth. The inviting architecture of the church sits juxtaposed to the clunky conversion of the remaining portion of the building into a cluster of unimaginative retail shops.

"Do you think he will show up?" Lana asked.

"I don't know. The better question is, do you want him to show up?"

"In some ways, yes, other ways, no."

Emily smiled. She understood her better than Lana could know.

"I get that. You shouldn't be too hard on Joey. You couldn't have really known him all that well when he disappeared. Some things may have been going on that you knew nothing about."

"It may have only been two official dates, but we had been friends at school and at church since sixth grade. And he was my go-to guy for all the school dances." Lana took a deep, exasperated breath. "You would think I would have rated at least a goodbye text."

"You would think so, but that may not have been possible for him. You just don't know yet."

"Why are you defending him?"

"A couple of reasons. You don't know what you don't know, so you must give him the benefit of the doubt until he proves otherwise. In some ways, I kind of get the desire to run away when life gets overwhelming. We don't all give in to that desire, thank God, but that doesn't mean it doesn't exist."

"I guess that makes sense, except for the part about you getting overwhelmed. I doubt that's possible."

"Anybody can get overwhelmed if the circumstances are right."

"What were your right circumstances?"

"Your mom and dad."

"What did they do?"

"They were madly in love and had a perfect relationship."

"How horrible of them!" Lana feigned.

"Yes, it was. I, on the other hand, only had my cat."

"Wow. You sound pretty pathetic."

Emily responded to Lana's jeer with a sigh. Not the burst of air that one gives to show displeasure. This sigh came from deep inside, with echoes of past tears.

"That's how I felt—a pathetic loser."

The words slowly made their way to the surface. Lana reached over and placed her hand on her godmother's. Emily patted a thank you.

"I was the one who needed to get away. Your mom and I were starting to bicker over your dad's disdain for our beliefs. She knew they were unequally yoked, but she thought he would come around eventually. I wasn't so sure. It only added to my poor self-image, especially her choosing to be happy with your dad over me. So, I ran away. I got caught up in the lie that promises distance will magically fix how we feel about ourselves. It never delivers. And you would think, as a literature teacher, I'd know this from a library full of books pointing this out. Guess that doesn't matter. Like all those characters, I acted as if whatever was happening in my life was so original."

"Doesn't the phrase 'nothing new under the sun' sound familiar?"

"Apparently not at the time. Without so much as a heads-up that I was looking, I took a teaching position abroad."

"I didn't know you did that."

"It was before you were born. I couldn't stand being the third wheel."

"Where did you go?"

"I spent three years at a school for American kids in Italy."

"That's not running away."

"It is if you don't tell anybody you are leaving."

"Not even Mom?"

"No. As far as your mom ever knew, I made an impulsive decision while touring Europe on a summer vacation. I had planned it for months but could never muster the courage to tell anyone."

"Did you meet any sexy Italian guys?"

"That's for me to know and you to never find out."

"Ahh, Auntie Em. You're no fun."

Emily smiled indignantly at Lana until an odd-looking character came into view. Without taking her eyes off him, her left hand stroked the armrest on the door until she found the button to lock the doors.

"Why did you do that?" Lana asked.

"Just an abundance of caution."

Her voice remained calm, something short of the teacher's tone that bristled students into compliance. Emily nodded her furrowed brow toward a man decked out in a garish court jester costume, or at least she assumed it was a costume.

Lana looked in the man's direction, quickly slapping her mouth with her hand to suppress a laugh.

"Remember, Auntie Em, we are not supposed to judge."

"Well, the correct reference is we are not to judge hypocritically, and I'm not. I'm being more like the proverb, which says a wise person is cautious and avoids danger, but a fool plunges ahead with reckless confidence."

"Do you think he is dangerous?"

"Maybe, maybe not. Experience has taught us recently that people may not be what they seem."

Lana looked at her cellphone. The time was 4:17 p.m.

"Joey should be here any minute. I'll text him we are in your car. He can hop in here with us."

"Sorry, this is only a two-seater."

"There's a back seat."

"For groceries, not people."

"I can fit back there."

A commotion outside interrupted their debate. They both looked toward the court jester. Lana recognized Joey.

"That's Joey."

"Get in the back seat!"

Emily lay on the horn as Lana clumsily navigated the narrow passage of the leather bucket seat obstacle course. She could see Joey swing his backpack at the man before dashing toward the car. He fumbled with the door handle.

"Unlock the door, Em!" Lana shouted.

"Oh, yes, I'm sorry."

Emily turned and fumbled with the buttons. She lowered the driver's window before finally hitting the correct button to unlock the door.

"Let's get out of here," Joey said as he plopped himself into the front passenger seat. Emily quickly complied. In her rearview mirror, she could see the court jester standing there like a lost little boy waving goodbye.

Chapter 18

CHARLIE DID NOT CARE for the so-called mellow sounds of smooth jazz. He considered it insulting to the soul of real jazz. His distaste for the genre amplified even more when someone forced him to listen to it while on hold. If he thought about it much, and he did, his anger stemmed not so much from the music itself, but from the arrogance the hold button represented. Charlie normally treated arrogance harshly, but that would be problematic today. Charlie needed the man not yet on the phone, at least for now. Despite his desires to the contrary, he'd have to continue tolerating this man's arrogance for a while longer. Or, at least until his usefulness runs its course.

"Charlie, I told you not to call me at this number." A scolding voice emanated from his phone.

"I'm so glad you could finally take my call." Charlie had to set parameters, even if he had to tolerate some of his undesirable behaviors.

"Like I have a choice."

"Doc, you have a choice. You just might not like the consequences."

"What do you want?"

"Just checking to see how our little mission is coming along?"

"On schedule."

"Yours or mine?"

"I didn't know there was a difference." The sarcasm barely hid the doctor's nervousness.

"I guess you need to ensure that there isn't."

"No worries. My final procedure for you should be uneventful."

"Final procedure?"

The lilt in Charlie's voice conveyed more than the simple surprise the doctor had expected. The tone reminded him more of his mother's "no, you are not" inflection, which betrayed the sweet words that actually left her lips.

"Yeah, it's time for me to retire, to fade into obscurity."

Charlie laughed.

"Like anybody knows who you are now."

"Maybe I just want to make my circle of acquaintances even smaller, definitely one smaller."

Charlie laughed again.

"You are an optimist, Doc, I give you that. You are an optimist."

"I'll let you know when we've addressed your request. Goodbye!"

The doctor did not wait for Charlie to answer. He wanted to slam the receiver, but he didn't want to alarm the staff. He wanted to get out from under Charlie's thumb, but he wasn't so sure now that was going to happen. His tormentor seemed too jovial, like he knew something was up.

Charlie hadn't always had the upper hand in their relationship. When they first met, his tyrant knew his place. He stayed in the background. More aptly, the doctor recalled, he lingered in the shadows and spewed humility. He portrayed himself as nothing more than a person fascinated with how the mind works. Charlie said his company wanted to give people a drug to overcome their fears and redirect their anger. This hooked the doctor. It appealed to his massive debt from medical school. It stroked his ego. Someone was offering him a heap of money to do something good for the world. How could he resist?

Initially, the subjects Charlie brought into the project seemed aware of their efforts. Their fears seemed minor, not truly enough to warrant any medical intervention. After a few months, just when the doctor was ready to throw in the towel from sheer boredom, Charlie shook things up. He had already set the stage with colorful comments about the tragic shooting at a Colorado high school.

"If we had our drug already, that wouldn't have happened," Charlie proclaimed. "Thirteen kids are dead because we are moving too slow!"

That was when the rules changed. Charlie transformed from a patient observer with idealistic dreams of a utopian cure for society to a man obsessed. He unearthed old records from the Central Intelligence Agency's mind control project. He implored the doctor to figure out where they had gone wrong.

Vanity propelled the doctor. The Senate hearings on the MK-Ultra Project dominated the headlines when he was in college. So much so that he authored a paper for his ethics class defending the actions of Canadian psychiatrist Donald Cameron. He painted the doctor as being singularly fixated on eliminating a mind disorder, which an unscrupulous CIA exploited.

"There is no doubt Doctor Cameron pushed the boundaries of ethical protocols, but that should not be our point of indignation," Callahan wrote. "We should reserve judgment for an even bigger question: Did he go far enough? I would argue that we should laud him for his courage in acknowledging the fallacies of the medical profession. He knew medical science could not progress while relying on past failures as a yardstick for today's ethical boundaries. Should not the ultimate aim, such as unburdening humanity from schizophrenia, take precedence? Society can absorb the inconveniences of the few in order to save the many."

Callahan could not imagine at the time that they would someday victimize him in the same way. In retrospect, he realized that he should have known flattery had a shelf life. A text interrupted his introspection.

"Bait delivered. May have a buddy for our fishing trip."

Chapter 19

AFTER HIS THIRD conversation with defense attorneys from the list of murders, the something-doesn't-make-sense meter went off in his head again. A low register on this meter usually turned out to mean Clark had an error in his facts, or he failed to ask that one extra question to fill in an information gap. A high register meant something nefarious, something intentional. His meter still only had a low reading. This puzzled Clark, but he was not sure why that bothered him. Regardless of his conflicted feelings, he kept plugging through the list.

"Hello. I'm Clark Solo, a reporter with the ..."

"Are you an existing client?" an obviously disinterested voice interrupted.

"No."

"What crime did they charge you with?"

"Ma'am. I'm a newspaper reporter."

"Your crime, please."

"Murder." Clark opted to play along. Clearly, this person did not know how to handle off-script inquiries.

"Where?"

"Vallejo."

"When?"

"2004."

"Thank you. Please hold."

Instantly, a faulty attempt at elevator music pelted him. A warped melody faded in and out, occasionally drowning out the static. After a couple of cycles of the disturbing noise, the operator returned.

"Sir, we don't show any record of a Clark Solo being arrested in Solano County."

"That's good to know. I'd hate having to write that story. Once again, I'm a reporter working on a story about a 2004 murder in Vallejo. I am looking to speak to Christopher Drake, please."

"Why didn't you say that in the first place?"

"My apologies. I guess I have a problem with my English."

"It doesn't matter. Mr. Drake left the firm about two years ago."

"Do you know how I may contact him?"

"Not on this side of eternity, sir. A former client murdered him."

"Oh my. So sorry to hear that. By chance, can you tell me the name of that former client?"

"Marcus Delaney."

"That's the man I wanted to talk to him about."

"Guess we won't be able to help you. Goodbye."

The conversation shocked Clark. He expected to learn a couple of lawyers had moved on, some might decline to talk with him, but not murder. Let alone murder at the hands of the specific client he called about.

A quick search of the newspaper's database turned up a series of articles, albeit sketchy on any substantial details that Clark could use. The out-of-town murder rated little space in his paper, but Clark pieced together that Delaney shot Drake after a brief showdown at the courthouse.

Witnesses reported Delaney was angry that his murder trial was going south—the murder Clark was investigating. Somehow, Delaney got a gun while they were in the defense conference room and shot the attorney. After a short standoff, Delaney surrendered to police and pleaded guilty at trial. Nothing from the newspaper archive helped Clark know how to contact Delaney or his new lawyer.

"At least this one may still be alive," Clark told himself as he dialed his favorite police contact. News from the other three calls had turned up dead clients—reported as either suicide or drug overdoses. The deaths seemed a little too convenient for Clark.

"Detective Maddox," came a gruff voice over the phone.

"Hey Bobby. It's your favorite reporter, Clark."

"Didn't know you could favor a reporter."

"Ouch. The donut shop ran out of bear claws today?"

"If only. Gayle is on a health kick again."

"Sorry to hear about that. I can drop off some supplies for you if you could run a name for me."

"Why?"

"I'm following up on a lead that claims to link the Kuzmin murder with seventeen other murders over the last couple of decades."

"Doesn't seem probable, unless Kuzmin started his killing spree around age nine."

"The person isn't claiming Kuzmin is the murderer in all those other cases, but asserts that somebody else is behind the scenes, pulling the strings."

"Oh, one of those conspiracy theorists stole your ear. Seems like a colossal waste of time, but that's what you reporters get paid the big bucks to do. What's the name?"

"Marcus Delaney. He should be in the system for murdering his lawyer in 2004."

"Is that a crime?"

"Sometimes."

"I see that wasn't his first time being a bad boy."

"I know."

"Looks like they are taking care of him up in Vacaville, the medical prison, not the regular prison."

"Still alive?"

"Odd question, but yes, he is."

"Thanks Bobby. I'll drop off supplies tomorrow on my way in."

"Make it an apple fritter, so I can honestly tell Gayle that I snacked on some fruit."

"Will do."

The something-doesn't-make-sense meter went off in his head again. So far, the tally of dead victims topped twenty-six, and he still had half of the list to go. This time, the reading seemed stronger, much stronger.

Chapter 20

"WHAT WAS THAT all about? And what was that thing you were fighting with?" Lana hollered from her cramped perch in the backseat of her godmother's sports car.

"I'm glad to see you too," Joey retorted as he struggled to insert the seatbelt while Emily sped down the street.

"You should see him. Just standing there like some sort of lost puppy waving goodbye. Wait. That's not a wave. I think he's wagging his finger at us. He is. Wow! That's weird, really weird. Is he a friend of yours?" You could hear the air quotes in Lana's tone around the word friend.

"No, not a friend of mine. More like a messenger from Satan."

Emily made a sharp right turn, punched it for three blocks and made an abrupt left turn on a yellow light.

"Hey! Fragile cargo back here."

"Yeah, I know," Emily replied in a wispy, retrospective voice that seemed more of an affirmation of that fact to herself than an effort to convince anyone else.

"Doesn't feel like it."

Joey turned around and blurted, "Do you want some cheese to go with that ..." He couldn't finish his prodding. Laughter interrupted as he took in the sight of Lana's contorted body sitting sideways in the back seat.

"Excuse me. You know, we could have left you back there with that freakazoid!"

"Okay, you two, that's enough. Guess we need to let Pastor Dan know about our change of plans."

"I'll do that." Lana pulled her arms from between her knees and shifted her body left and right. Despite her struggles, she could not squeeze around herself enough to retrieve the phone holstered in her hip pocket.

Joey, still turned and gawking over the seat, laughed again.

"You sure about that?" he said.

"Stop it! This is not funny!" Lana swatted awkwardly in Joey's direction. Her arms moved mostly from the elbow. Her shoulders were now wedged firmly in place.

"Yes, it is."

He turned around and pulled out his phone.

"What do you want me to say?" Joey asked.

"Just tell him something came up, and I'll call him back later," Emily instructed.

"Okay. Done," Joey said as Emily pulled into a parking spot in front of a coffee shop.

"Now help me peel her out of the backseat."

Emily turned and got out of the car. Joey's exit was not as easy. The sports car sat low to the ground, and Emily's parking hugged the curb. He unfolded his long legs, turned to place his feet on the curb, and found his knees beside his ears.

"Come on, contortion boy. Get out!" Lana teased.

A giggle consumed her as Joey rolled to the right and pushed himself up off the sidewalk. When he finally uprighted himself, he looked at Emily and smiled. They shared a mischievous glint and, without saying a word, their actions became synchronized. Both seats flipped forward in tandem, sending Lana to the floor. Engulfed in laughter, the teenager crawled backwards toward the curb. Joey reached down to help her up, shielding her head as she rose.

"Thanks," Lana said.

She was standing uncomfortably close to Joey, yet she liked it. Joey locked eyes with her, not knowing what to say or do next. The adult stepping onto the curb interrupted the moment.

"You know, this cute little car is all about me, not my passengers," Emily said.

"We noticed," Lana said.

Joey looked over at his former English teacher, smiled and returned his gaze to Lana. The uneasiness of the moment suddenly started glowing on his face. He struggled to find a way out of this situation. Finally, he pointed to his backpack on the floor of the car.

"My backpack," was the most eloquent phrase he could muster to his lips. Lana seemed to understand his grunt and sheepishly stepped aside. He snatched the bag, closed the door, and turned toward the coffee shop.

"I think chocolate, lots of chocolate, is in order. How about you two?" Joey asked.

The words sounded bold and funny, but the former runaway knew there was no confidence, no humor behind them. He was at a loss about what to tell them about his absence. All his rehearsals of this moment became moot when Candle showed up.

* * *

After a few sips of a caffe mocha and half of an indulgent chocolate brownie, Joey could no longer avoid the obvious conversation he needed to have with Lana. Having his English teacher there, too, did not make it any easier.

"I guess you figured out that I'm back," Joey offered lamely.

"Yes, Captain Obvious, we figured that out." Lana gave him no mercy.

"Lana!" Emily scolded her. "I'm sure your mom is glad to know you are home safe and sound."

"To be perfectly honest, I haven't talked to her yet."

Joey stared into his mocha, avoiding eye contact, hoping it would mask his embarrassment. He did not have the courage to say he had chickened out earlier, and he certainly could not say that it was not part of the strategy Charlie laid out for his return home.

"You haven't. Why not?" Lana asked. The confession surprised her, but her words sounded more like a scolding.

"I figured I owed you more of an explanation. At least I left my mom a note."

"Oh." Lana's voice was now tinged with guilt for her abruptness. "I'm ready to hear why you disappeared."

"Believe it or not, it has everything to do with that weird man you saw today. His name is Candle. He started stalking me a few weeks before I left. He showed up everywhere I went and spouted stupid riddles."

"Did you tell your mom?" Emily asked.

"No. What he kept telling me complicated things."

Emily and Lana looked at each other, sharing confused expressions over the cryptic nature of Joey's answer.

"What does that mean?" Lana asked.

"I can't get into that right now. I just wanted you to know that my leaving had nothing to do with you, except maybe to protect you."

"Protect me from what?" Lana's voice did not hide her growing frustration with Joey's almost answers.

"I didn't know, but Candle had me pretty freaked out. He kept telling me stuff that made it so I didn't know who I could talk to or who I could trust. When I left, I wasn't even sure I could trust myself."

"Sounds overwhelming, Joey. I can't even imagine what you were going through," Emily said in her calming, maternal voice. Lana had come to appreciate that voice. "Would you like some company when you see your mom again?"

Joey sat in silence. Her tenderness swelled his emotions. He eventually choked out a quiet thanks as he shook his head no. Emily placed her hands on top of his. After a few moments, Lana's hand joined the pile. Joey shared glances with the two and smiled. The embarrassment seemed lifted, even though a few tears strolled down his cheeks.

"Well, I can at least give you a ride home," Emily said, breaking the silence.

"I call shotgun," Lana proclaimed.

Chapter 21

JUSTIN STOOD IN FRONT of the large picture window of his Russian Hill home, staring into the nightfall slowly engulfing the city below. His mind ignored the classic postcard view of the fog-wrapped bridge; its focus was on Alicia and kept replaying her words.

"I want us to start over. I want to fall in love with you again. This time, I want to do it right. ... If we somehow don't fall back in love again, then it will hurt a lot, but less than if we rush back into something built on lies."

He kept wondering if this would be the undoing of their relationship. After all, it was her manufactured intrigue that attracted him to her. A muffled laugh accompanied his recollection of how they met. Even though their eyes locked momentarily while sitting at a bar in North Beach, nothing motivated Justin to pursue her. It was not until she confronted him with a portrait sketch and a cockamamie story about him being the man of her dreams that Justin relinquished control to his hormones. His intellectual side suspected the well-rehearsed pickup line, but he let the flattery to his ego drown out the warning sirens. As their relationship progressed, her control of the details and the pleasures outpaced his instinctive cautions. That was the woman he fell in love with. That was the woman he risked life in prison to rescue from a crazed killer. That was the woman he inadvertently unveiled her criminal past to the police. The woman sitting in jail today, according to his runaway doubts, lacks that intrigue.

"To be honest, I can't guarantee you how much longer I will be part of her life," Justin told the linebacker of a man sitting on his couch. It wasn't just his doubts. He wasn't sure this new woman, as she continues to break out of her old cocoon, would still want him.

"Life does not come with guarantees. If it did, we wouldn't be the men we are today," Frankie Zimmerman said.

"I'm not sure that's the best sales pitch," Justin said.

He walked from the window and sat back down in the high-back leather chair that he had bought on one of Alicia's excursions to the Napa Valley.

"Probably not, but it's the best I've got."

"I'm still not sure I understand why you are here. I already told your funky lawyer friend over there I didn't want to talk to you. Haven't even opened the certified letter he sent."

Justin wanted to send Frankie and his lawyer packing when they showed up at his door, but the look on his former mentor's face convinced him otherwise. The tough facade he had always known was gone. A more malleable expression, something akin to a person facing their ultimate finality on this earth, replaced it.

"Well, you don't survive the things I've done without knowing a few people who've done a lot worse," Frankie said. "The feds, well, they made me a deal I couldn't refuse."

"I don't capeesh."

"I'm sure Annie has told you about her plea deal."

"Yes."

"Well, it came at a price."

"Throwing your money around again?"

"If it were only that easy. I have to roll over on a few of my associates back in Chicago. If I do that, I'll need to disappear, and I'd prefer that it not be at the bottom of Lake Michigan."

"All this just sounds like another stop on your father of the year comeback tour."

"Why are you so cynical?"

"A job, a spot in a prestigious art school and a get-out-of-jail-free card. Of course, the daughter you abandoned has got to love you now."

"You got me all wrong."

"Yeah, sure."

"Give me a break. I'm not trying to win her affections; we both know I do not deserve that. I'm just trying to make a few amends. Besides, with the deal I just made, I won't ever get to see her again."

Frankie paused for a moment, then continued.

"I left her behind back then because I didn't want to put her in harm's way. I know I didn't do enough to protect her. I'm not sure there was much else I could have done, but there is a lot I can do this time."

"I hope you won't feel disappointed if I don't shed any tears over your leaving."

"I'm not expecting you to. I am expecting you to take care of my Annie, even if this thing between the two of you doesn't work out."

"Of course, that goes without saying. I'll be there to help Alicia— you know that's her name, not Annie—pick up the pieces after you're gone again. Does it feel special to be the father who abandoned his daughter twice?"

"I'm going to just ignore that because I need you to listen, to understand how I set some things up to help you take care of my Annie."

"I don't need your help."

"No, I guess you probably don't, but I insist. In the letter you haven't read, you'll discover that you now own the building where her new art studio is located. You should also get a call in a couple of days from the art school asking you to serve on its board of trustees."

"Is that how they are thanking you for a sizable donation?"

"They said you were already on their list."

"I'm flattered."

"The most important item is the key to a safe deposit box."

"The family jewels?"

"It's more like an insurance policy. You might even call it another get-out-of-jail-free card."

"Sounds intriguing. Are you holding back from the feds?"

"Not exactly. They didn't know enough to ask about some things, and I didn't feel compelled to tell them either."

"Why do you think I'll need it?"

"The feds' record on protecting the families of snitches isn't perfect."

"You expect me to use your little insurance policy to threaten one of your mob buddies back in Chicago?"

"Not directly. I've just provided you with a contact who can resolve the matter for you."

"Nice friend. Are these services prepaid?"

"In a manner of speaking. Let's just say he knows how to get compensated."

"Convenient. A self-paying hitman. I don't suppose you invented a perpetual motion machine, too?"

"I didn't invent him. Ironically, I think the feds did it. Regardless, Annie can't know anything about this. Let's just keep this conversation between us."

"Don't worry. As far as I'm concerned, you were never even here. You never even existed."

Justin returned to the window and stared at the cityscape below. Frankie took the hint. He and his attorney made their way to the door. Halfway through his exit, he paused and looked back at Justin.

"I hope you and Annie can work things out." Frankie's voice wavered, so he stopped and collected himself. "I would be really proud to call you son."

Chapter 22

OUT HER FRONT WINDOW, Gloria Maldoon noticed a tall, slender man stop his bicycle in front of the house, look around and then fiddle with his cellphone. She bristled. Her comfort with out-of-the-ordinary activity had decreased markedly since the light scare this morning. She kept hearing strange noises, noises she finally convinced herself were always there. But she never quite shook the feeling that somebody was watching her. This was the first time out of a dozen or so inspections today that she clearly saw anybody out her window. Earlier, she would have sworn a hat of some sort bobbled momentarily in the tall grasses at the top of the terraced backyard. The fifty-something man out front looked familiar, but before she could really digest his appearance, he tucked away his cellphone and rode away.

"You know, Joey," Gloria spoke into the empty living room as if her son was still there. "You are supposed to be here to protect me from my motherly paranoia. That man was just being responsible. Texting and peddling are an unpleasant combination."

She chuckled momentarily at her own humor, but it failed to thwart the burst of sadness that pushed its way through her body. Tears welled up in her eyes, and she wrapped her son's black-and-gray cardigan even more tightly around her body. She could still smell his cologne; the one she often complained that he doused on a little too strong. She wallowed in self-pity, something of a luxury she allowed herself today. After all, it was the anniversary of her son's disappearance. Tomorrow, she will once again neatly pack up her emotions just as the world expects of her, and life for everyone else will be back to normal.

Gloria returned to her recliner facing the window. On the coffee table lay the tear-stained note from Joey. Its inconsistency with the son she knew still bothered her. Her push to figure out its mystery, to understand the secret meaning he was trying to convey, had faded into something scarier. Her thoughts now acquiesced to the possibility that the son she remembered was not the son she lived with. To the mom who gave up so much to make Joey a part of her life, this notion felt devastating. It meant she had failed as a mother. She tried redirecting this torture to a more rational reality, but her emotional roller coaster thwarted the attempt. Her mind would not accept a reality where her son was just a normal teenage boy who experienced change at such a rapid pace that even he couldn't know who he was. She was his mother.

Another distraction outside her window interrupted her lamentations. Two women got out of a small teal blue car, much like the little two-seater sitting in her garage. They were laughing at a third person struggling to get out of the undersized backseat when the gentleman on the bicycle returned. The women blocked much of her view of the comical scene, but the person getting out was ungracefully tall and thin like her Joey. The older man motioned with his hands for the group to huddle. They leaned in and wrapped their arms around each other. They stayed like that for what seemed like an incredibly long time to Gloria, then they parted to let the man from the backseat take the lead. He took a few steps toward the house when Gloria let out a high-pitched screech.

"Oh, my God! Oh, my God! Oh, my God!"

Gloria's brain had her body racing out to the crowd coming toward her, which now seemed to be laughing and holding back tears of their own. Her feet did not comply. They ran in place. She did not let her eyes drift from the man in the backseat, lest he might disappear like the hat did earlier today. This could not be a mirage. That would be too cruel. When the man disappeared and someone struggled to open the front door, Gloria instinctively held her breath in anticipation.

Her heart skipped a beat when she heard someone pounce up the steps, landing loudly on every third step despite being told many times not to do that. Finally, the man, just a teenage boy, stood at the top of the stairs. He seemed unsure of what to do next. Tears streamed down his face as he watched the frantically jumping woman suddenly stop moving. Her body trembled in utter confusion, unsure whether to laugh or cry, to run over to him or stand there staring at her returning child.

"Mom!"

Joey ran to catch Gloria as she crumbled from the weight of her emotions.

* * *

When Gloria opened her eyes, she saw a strange woman dabbing a cool rag on her face. Her mind struggled to figure out why this was happening. She tried to speak, but words eluded her as well.

"Mrs. Maldoon. Are you okay?" the woman asked.

Gloria stared at her for a moment, still unsure of her surroundings. She could now tell that her head was in the lap of this woman.

"Why are you taking off my makeup?" Gloria asked.

The sound of laughter filled her head with a new confusion. This small, but stout woman holding her head has the deep laugh of a man.

"That's my mom."

She can talk without moving her lips. How can that be? Something is not right.

"I'm going to help you sit up, Mrs. Maldoon," the woman's voice now had a soft, feminine tone. "Do you know where you are?"

Gloria looked around the room. Her eyes fixed on a shiny trophy with ribbons hanging from it, and she smiled. It reminded her of the only sports trophy her little Joey had received. Next to it was her favorite memory of her mother—baking cookies for the holidays. She let her mind taste the spicy oatmeal, cranberry, and walnut treats.

"Are you coming back to us, Mom?"

Gloria turned her glazed expression toward the deep voice. It was not coming from the woman this time. She stared intently at the man standing beside her. Her eyes and brain were not yet in sync, but the veil of confusion seemed less murky.

"Joey?"

"Yes, Mom, it's me."

Another wave of emotions welled up in Gloria. She motioned for Joey to come closer. The lanky teen kneeled on one knee. His mother's hug pulled him even closer, tipping him over onto the floor. More laughter filled the room.

"Let's move Gloria to the couch," Emily instructed the room.

Joey rolled over, and Pastor Dan extended a helping hand, but the teen declined. He pushed himself up into a squatting position, wrapped his arms around his mom, and slowly stood up. With slow, methodical steps, they made their way to the sofa.

"Drink this," Lana said as she inserted a glass of water into Gloria's hands. Lana held on until she felt a firm grip on the glass.

"What are all of you doing here?" Gloria asked as she set the water on the coffee table.

Joey reached over to the decorative coaster caddy and slipped the cork-filled book under the drink. Gloria smiled and grabbed his right hand, pulling it tightly toward her and kissing it.

"We heard there was going to be a welcome home party and did not want to miss out on the celebration," Pastor Dan offered.

Emily slugged him.

"What?" he challenged. "You mean there is no cake?"

Gloria laughed, then shifted her body so she could sit up straight.

"Did I pass out?"

"Sure did," Joey affirmed. "I almost didn't catch you in time. That lamp would have left a mark."

"Well, thank you for being there when I needed you."

Joey blushed and lowered his head for a moment.

"I'm sorry for leaving you."

Gloria kissed her son's hand again and gave him that subtle nod of approval that mothers possess. The one that instills comfort, letting their children know everything will be alright.

"Well, Mrs. Maldoon, it looks like you've gotten over your shock, so we'll take our leave. I will offer one piece of advice. Just enjoy the moment tonight. There are obviously many questions that deserve answers, but they can wait," Pastor Dan said.

Mother and son nodded in silent agreement.

"Good. And do you mind if I stop by tomorrow morning to check on the two of you and chat for a while? Say ten o'clock?"

"That would be good," Gloria said.

"Alrighty then. I left my card on the counter there if you need to talk before then. Call anytime."

Pastor Dan motioned for Lana and Emily to follow. As the door closed behind them, Emily released the thoughts swirling in her head about the mother-son reunion she had witnessed.

"I hope the prodigal son in there understands what just happened."

"I was just thinking about that parable, too," Lana said.

"I think he does," Pastor Dan replied. "But I don't think the prodigal son is the right passage to guide them. A passage from Corinthians comes to mind. *Love is patient and kind; love does not envy or boast; it is not arrogant or rude. It does not insist on its own way; it is not irritable or resentful; it does not rejoice at wrongdoing, but rejoices with the truth. Love bears all things, believes all things, hopes all things, endures all things.*"

"Yeah, I think you may be right. Whether Gloria wants to admit it, her son broke her trust, and that's going to affect how she reacts to him for a long time." The matter-of-fact tone of Emily's voice conveyed a sense of sadness and impending doom.

"I can't believe I'm going to be the one defending Joey, given he ran out on me, too. But clearly Joey didn't trust his mom enough to work out whatever caused him to run." Lana paused for a moment, then added. "Apparently, he didn't trust me either."

"Trust is going to be an issue for them. Others as well. The reunion process can be difficult under good circumstances, but it gets exponentially worse when you add in feelings of betrayal and guilt. There is not much we can do to fix the past issues, but we can help address them as they move forward," Pastor Dan said.

"Thank you for getting involved," Emily said. She had secretly texted the youth pastor after Joey declined an offer to let Lana and her accompany him.

"It's all part of my superhero service," he said, striking a less-than-impressive comic book pose.

Chapter 23

AS EMILY PULLED up to the Solo house, it suddenly struck her just how much the neighborhood had changed since Clark and Lois had moved in. Then again, it was not the same city either. It was the wrong kind of silence that bothered her. It did not seem like children played on their street anymore. Few of the homes had kids, but the parents locked them indoors, hiding them away from all the dangers they could imagine.

She and Lana arrived at the house later than planned, thanks to an unimaginable afternoon. Clark had texted he was running late as well, so Emily knew it was Mandarin to the rescue. The bag of red and white containers had barely touched the table when Clark opened the door.

"Good timing, Dad," yelled Lana.

"It was all part of my evil plan," he replied with a ghoulish laugh and the wiggling of his fingers together under his chin.

"Hope you had a good day. Ours was certainly interesting," Emily said as she shared a polite hello kiss with Clark. They both felt uneasy about being more amorous in front of Lana.

"My day was interesting, all right. Let's hear yours first," Clark said. He still did not know how he wanted to broach his question.

"Do you remember a friend of mine, Joey Maldoon?" Lana asked.

"Yeah. The boy who made you cry," Clark said. His inner voice answered, "You mean the boy who made me feel like a failure as a father?"

Clark thought Joey seemed like a good kid. He had met him before, but he still grilled him with questions while they waited for his baby girl to make an entrance for her first official date. The nervous teen quivered on the couch and choked out answers to the questions Clark lifted from a website on questions to ask your daughter's date. The concerned father liked how the boy did not hesitate with his answer to the question: "Are you willing to watch out for my daughter's wellbeing tonight?"

"Absolutely sir. Not just tonight, but forever. We've gone to all the same schools. We are in the same youth group at church. You know, we've been good friends, really good friends for like forever, since like sixth grade. I can't ever imagine doing anything to hurt any of my friends, especially not Lana."

"That would be the one," Emily affirmed.

"It turns out that he didn't dump me. Well, not only me, anyway. You could say he ghosted me, but you can't ghost everybody. At least I don't think so. It turns out that I didn't see him anymore because he ran away," Lana said.

"Oh my, that's not good. And you are just finding out today?" Clark asked.

"Yeah."

"Do you know why?"

"Joey said he couldn't tell me everything about why he left just yet, but he wanted me to know ..."

"Excuse me," Clark interrupted. "Joey said what?"

"Yeah. He texted me this morning. I showed the texts to Emily. And the next thing you know, Joey is jumping into Emily's car after almost getting into a big ol' fight with some weird-looking dude out in front of the church."

"Umm. Slow down. You kind of buried the lede to the story."

By the time Clark reached for his fortune cookie, Lana and Emily had fully recounted the events of the day in that circuitous way that only non-guys can do. He felt informed but confused. That confusion was making it more difficult for him to figure out how to broach the topic he needed to talk to them about. He sought guidance from the cookie.

"Seek a wise friend or a tough decision may be your doom."

Clark burst into laughter. Not the gentle ha ha that's funny kind, but the all-consuming laughter that shakes through your body and makes it difficult to breathe.

"What does it say?" Emily asked.

He tried to read it aloud, but he could not push out any words. Lana snatched the fortune from his hand and read it aloud. She glanced at Emily, then both looked inquisitively at Clark.

"I don't get what's so funny," Lana said.

"Me neither," Emily echoed.

"You will."

Clark tried to shake off the giggles. He wiped his eyes and took a deep breath.

"I needed the silliness." He took a couple more deep breaths to fully regain his composure. "I needed to remember what it is like to enjoy moments like these before I tell you about my day."

"That's a rather ominous start," Emily said.

"That's because I have a rather ominous question. Are you okay with me taking on a story that has the potential to upset some very nasty people, people who've been behind a couple dozen murders over the last two decades?"

"Aren't most of the people you write stories about bad people?" Lana asked.

"Yes, but these people are more sinister than that. They've been very good about covering their tracks, even killing people to do that." Just saying those words out loud gave Clark the chills.

"What tracks are they covering up?" Emily asked.

"Not sure yet. Whatever it is, it's worth killing over."

"And you are asking us because?" Lana cut to the chase.

"Because it was just a few months ago that some wackos held us at gunpoint and threatened our lives." Clark could not believe he could just say that so calmly. It kind of scared him.

"You had no way of knowing that could happen." Emily reached out to reassure Clark.

"Yet it did. I can't predict the future, but if a routine story can turn into a made-for-TV movie, then I should think twice before I put you two at risk for a story where the bad guys may wear badges."

"Can somebody else do the story?" Lana asked.

"Possibly. To be honest, I'm not sure it would necessarily protect us. The story came to me, and that would make a loose end that these guys would want to take care of."

"Well, you're doing a good job of scary us," Emily said.

"I'm sorry."

"Nothing to be sorry about. You did nothing wrong, and we should feel scared. The truth is, though, you don't need us to answer your question. Whoever sent you the story already did. Might as well expose the bad guys. We are already at risk," Emily said.

"Does this mean we have to go into hiding?" Lana asked.

The question stunned Clark. He hadn't considered that possibility. The fact that Lana made such an observation impressed him as well.

"Don't think so, sweetheart. For now, I think we just need to be more vigilant. Be aware of your surroundings and anything that seems out of place."

"Like that court jester today?" Lana asked.

"I don't think he had anything to do with my case, but you get the idea."

"Do you have anybody you trust in the police department that you can talk to about this?" Emily asked.

"A couple of folks, but I'm not that far along in the story yet."

"Have we heard of these murders?" Lana asked.

"Probably not. Technically, all the people who committed the murders have been sent to jail. What I learned today suggests that someone else may be involved. How? I don't know. At this point, it just seems there are just too many coincidences between these murders from all across the Bay Area and an outlier in the foothill town where I worked before coming to San Francisco."

"An outlier?" Emily asked.

"Yes, it's the only one not in the Bay Area proper. It's also the first one, so that could mean it is case zero. Ironically, that case was my first big trial to report on. And it was a doozy of a case—Tory Avlah murdered a woman he picked up in a bar."

"Did you say Tory Avlah?" Lana asked.

"Yes, why?"

"I've seen that name before," Lana said.

"Not likely. That case was way before you were born."

"No, I've seen it recently. I think I saw it in Mom's old letters. I've been reading through them," Lana said.

"Why would your mom be writing about him? Can you go find those letters?"

"Okay."

Lana ran off to her room.

"I'll let you two figure that one out. I have papers to correct," Emily said.

"You have to go?" Clark asked.

"Yes. I should go," Emily said. She gave Clark a quick kiss, grabbed her purse, and yelled over her shoulder. "Tell Lana I'll see her tomorrow."

Emily was not being completely honest. As a teacher, she always had papers to correct. She had to leave before the letters came out and the conversation shifted to Lois. It was already a little weird that she was dating the widower of her best friend.

Chapter 24

COMING TO SCHOOL seemed like a letdown after yesterday's excitement. A midweek algebra quiz from Mr. Cobb or a lecture on the three laws of thermodynamics by Mr. Parsons did not tingle Lana in the same way as a high-speed getaway. Well, at as high a speed as one can get with Auntie Em behind the wheel.

Even more important, or at least that's what she wanted to believe, she had Joey back in her life. He had been her second-best friend after Maggie since sixth grade, and for a brief moment, she thought he could be her boyfriend. The romantic, optimistic side of Lana kept telling her that this should be a stupendously joyous occasion. The kind of happiness you scream about to the world at the top of your lungs. She did not want to scream. Maybe a little yahoo. Definitely more than a whisper. And the only reason she wanted to scream was to yell at him for being such a jerk. It made her insides confused. She still felt the bitterness of the heartache that she endured when Joey left abruptly, without any type of goodbye. Her stomach seemed to battle back with a fluttery feeling that made her feel excited, nauseated, and scared at the same time.

She tried to avoid overthinking this new emotional dilemma, but her mind would not cooperate. The little reel in her head kept replaying yesterday over again and again until she practically had the entire script memorized. Nothing said between the two of them told Lana that Joey wanted to pick up from where they had left off. Nothing said made her think he did not either.

Lana felt the buzz of her cellphone, triggering a spark of joy that suggested her romantic nature might win her internal battle. Like a kid in a candy store, she reached for her cellphone with the anticipation of getting the treat of hearing from Joey. She just knew it was going to be from him. It was not. Her body slumped like a child discovering the cookie jar corrupted with Brussel sprouts. Her phone told her the texter blocked their identity. That always concerns Lana, but not as much as the message itself.

"Tell Joey I'm watching you."

Lana spun around. She saw nothing but a sea of purple, yellow, black, and green polos ambling along toward their second-period class. Lana slowed down and looked across the campus more methodically for something out of place. Across the street, she spotted the anomaly. The strange little man from yesterday hung off a lamppost like a sail on a mast. He waved to Lana with his free hand. She wanted to panic and run away, but something her dad had said last night took over. Lana snapped a picture of the court jester.

As if on cue, he jumped high into the air and landed on the sidewalk, seamlessly going into a little jig that drew the attention of the crowd. He stopped, resting his right foot on his left knee, and reached under the right lapel of his garish jacket.

"He's got a gun!" screamed a chorus of students, plunging the campus into a blur of panicked teens running for shelter.

Lana wanted to join the fray, but her body resisted the fear pulsating through her veins. She stood her ground, facing the man. He smiled, tipped his head toward her gallant posture, and pulled out of his jacket a black wand that puffed into a colorful bouquet of silk flowers. The strange little man thrust the bouquet toward Lana several times. When she repeatedly rebuffed his suggestion to take the flowers, he stomped both feet and made an exaggerated frown. The little man then ran his left index finger down from the corner of his eye, mimicking a mime gesture for tears.

Lana took a second picture before a group of students walked between her and the show across the street. Blind normalcy had returned to the campus, evaporating the temporary panic as quickly as the suspected gun bloomed into the colors of the rainbow. When her view returned, Candle was gone. She stood there searching for signs of where he might have gone until a clamoring bell announced she was now late for second period.

"I guess I'm going to be even later to class," Lana thought as she forwarded the photo and the details of what had just happened to her dad.

Chapter 25

A LITTLE SHAME TOUCHED Clark as he carried a small pink box up to the reception desk for the city's Bureau of Investigations. He was playing into the stereotype, and everyone here knew he was a mule for one of the cops in the building. The newspaper reporter would have felt worse except the sweet treats got the job done.

"Good morning. I have an appointment with Detective Maddox," Clark told the officer behind the reception desk.

"You sharing?" She sniffed the air and pointed to the box.

"That's up to the good detective." Clark returned her smile.

"I'll let him know you are here."

Clark took a seat and tried to make some sense of last night's discovery in the old letters Lana was reading. He had never read them before; they seemed too personal and too painful for him to experience a second time. Aunt Ruth wrote a few times about an Uncle Tory in her weekly chronicles of life to Lois. Her first reference to him focused on his apparent disappearance, which had the aunt a little worried. She lamented about how Tory had more than his share of vices, even more than her dead husband, but he was still family.

"Your Uncle Tory's landlord reached out to me to see if I had seen him. This unpleasant man wanted me to pay Tory's back rent. I declined, which did not make him happy. I called Tory's neighbor, the one your uncle used instead of getting his own phone, and he shared some unpleasant details of his own that I won't bore you with. The bottom line is your uncle is missing, and nobody seems to have a clue why. I called the police, but they were of no help. I got the impression they were glad he was gone. Still, I pray Tory is okay and will turn up soon.

"This news about Tory got me thinking that I never really told you why I took my maiden name back after Victor died. It was not out of shame, although I know that was the claim about town after his drunkenness stole three lives that day. Despite his flaws, I loved him very much. I abandoned his name because he said the shadow of his business shouldn't burden me. I'm not sure what that means, but I did what he asked. I feel silly confessing that I never quite understood what he did, but that was just the way things were back then. Victor made it clear that I should never talk about his job. With the Air Force base nearby, I thought nothing about his job being very hush-hush."

A letter about three months later clinched for him that Aunt Ruth was talking about the same Tory Avlah that Clark had reported on so many years ago.

"I received news about your Uncle Tory today in a very unexpected way. A lawyer named Greg Vernier called to ask if I could be a character witness at his trial. Once again, the police think Tory killed a woman he met in a bar. Mr. Vernier changed his mind about my testifying after I explained a few things I knew about that other trumped-up murder charge. I don't know what to think. Trouble seems to follow Tory. Victor thought so, too. I overheard him grumble to someone on the phone once that he should never have let his brother get involved in his business."

"Clark." The gravelly sound of Detective Bobby Maddox's voice jarred him back to reality. "I see you brought me some tasty fruit like you promised."

"Nothing but healthy stuff for you." Clark played along, but the unapproving shake of the young officer's head said she was not buying the detective's little charade.

"Let's walk."

Maddox grabbed the box and strode half-way through the lobby before Clark could get up from the chair. Clark groaned silently and examined the feet of the man who towered over him. The detective's stride extended a full tile more than Clark's, making the reporter question whether he could walk and talk at the same time.

"So, why are you really looking into Delaney?" Maddox asked once both were out on Bryant Street.

"I told you. I'm working on a tip."

Maddox stopped and looked straight at Clark.

"Eighteen murders?"

"At least."

"There's more?"

"I've just started looking, and so far, eight more people are dead."

"Twenty-six murders? Connected? That's hard to believe unless you are suggesting we have another Manson-like character on our hands."

"I'm not jumping to conclusions, but think about it. It's not like they are giving predictable excuses, like the neighbor did it. We've got defendants claiming they were trying to rescue their murder victims. That seems a bit much for random probability to explain."

"Copycats?"

"Why would anybody copy a defense that hasn't worked?"

"Our jails aren't filled with the smart criminals."

Maddox resumed his walk down the street. Clark scurried to keep up with him.

"You know, I'm more afraid someone or something in law enforcement is pulling the strings," Clark confessed.

"If that's the case, how can you trust me with this information?"

"Whoever this guy is, is pretty smart and resourceful."

"So, you are saying that leaves me out?"

"Not just you, but any local jurisdiction."

"Why?"

"This is too widespread, across too many jurisdictions for it to be a local cop. My hunch is something federal. Maybe the CIA. It's not like they have a stellar record with their clandestine operations on the American people."

"Don't tell me you are one of those MK-Ultra conspiracy theorists?"

"You can't call it theory, if they fess up to it, or at least to some of what they were doing to control minds. Who could make up something that horrific?"

"So, you think there is more to the MK story?"

"There is always more to the story. Always."

"How much more?"

"No telling. Frank Olson. Sirhan Sirhan. Unabomber. Those names sound familiar?"

The buzz of Clark's cellphone spoke before Maddox could answer. He could see it was from his daughter.

"Do you mind? It's my daughter, and it's during school hours."

"No, go ahead."

Clark opened the text to see the picture of Candle hanging from the street post. A chill ran up his spine as he read the narrative Lana sent.

"OMG, thanks for letting me know. Please catch a ride home with Emily," he texted back.

The expression on Clark's face told the detective that he had not received good news.

"Is everything okay?" Maddox asked.

"No. And I'm going to need another favor."

Chapter 26

JOEY STEPPED UP into the living room and could see a bunch of ingredients stacked on the counter. His mom organized them for efficiency and minimum dish usage. Flour, almond meal, ground flax, cinnamon, and baking powder in one cluster. Bananas, vanilla, eggs, milk, avocado oil, and lemon juice in another. A third pile had chocolate chips and chopped walnuts. The goal of the efficiency expert: make her son's chocolate chip pancakes with the fewest number of dishes and utensils.

He loved her pancakes, and not just for their sweet, nutty, and spicy flavor. They reminded him of the great family moments they had shared. His brain could not hold on to the nostalgia. Questions about his parents pushed the sentimental aside, thanks to Candle's wild accusations. His mind wanted to know if his dad had really abandoned them, or was there something more to the story than his mom had shared? Was his family bigger than just the two of them? Candle pointed out somebody a few years older than Joey that had many of the same features. He kept saying that guy is probably your brother. Joey could not tell. The kid could have been somebody who just happened to look like Joey. Charlie promised to provide answers once he had done his little task.

"Good morning, sleepyhead."

Gloria smiled at the sight of her boy back in her home. Joey reciprocated with a full-body yawn.

"You making cheesy scrambled eggs, too?" he asked.

"Yep, just the way you like it—with a little salsa verde and cottage cheese whipped in and a handful of chopped black olives and shredded Italian blend cheese on top."

Joey slipped into a familiar routine. He opened the cabinet door, grabbed the breakfast dishes, and strolled over to the table. The teen nearly dropped the stoneware plates when he saw the brightly colored centerpiece on the table.

"What's that?"

A tremble reverberated through his voice. Gloria's mother instinct engaged, and she scurried to Joey's side.

"What's what, dear?"

"Where did those come from?"

He pointed to the flower arrangement filled with white, red, and blue cup-shaped anemones and purple hyacinths. Three black towers poked up through the arrangement. The tallest middle spire held a single yellow daffodil. The two outer ones held slightly used black candles, which seemed to drip red wax.

"You mean the flowers?" Gloria answered with a slight chuckle. "I don't know. The delivery boy said you would know who they were from."

"What did he look like?"

The question and the panic in Joey's voice caught Gloria off guard. She stood there looking at Joey, her face crumpled in confusion. She pulled the dish towel off her shoulder, its resting place when she cooked, and mindlessly started wringing it.

"What did he look like?"

Joey's panic intensified with tinges of anger as he repeated the question, pushing out each word slowly and deliberately.

"I don't know!" The words burst from her lips with more emotion than she expected. "Kind of short, white guy. You know, I was kind of distracted by that silly costume he had to wear."

"Costume?"

"Yeah. The poor kid had to wear this garish court jester outfit. The marketing ploy to make the florist memorable might have worked if they had had their name somewhere on his uniform, on the delivery truck or something. I didn't see anything."

"There was a delivery truck?"

"Umm, come to think about it, no. I didn't see one. That's odd."

Joey slipped down onto a dining room chair. Resting his elbows on his knees and his head in his hands, he took deep, loud breaths.

"Sweetie, what's the matter?"

Gloria kneeled in front of her son and gently lifted his chin so she could look him in the eyes. Her penetrating stare pulled tears down Joey's face.

"Tell me what's wrong."

She dabbed the towel on his wet cheeks. Her voice became even softer.

"Whatever it is, we can work it out together."

Joey shook his head back and forth.

"No! WE can't."

Chapter 27

VERNIER USUALLY RELISHED the day of opening arguments. Laying out a defense to the jury after weeks of preparing for trial invigorated him, much like a child who feels like they can run faster and jump higher when they get new sneakers. Today, he had no such illusions. He could not outrun the fact that his client, Mikhail Kuzmin, had murdered Teri Marcos in his apartment. That was not the real problem. He had been in that position many times before. His inability to jump to the high ground, to argue zealously a defense that most resembled the whole truth—that was the problem. A clear conscience for the defense attorney rested on a newspaper reporter's ability to expose in time a similar truth about the other murders.

Opposing counsel also dampened his enthusiasm. Vernier had volleyed legal arguments with Mark Waltrip before and did not relish battling the zeal of this legal pharisee again. Vernier could not figure out if the assistant district attorney had lost or never had a legitimate under-standing of his side of the legal covenant. Even his fellow district attor-neys could see how the letter of the law consumed Waltrip. They could also see how the actual spirit of the law eluded him, something he re-proved during the recent pre-trial hearings. Despite experiencing Mi-khail Kuzmin's mental issues first-hand, Waltrip mocked any requests for a plea deal. Instead of manslaughter and mandatory psychiatric treat-ment, he pushed for the maximum allowable charge of first-degree mur-der.

"Ladies and gentlemen of the jury," Vernier took to the courtroom stage and hid his doubts from the audience of twelve. "The prosecution would like you to believe this is a simple case. On the surface, it might seem that way. Then again, on the surface, a lie sounds like the truth."

Vernier paused for dramatic effect and to examine the reaction of the jury. He could see a few jurors struggling to suppress a smirk, which gave him a glimmer of hope.

"The prosecution would like you to believe this crime started on the night of April 14, but that would not be true. Months earlier, someone planted the roots of this crime, and Miss Marcos is its second victim. My client is the first victim of this crime. I know, I know that is an in-credibly bold statement, and I apologize if it sounded like I was dimin-ishing in any way the tragic death of Miss Marcos. Rest assured; I am not. The tragic consequences of Mr. Kuzmin's actions that night are not in dispute. But if you go below the surface, where the truth hides, you'll discover that the actual crime here is the one that stole the normal brain functions you and I enjoy. As you come to understand this crime, you will realize that the proper decision before you in this trial is: what was the intent behind my client's actions on that fateful night?

"I know we are asking a lot of you. We lawyers have the simple part. We are going to parade a lot of experts up here to convince you of this fact or that fact. In the end, it is you, the jury, who will have to decide if Mr. Kuzmin intended to kill Miss Marcos. I can tell you right now, the simple answer is no. Mikhail did not intend to harm Miss Marcos in any way that night. In fact, we will show that—in his altered state of mind—

Mikhail thought his actions were life-saving actions. He thought he was saving her. I know you are thinking right now; we have a conundrum before us. The district attorney has already made it clear he is going to show Miss Marcos died from injuries inflicted by my client. We will not dispute that fact. We will, however, show that despite the consequences of his actions—in Mikhail's altered mental state—he genuinely believed his actions could save her life. How can that be? I'm pretty sure your gut reaction to my statement is nobody in their right mind could think Mikhail's actions that night could save anybody. And you would be right. Nobody in their right mind would, but Mr. Kuzmin was not in his right mind.

"If I know opposing counsel, and I dare say I do, he will probably point out in dramatic fashion that my client does not show any signs of the mental defect necessary for this defense. He would be partially right, in so much as that the temporary insanity of that night was just that, temporary. However, he cannot deny what the responding officers saw. Mikhail's altered state of mind was so consuming that the police could not question him that night. In fact, they could not question him for several days. Something caused his mind to snap. Something caused his brain to stop functioning correctly. Something caused him to think right was wrong and wrong was right.

"As I said at the beginning of my remarks, this is not a simple case. You will hear complex testimony about the inner workings of the human brain. It will probably cause your own head to spin. I apologize in advance for that, but it is the only way to get below the surface where the truth hides. I am confident that by the time this trial is over, you will see that there were two victims that Friday night and that your only option that serves justice is to find Mikhail Kuzmin not guilty."

Vernier let his words linger in the air for a moment before turning his focus away from the jury and returning to his post at the defense table. He glanced toward the gallery and spotted Clark, who quickly motioned that he needed to talk to the defense attorney.

"Mr. Waltrip, you may present your first witness," directed the judge.

Vernier stopped mid-step and did an about-face.

"Your honor, the defense requests a brief recess."

Vernier hoped the judge would not ask for an explanation of his sudden request. He had to take a chance. Something told him—maybe it was his gut, or the way Clark signaled—that he needed to respond to Clark sooner rather than later.

"Very well. The court will take a 15-minute recess." The bang of the gavel echoed the judge's annoyance at the interruption in the trial's pace.

"Thank you, your honor."

Vernier turned around, ignored the confused body language of the assistant district attorney, and made his way out of the courtroom to a nearby conference room. Clark chased after him.

"I didn't mean right now," Clark said as he closed the door.

"I know, but I've been thinking about our conversation the other day. The one about your peculiar list of names." Vernier motioned for Clark to sit.

"Yes."

"I want to apologize for essentially giving you the brush-off."

"Okay, apology accepted. But you had to know that doing this meeting right now clearly upset the judge in there."

Vernier shrugged his shoulders, then leaned in toward Clark.

"This conversation needs to be off the record, at least for now."

"I think I can do that. We'll see if this conversation allows me."

Vernier laughed.

"I appreciate your commitment to a noncommittal answer. I'll accept your terms."

Vernier stuck out his hand toward Clark, signaling he wanted to cement their verbal agreement with a handshake. Clark accepted.

"I'm assuming you heard my opening remarks?" Vernier asked.

"Yeah."

"I wish I were as confident about the outcome of this trial as the guy in there sounded," the lawyer confessed.

"It was a little optimistic. I don't know how you are going to pull the proverbial rabbit out of your hat on this one."

"I'm not. You are."

"Yeah, right. The timing just doesn't align. This trial will last, what, a few days. That story on the peculiar list of names will easily take weeks just to gather all the information."

Vernier scrounged his face and stroked his anchor goatee, as if he needed to ponder his response. For added effect, he parted his lips as if he wanted to speak but stopped. When he felt he had played the role of a reticent attorney long enough, he continued.

"I can motion Mr. Waltrip in there six ways to Sunday and slow the pace of this trial. And my staff can help speed up your process."

"Why are you doing this?"

"To win my case, of course. As you pointed out yesterday, this story has the potential to change the outcome of this trial."

Clark did not buy that answer, but he still was not ready to tip his hand just yet on his near truths. He needed answers to his own questions.

"I'll accept, for now, your commitment to a vague reply that dodges why you are really doing this."

"You're funny, Mr. Solo, really hilarious. Stop by my office tomorrow morning. What did you need to talk to me about?"

"Your conversation with Tory Avlah's sister-in-law. You changed your mind about her testifying. Why? And something tells me it's going to sound familiar to what happened to Kuzmin."

Vernier slipped out of character and let his body language display the shock he felt at Clark's discovery and intuition. He wanted to ask how he knew about Ruth Avlah already, but he held back.

"That answer will take more time than the judge gave us. In short, both of them disappeared for a few months and suddenly popped back up. Friends and colleagues described them as different somehow but could not put their finger on what it was."

"That's interesting," Clark said. "Very interesting."

"Is that everything? I should get back in there."

"Yes. How much longer is this going to last today? I need to run up to Vacaville and see one of the peculiar names."

"Not long. Did you notice how my client seemed like he was coming down with something?"

Chapter 28

FROM THE MOMENT Gloria opened the door, Pastor Dan could tell tears had filled the morning. Her face, devoid of the usual décor that smoothed out imperfections, showed obvious signs that little sleep had come last night. Puffy, red eyes betrayed Joey's assertion that he was okay. The mood was no longer jubilant. An air of uncertainty hung in the air like the city's thick fog. The reality of reunification had sunk in.

None of that surprised him.

"The emotional turmoil you are feeling now is normal," Pastor Dan explained as he saddled up to the breakfast bar and the cup of coffee Gloria had poured for him. "That doesn't mean it is good, just painfully real. To be honest, if either of you was going around happy-go-lucky, I'd say you were lying—to each other, to yourselves."

"I get that," Gloria whispered. She pointed to her son, who was wearing earbuds and listening to his music in the recliner. "He doesn't."

"Why do you think that?"

"He got really upset when he saw the centerpiece on the table."

"I can't imagine flowers doing that. There must have been something on the card that upset him."

"Here's what's left of it. I didn't see any words on it."

Gloria pointed to the torn fragments of a smoky red card. Pastor Dan assembled the pieces to reveal the gold-leaf artwork. The card was slightly thicker than he expected, but his eyes were distracted by the plate of leftover pancakes Gloria was sliding in his direction.

"Something clearly happened while he was gone, but he will not talk about it. He won't let me in on his feelings, what happened or anything. I just know it was something awful," Gloria said.

Pastor Dan nodded in solemn agreement while reaching for a pancake. He rolled it slightly and took a bite.

"It is going to take a lot of patience on your part as he works, make that the both of you, work through this. There are a lot of unanswered questions. Why did he leave? What happened? Where was he? What caused him to return now? The only thing I know for sure is he didn't leave because of these chocolate chip pancakes. These are awesome."

"Thanks. That's my mother's recipe. She was not what you'd call a traditional mom, but she did like to cook. Almost all my comforting memories of her were in the kitchen."

A different sadness overcame Gloria. Pastor Dan noticed and placed his hand gently on hers.

"How long has it been?"

"Almost eighteen years now," she said as new tears welled up. "I still can't believe he took her from me."

"It is sometimes difficult to understand God's timing."

Gloria pulled back her hand and stared at the pastor.

"Oh, it wasn't God who took her. It was Tory Avlah. That evil man beat her to a pulp and then tried to claim he was trying to save her. Thank God the jury did not buy his lies."

That news surprised him.

"Did that happen up in the foothills?"

"Yeah. Why do you ask?"

"I think I know Tory."

"Part of some prison ministry?"

"Not the kind you are talking about. His prison was alcohol."

"Am I supposed to feel sorry for him? Did he tell you about his plans to dispose of her body? How he was going to cut her up into little pieces and put them in an old trunk?"

"Yes, he did. He told me lots of things when I visited him at the homeless camp. From what I can tell, Tory held back nothing. I can tell you there's more to that disturbing tale than you can ever imagine. I know this may be of little comfort to you, but he confessed his sins and repented for what he did to your mom."

"Well, good for his undeserving soul."

There was no charity in her voice. Gloria knew it, but she could not bring herself to act any other way. Forgiveness seemed just beyond her reach.

"Yes, it was," Pastor Dan agreed, opting not to react to her sarcasm. "Just like it is good for the rest of us. We are all undeserving souls in need of repentance."

Gloria turned and rinsed her coffee cup in the sink. She stood there quietly, resting her hands on the sink apron. Twice she stole glances at the pastor but said nothing. Finally, her words returned.

"I know I am supposed to love him as a brother in Christ, and don't get me wrong, I am glad he accepted grace, but I can't ever excuse what he did."

Pastor Dan smiled.

"The Bible only asks us to love our brother, not to like them. To forgive, not to excuse. He suffered from the consequences of his poor decisions. Only some of that suffering, though, came from the justice system of man."

Gloria shrugged. Over time, she had boxed up his memory and kept it tucked away. Every once in a while, generally at an inopportune time, the lid would pop open, and that emotional scar would rear its ugly head. He did this to her. Her punishment for his sins.

"There's an irony in our memories of Tory. To me, he will always be the selfless hero who saved my life and died trying to save my fiancée."

The roles of the comforter and the comforted changed. Gloria placed her hand on his.

"I'm so sorry for your loss. What did he do? Tory, that is."

"My fiancée volunteered at the same homeless shelter as I did. She said it kept her grounded, a there but for the grace of God kind of thing. She was a doctor, an OB/GYN, so she normally worked with pregnant teens. That Saturday, we were doing outreach to those who couldn't or wouldn't stay at the shelter. Rebecca carried a little black bag like old-time doctors used to do. She joked about making house calls to the homeless. Some addicts must have thought she carried narcotics in that bag. They got really upset when they found out it was nothing more than basic first-aid supplies. They attacked her as we walked through this one area that was hidden from the street view, near Tory's makeshift home. One of them pulled out a gun. Tory tried to calm him down and stood between the gun and Rebecca. The addict wasn't listening to reason and opened fire. Tory caught most of the bullets except the one that pierced her heart. When the gun was empty, they ran away."

"Oh my," was all that Gloria could muster.

"What am I doing?" Pastor Dan said, getting slightly flustered. "I am here to provide you comfort, not to unload my past woes on you."

"No. No. You did nothing wrong. In fact, it helped me put things into perspective. Thank you."

Then she nodded toward her son.

"What about him?"

"You know I can hear you if I'm only wearing one earbud," Joey interjected.

"Then why didn't you say something?"

"Because you taught me it is rude to interrupt."

Chapter 29

"I DO NOT KNOW what Vernier did, or if he did anything at all, but shortly after our meeting, Kuzmin started puking his guts out. The judge couldn't recess the trial fast enough," Clark told his editor as he sped along Interstate 80 out of the city.

"Guess I'll cancel my dinner reservations at the jail tonight," Bill Buckley joked.

"Weird things definitely seem to follow that man. You know, the more I dig into this story, the more confusion I seem to uncover about Vernier. He's wrapped up in all this way more than he is letting on. I know he thinks he is manipulating me. The weird part is I think he is trying really hard to ensure I know he is up to something."

"Why would he do that?"

"I don't know. Maybe he is using my reporter instincts against me." Clark paused for a second to mull over his own words.

"Actually, that's a pretty smart ploy," Clark continued. "He knows I'm going to zero in on the inconsistencies, and what better way to focus my attention than to make something seem out of place."

"That means there is something in this for Vernier. What do you think it is?" Bill asked.

"Depends on whether he is the author of the list."

"Why does that matter?"

"Is he exploiting an opportunity that my sharing of the list provided him? Or, and I'm leaning more in this direction, is he exploiting me to make an opportunity for himself?"

"If he is exploiting you, is it all about the current case?" Bill thought it was not likely but waited to hear Clark's perspective.

"Yes, it would definitely benefit this case, but I don't think that's his primary motivation. If it were just about this case, he could toss his conspiracy out there unchecked to muddy the waters. He wants to get something out in the public arena in a verifiable way without attaching his name to it."

"Don't suppose he is doing an end run around attorney-client privilege, do you?"

"That thought hadn't occurred to me. It would make sense. I'd also have to assume that he's smart enough not to set up a situation where he gets embarrassed."

"Sounds reasonable, but we both know smart people do stupid stuff. Don't be surprised if the facts do not bear out your assumption."

"I get that, boss, but something definitely surprised him when I asked him about his conversation with Lois's aunt."

"Such a personal connection to this story makes me worried." Bill's tone switched from analytical to compassionate. "I'm concerned about the dangers involved. You can unearth something you can't bury again."

Clark laughed.

"There is no way Aunt Ruth was mixed up in anything bad. She was just the sweetest lady."

"You also said nothing exciting ever happens out in the boonies. Besides, it's the uncle that sounds fishy."

"You got me there, boss."

"What do you hope to learn from Marcus Delaney?"

"I want to know if he disappeared for a while before his murder episode. If so, then what happened while he was gone? Aunt Ruth's letters suggest Avlah changed after his disappearance. Kuzmin disappeared, and his friends claimed he had changed, too. They just couldn't explain exactly what was different. I'm hoping Delaney will give me insight into what to ask in that interview."

Chapter 29

ONE OF THE CARDINAL RULES of law enforcement is to keep your work life as separate as possible from your personal life. This time, Detective Maddox could not. The lines blurred months ago when Gloria Maldoon reached out to her best friend after her only son disappeared. Bobby Maddox had already witnessed the tears she shared with his wife, Gayle. He kept tabs on the investigation, though it was a futile task given the division's resources and the grim fate of teenage runaways who had been missing for more than a few days.

Joey Maldoon's return would not normally be a police matter. However, it appears the wayward teen did not come home alone. The strange character that stalked Joey just before he left was now stalking Lana Solo, and that made it a police matter. Unfortunately, a detective strolling in and asking tough questions could push emotional buttons Maddox preferred to leave un-pushed. Hence, he brought Gayle along.

"If this goes wrong, it's all your fault," Bobby told his wife as he rang the doorbell. She replied to his boyish smile with a familiar scowl that often confused Maddox. He never knew when it was playful or serious.

"You keep telling yourself that," Gayle said.

The door opened, and Gloria did a little jig as she reached out to hug her friend.

"My Joey is back home!"

"I heard," Gayle squealed back.

Detective Maddox stood there quietly, feeling a little uncomfortable as he waited for the emotional exchange to end. When Gloria stepped back, she looked inquisitively at the man she knew did not have an inkling of how to play hooky. He had to be here on police business.

"Bobby, don't take this the wrong way, but why are you here?"

The detective laughed.

"That's not the first time I've received that reaction at somebody's door. I'm just being a chauffeur today and, if necessary, a sympathetic ear."

"The pastor just left, so we may be tapped out on sympathetic words, but please come on in. The coffee is still hot, and there are a few pancakes left."

"Chocolate chip pancakes?" Maddox's body perked up and his nose went into action.

"It doesn't matter, you can't have any," Gayle said. "You already had an apple fritter."

"I don't know what you are talking about."

"Who are you kidding? Your mustache tells all."

Maddox instinctively started brushing his hand across his thick lip carpet. Gloria placed her hand on his chest and started laughing.

"There's no point in trying to hide evidence now."

He turned toward Joey and stuck out both hands.

"Joey, help me out. It's two against one here."

"Uncle Bobby, you are on your own."

"Coward!"

Maddox cradled Joey's head. Lumbering away with the teen in tow, he leaned in tightly, like he was doing a wrestling move, and whispered.

"We need to talk about Candle, but not in front of your mother."

Joey's body stiffened, and his heart sank. He figured something was up. Uncle Bobby did not make social calls in the middle of the day. He was too busy trying to catch the bad guys, and now he wants to talk to him about one of them.

"Okay," Joey whispers back.

Maddox let go of his hold on Joey, and the teen stood up.

"Uncle Bobby, come check out this new game I found."

"Okay. Am I going to be able to keep up with the game?"

"Sure. It's not as slow as those ancient games from when you were a kid, but you'll get the hang of it ... eventually."

Gloria smiled as she watched the two of them bounce down the stairs.

* * *

"That was a crafty deception up there. Should I be concerned that you are getting good at it?" Maddox asked.

"It wasn't really a deception. I have a new game," Joey said, flashing his smartphone to his uncle.

"Ah. They say the best lie starts with the truth."

Maddox stood there for a moment, staring at Joey. He thought of the boy as more than the child of his wife's best friend. He had been there for all the birthdays, science fair projects, and the season Joey rode the bench in soccer. Maddox considered him the son he never had and thought the feeling was mutual.

"How do you know about Candle?" Joey interrupted the silence from his perch at the end of the bed.

"A friend of mine called to say your weirdo spooked his daughter this morning."

"Lana?"

The detective could hear the fear in his voice. He nodded yes.

"What did Mr. Solo say happened? She is all right, isn't she?"

"Lana is fine. The weird guy just spooked her," Maddox said calmly.

"Good. I'm glad she is okay."

"Something happened yesterday, too? A little tiff between you and this Candle guy?"

"Nothing I can't handle."

The answer concerned the detective, and he let his facial expression give away his reaction. He patiently waited. The experienced detective knew that imposed silence screamed louder than any words, especially if the person being questioned could still hear their conscience talking. Joey squirmed. He felt the detective's eyes peering directly into his soul.

"Lana is safe. Candle won't hurt her. He is just trying to get at me because I came back home. He thinks I'm his, and that's just not so," Joey purged. Maddox could tell this conversation revealed more than Joey wanted anybody to know.

"I don't mean *his* in a prison sort of way, just that he is kind of possessive about his friends."

"So, you are friends?" Detective Maddox asked.

"Well, he thinks so."

"So, you are not friends?"

"Not best buds or anything."

Maddox grabbed the desk chair and placed it in front of Joey. He sat as low as he could and leaned in close.

"You know I want to believe you, right?"

The gentle tone made Joey feel like his Uncle Bobby was talking, not the detective. Without taking his eyes off the floor, Joey nodded yes.

"You also know I can tell when you are not telling me the truth."

Joey continued staring at the floor but did not respond.

"Okay. I guess I'll just have to talk to Candle directly."

"No!"

Joey jumped to his feet, nearly tipping Maddox off the chair.

"That's a bad idea. A really bad idea."

"Why? You said Lana is safe."

"He doesn't like cops."

"So? I don't take that kind of thing personally anymore."

"I mean, he *really* does not like cops." Joey stretched out his words for dramatic effect.

"Umm, Joey. You are sending mixed messages here. Is Lana safe or not? If he has the possessive issues you're describing, you have to realize that he will not stop at just Lana. Your mom is at risk. Pastor Dan and Aunt Gayle are too. Anybody you have come in contact with since you've been back could be the one that sets him off."

"There's just nothing you can do, Uncle Bobby. This is my problem, and I have to solve it by myself."

"Yes, it was your problem, but it's not *just* your problem anymore. Lana and your mom are mixed up in this, too. And no, you don't have to solve this by yourself. I'm here; let me help you."

"No, it's not as bad as you might think. I know what I have to do to take care of Candle."

"That doesn't sound good at all."

A scream from the top of the stairs startled both of them.

"Bobby! Come quick. The man from the flower shop is standing on your truck," yelled Gloria.

Chapter 31

DESPITE DOZENS OF JAILHOUSE interviews, Clark never quite got used to seeing someone in chains. Their presence raised the hair on the back of his neck. He could feel his anxiety rise as his body shifted into a primitive fight-or-flight mode. He could tell himself that prison protocols would have even delivered Mother Teresa in chains. That bit of intellectual nuance did little to calm his fears. His only choice was to push through it.

"Thank you, Mr. Delaney, for agreeing to see me today," Clark said from his side of the cold steel table.

"You were in luck. There was an unexpected opening in my busy social calendar," Delaney said, as the guard locked the chains to the prisoner's side of the table and to the floor.

Delaney did not look at Clark. His eye and head movements suggested something circling behind the reporter. Clark struggled to comply with staff instructions to ignore this behavior. Failure to do so, they claimed, would set Delaney into a delusional tailspin. This seemed hard to believe, but Clark did not want to test the validity of their advice.

"Did they explain why I wanted to see you?" Clark asked. His tentative voice echoed the uneasiness he felt.

"They just said you were a newspaper reporter."

"That's right. I'm looking into a few old cases where defendants like yourself claimed they were trying to *save* the people they were convicted of murdering," Clark said, emphasizing save with air quotes.

"You make it sound like I was lying."

Delaney stopped moving. He kept his focus on something imaginary above Clark.

"That was not my intention." Clark knew better than to apologize and pushed some hidden strength into his voice.

"They said you would do that. They said you wouldn't believe me."

Delaney returned to swaying his body in apparent rhythm to the invisible creature flying behind Clark.

"Who said I wouldn't believe you?"

"You know."

"The guards?"

"No. You know who I am talking about. The same people who sent you here to get inside my head."

Clark played his best poker face. He raised an eyebrow and tilted his head slightly to show his confusion over Delaney's statement. Beneath that projected illusion, Clark held back his desire to bang on the table and demand that the guard get him away from this nut job.

"Mr. Delaney, I don't know what you are talking about. I just wanted to hear from you what happened on the night you killed Molly Milton."

"I didn't murder that woman. I just followed their instructions."

"Whose instructions?"

"The same people who sent you here."

Clark took a deep breath. He felt like a straight man in an old vaudeville routine. Saying third base would probably make the guard laugh, but Clark did not know how Delaney would react.

"My editor is old school. I must attribute everything in my articles to somebody. So, can you tell me about the people who you think sent me? Then I can quote you and make my boss happy."

"Everything?" Delaney paused his swaying as he tried to process the concept.

"Yes, everything. If the sky is blue, he wants to know the people in the story saw the blue sky."

"But ... it is your story?" Confusion still marred his face.

"I am only the scribe. It is their story. So, can you tell me your story?"

"Who am I? You sure you wanna know?"

"Yes. I want to know about that night and what led up to that night." Delaney smiled.

"The moon did not shine. It was too dark, not bright. So, we sat in the house all that hot, hot, dry night. I sat there with Molly. We sat there; we did. And I said, how could I be bold if she forbids?"

Clark stifled a groan. He recognized the cadence and rhyming rhythm of the classic children's story he had read to Lana a hundred times before. This annoying response, too clever for a disturbed man, pinged his something-doesn't-make-sense meter.

"You are a fake," Clark interrupted. He hadn't really thought the idea through before the words burst from his lips.

Delaney stopped speaking, sat rigid in his chair, and looked directly at Clark.

"The last man who said that to me was Archie Leach."

"Archie Leach?"

"Yes, he's as real as you and me."

"So existential of you. Just answer my questions with no theatrics, please."

"I'm confused," Delaney said, then he leaned forward as much as his chains would allow. "Don't you know that this world is but a stage, and we are mere actors?"

"I don't buy that," Clark bristled at the notion and allowed himself to react to the comment. "For us to be mere actors, then you have to accept the implication that there must be a director out there calling the shots. I don't. I don't see any evidence of that, and the level of stupid out there says, if there is a director, he is not a good one."

"Now who is being existential? You need to think smaller to figure out who the big kahuna is."

"That sounds interesting, but what does that mean?"

"You're the reporter. Find out."

"That's why I'm here talking to you."

Delaney did not answer. He returned to his swaying motion, moving in rhythm with the motion of the invisible object flying behind Clark.

"Are you saying somebody told you to murder Molly Milton?"

No response.

"Did you disappear a few months before the murder?"

No response.

"Who is this *they* you keep talking about?"

No response. Clark's frustration exploded.

"Don't you get it! If I can prove that somebody else pulled the strings, it will improve your chances of getting out of this hellhole."

Based on Delaney's movements, the object behind Clark seemed to fly in a more erratic pattern. Instinctively, he turned around to look. As foretold, Delaney started banging on the table and chanting repeatedly.

"The doctor do not mind. He just makes candles, you see. Knock, knock on my door. See the mister, see me."

Chapter 32

ALICIA FELT GUILTY as she stepped out of the jailhouse as a free woman. She did not quite understand how her release date got abruptly pushed up, but she was grateful for the plea deal her lawyer finagled. Her guilt was not over her crimes, but over whom she had called first. It was not Justin; that call would come later. She turned to the man she relied on for counsel during her too long, but technically brief, stay at the county jail. As she emerged onto the corner of 7th and Bryant streets, she could feel the warm midday sun. She stood there for a few moments to soak it in. Then, a gentle cool breeze and the roar of interstate traffic nearby reminded her she was still in San Francisco.

"Annie."

She recognized the voice and turned toward it.

"Pastor Dan, I told you that Annie doesn't exist anymore. Please call me Alicia."

He bowed his head and slumped his shoulders to express his penance. His self-deprecating posture made her laugh. She was not sure if it was the goofy pastor that made her laugh, or that he was standing in front of a massive twisted abstract tube sculpture that conjured up mental images of a giant colon on stilts.

"Apology accepted," she finally offered.

Pastor Dan perked back up and joined her on the sidewalk. Alicia pulled out her phone and squeezed in tight beside her counselor. She wanted something to commemorate her new freedom.

"Well, Miss Alicia, where do you want to go?"

"If it's okay with you, I'd be happy just walking around. I really missed this being outside thing."

"That's perfectly fine with me."

He motioned for her to lead the way down Bryant Street. They walked silently until the Hall of Justice sculpture no longer towered over them.

"How do you feel?" he probed.

"To be out of jail? Awesome," she said. "To be back in the real world? I'm not so sure how I feel."

"If you had said anything else, I'd be figuring out a way to tell you that you are lying."

"You sure about that? I'm pretty good at that lying thing. Sometimes, I'm so convincing, even I can't tell for sure when I'm lying."

"In another time, I would have said that sounds like bragging. Now, I'm more inclined to think that shames you."

"More like scares me."

Alicia had never really given it much thought before. She would not have even labeled what she did as lying. It was just what you needed to do if you wanted to gain and maintain the advantage.

"To be honest, no pun intended, it scares me how comfortable I am with deception. Operating only in the truth arena, well, it's not as easy as you Pollyannas make it out to be."

"You'll get used to it. It's like a forgotten muscle that needs constantly worked to build its strength."

"How would you know? It's not like you are the type of person who struggles with telling the truth."

Pastor Dan laughed.

"Not now, my friend, but that has not always been the case. Thank God, but telling the truth is just part of who I am now. Every once in a while, though, I discover that the lying muscle never loses its strength. Those rare occasions scare me, too. A lie can slip out without my even thinking about it. In my line of work, they call that our sin nature."

Alicia stopped and stared at the pastor. He smiled.

"Oops. I did it again," he said.

"Umm, you sure did, Britney. And we both know it wasn't an accident, either."

"What you talkin' about, Willis?"

"You know way too much pop culture to be a man of the cloth."

"You can still be in the world without being of the world."

Alicia started walking again.

"Maybe some other time you can enlighten me as to what that means. Right now, I need your advice on what to do with Justin."

"Okay."

"Am I nuts for wanting a do-over, to start this relationship over from the beginning as if we never met?"

"Nuts? No. Unrealistic? Maybe. It depends on how demanding you are about ignoring the past the two of you already have."

"I'm not like wanting those memories to be totally erased. A lot of good stuff happened. I just want a do-over on the whole commitment for life part. Now that he knows who I really am, or hopefully, who I really was, does he love me for who I am now?"

"Who is that?"

"Who am I now? Other than I want to stay Alicia, I'm not sure."

"Then how can he know who he loves?"

Alicia smacked her counselor on the shoulder.

"And that's my problem in a nutshell. So, am I the nut?"

"Not completely."

Alicia turned her head to see Pastor Dan's smile.

"Over the last few weeks, you have shared a lot. You've been brutally honest about your past. So, let me be brutally honest about your future. If you truly want this to be a new relationship, then you need to keep it out of the bedroom. That arena will only ferment old habits and make it difficult for either of you to make an honest assessment of your feelings."

"You can't be serious?"

"Yes, ma'am, very serious. You can't send mixed signals and expect him to understand. You are asking him to reassess his commitment to you. At the same time, you want him to join you on this journey with no clear end destination in mind. That's a lot to ask of Justin, but I think he might be willing to try. If you include the bedroom, though, you are telling him nothing has really changed."

"For how long? Are you saying not until we get married?"

"That would be the least confusing answer. You need to wait until you both are clear about where the destination is and when you expect to arrive."

"What does that mean?"

"I realize that sounds like a bunch of pop psychology mumbo jumbo, but it doesn't have to be. You know, I could just tell you what the destination should be, but I'm not sure you are ready for that revelation."

"No, padre, I'm not."

"Then I'll save it until later. I believe that makes your debt up to what, seventy-seven sermonettes, is it?"

Alicia laughed. She appreciated his bluntness about his faith, and his willingness to let her hear about it at her pace.

"What if I never pay my debt?" she asked playfully.

"Then you'll have an eternity of regret," he responded seriously.

"Wow! That's kind of harsh."

"Welcome to the world of truth. We can't ignore some truths just because they do not feel like flowers and bunnies."

"I thought you were peddling for a god of love."

"I am. I just understand that God's love is bigger than most people want to give him credit. People want to ignore that justice and wrath are part of love. They'll readily accept it in their own actions but deny God the same virtues."

"I'm not sure I like this god of yours."

"Why? Just because his love of justice requires that he dole out consequences for injustice?"

"Every little mistake has to be punished, no matter how minor?"

"To be perfectly just, yes, a payment for absolutely every sin must be paid. However, God also has a plan where he puts all that debt you rack up on himself."

"Now you are really talking mumbo jumbo. Nobody would do that?"

"What do you mean? It's not such a foreign concept. Who paid your debt so you could avoid the consequences of your crimes?"

"Nobody, I guess. They just didn't have enough evidence to guarantee a conviction at trial, so they went for a sure thing—a plea deal."

"Are you sure about that?"

"Yeah, unless you know something I don't know."

Alicia's voice appeared more confident than her reality. The question had been plaguing her. Why did the district attorney suddenly shift gears and offer her a sweetheart plea deal?

"No, I'm not in the know," Pastor Dan confessed.

"You know, they made me give up my stash of money."

"You've mentioned that a few times. Did that cover the entire debt?"

"No. Not even close."

"So, somebody, say the district attorney, paid your debt for you."

"Maybe, but I think that's a stretch."

"Not as much as you would like to think."

Alicia pondered for a bit. She was not sure how the good pastor did it. Once again, he walked her down this path where her old sense of right and wrong faltered. She tried to steer him away, but he managed to crash her back into the same wall.

"You know, all this religious stuff doesn't help me know what to do with Justin."

"Technically, it is the gospel, not religion, but I digress. I think there is a link. You can't find truth without coming to terms with the truth maker. If you want to have an honest relationship with Justin, then you must be honest in all aspects of your life."

"Are you saying I can't be happy with Justin without your god?"

"You say that as if you are the one who determines if God exists."

"Don't I?"

"Your choice to believe or not has no more bearing on God's existence than your choice to believe in the existence of gravity."

"You are doing it again."

"Doing what? I'm just following your lead."

"My lead?"

"Yes. You keep bringing up questions about God."

"No, I don't!" When the ring of her emphatic tone quieted, she placed her hand on his forearm.

"Really? Do I?"

"Yes, you do. It is normal when you embark on a truth quest."

"I'm not on a truth quest. I'm just looking for answers."

Pastor Dan snorted.

"Are you really looking for answers? Aren't you really hoping for familiar lies to your questions?"

"Well, no. That would be stupid."

"See, you just found another nugget of truth."

Alicia took a deep breath in exasperation.

"What about Justin?"

"I guess you'll just have to talk to him."

Pastor Dan pointed to something over her shoulder. Alicia turned to see the nameplate on the building—Justin's building.

Chapter 33

DETECTIVE MADDOX COULD NOT BELIEVE his eyes when he landed on the stoop of the Maldoon house. A strange little man, clad in brightly colored theatrical garb, stood in the bed of his truck. He was not hiding. He clearly wanted to be noticed—waving his arms and jumping around like an orangutan at the zoo.

"Sir, this is Detective Maddox from the San Francisco Police Department," he said, displaying his badge as he walked methodically toward the truck. "I don't know why you are in that truck, but I need you to stop and slowly place your hands on the side of the truck."

Candle stopped his commotion, curved his right arm up, and placed his fingertips on the top of his felt cap. He cocked his head to the left. His chin pushed forward. The right eyebrow raised in mime fashion, trying to convey his confusion over the detective's actions. Maddox ignored his shenanigans. He continued walking forward. He pushed his sports coat back so the little man could see he was ready to draw his weapon.

"Don't look at me like you don't know what's going on. I said, get your hands on the side of the truck."

Candle did not move from his pose.

"Why are you in my truck?"

Silence. Candle shifted his stare toward the house.

"What do you want?"

No change in pose. Candle continued to stare toward the house.

"Joey?" Detective Maddox called out.

"Yes, Uncle Bobby."

Joey stood in the doorway. He could not understand what was happening. This was not part of the plan that Charlie drilled into him.

"I'm assuming this is your friend, Candle."

"He is Candle."

The answer sent a familiar vibe through the detective. It did not sit well with him, but he hid its effects. He maintained his stern demeanor—an I'm-in-charge-of-this-messed-up-situation façade that gives law enforcement an upper hand despite their natural fears.

"I can arrest him for harassment, but that means you'll have to file a complaint. Is that what you want me to do?"

Before Joey could respond, a crackly voice emerged from Candle. "Tell tale tit! Your tongue shall be slit. And all the dogs in the town shall have a little bit."

He repeated the chant three times, adding more volume and drama each time, then stopped. His gaze fixed on the teen. He slowly lifted the index finger of his left hand to his lips.

"Don't pay any attention to this character. He is just trying to mess with you," Detective Maddox hollered.

Despite the warning, Joey panicked. He understood the threat tucked inside the nursery rhyme about tattletales. The whispered rumors about Charlie and his minions rampaged through his head. He could not let them come true again. He had to stop Candle.

"Let him go!"

"You can't let him scare you. I can protect you," pleaded the uncle side of Bobby Maddox.

"Just let him go. Please Uncle Bobby, just let him go."

The detective shook his head.

"I can't. You are not his only victim."

Detective Maddox took another step forward and barked at Candle.

"I told you to put your hands on the side of the truck!"

Candle twisted his body to the left, building momentum with each rotation until he spun like a top. With his hand still placed on his hat, he continued to spin faster and faster.

"Look out!" Joey hollered. He knew what was about to happen.

Candle yanked off his hat, and an orange fog sprayed. Maddox rushed the truck. A few more rotations of this strange little man and the fog thickened. Detective Maddox could no longer see his suspect. He systematically swatted his way through to the bed of the truck, but to no avail. Candle had disappeared.

Detective Maddox jumped out of the truck and ran up the sidewalk, hoping to clear the fog. Five strides later, his surroundings returned. He scanned the area, but there was no sign of Candle. He marched back to the Maldoon home.

"Why did you warn him?" he barked at Joey.

"I didn't warn him."

"Well, kid, that does not bode well for you either."

Chapter 34

DOCTOR AMBROSE CALLAHAN LOOKED in the rearview mirror of his boxy sedan and saw a chiseled black SUV roll up to a stop behind his parking spot. The doctor huffed when he looked around and did not see anyone blocking its path. A colleague had already made him late, and he was not in the mood for another lecture from his wife about how he had once again put his job ahead of her. He tapped the horn.

"Come on, let's get moving," he begged the vehicle impatiently.

The SUV did not move, so he hit the horn again. This time with a little more gusto.

"If you don't move, you're going to have dinner with my wife," he hollered.

The doctor jumped at the sudden sound of something tapping against the passenger window. His heart skipped a beat. He recognized the man standing there. He took a deep breath and lowered the glass.

"I'd love to share a meal with your wife," Charlie said.

"Stay away from her!"

"But you offered? Or was that a threat?"

"Charlie, don't play your games with me."

"As long as you don't play games with me."

Charlie reached inside and opened the passenger door. The doctor could feel his body push itself into full panic mode. He tried to mask it, but he could not keep the beads of sweat from forming on his brow.

"I don't know. I don't know what you're talking about. I'm not playing games with you."

Despite his best efforts, Callahan knew the sound of his words lacked sincerity. Worse yet, he could tell Charlie thought so as well. He responded in an equally insincere tone.

"That's good to hear, good doctor. Then you will have no problem explaining why your little mission is not performing as requested."

The doctor's nervousness turned to anger. Charlie had trodden on something sacrosanct.

"You know, this isn't factory work. We are dealing with people. I can't just tweak some widget to make it work."

"Oh, I understand, but you've been so productive in the past."

"Past results do not guarantee future outcomes. You know, just like my stockbroker says." Callahan's voice wavered. His boldness disappeared with a nervous laugh.

"You seem uncomfortable, Doctor."

"As you know, I am running late, and that makes my wife unhappy. You know, a happy wife makes a happy life."

Charlie shook his head.

"Dear doctor, it's not an unhappy wife that you need to worry about."

Callahan pushed back.

"This isn't what I signed on for!"

Charlie laughed.

"Sure, doc. If you believe that, I've got a bridge to sell you."

"There was a time, Charlie, much longer than I care to admit, when you seemed genuinely interested in helping people."

"Yes, I'm people, ain't I?"

Callahan just stared at Charlie, trying to squelch feelings of guilt. His tyrant was right. He should have known that do-gooders could not afford the money they threw at him. They got what they wanted: a solution to the MK-Ultra failures. He got what he wanted: money and prestige, even if the project's secrecy meant he was an accolade crowd of one.

The solution was not that complicated. The CIA had previously taken a heavy-handed approach. He likened the use of LSD to using a sledge-hammer when a feather would suffice. Stimulants chemically alter the brain and make it malleable to the power of suggestion. The results, however, were too unpredictable and unproductive. After the last couple of decades working for Charlie, he found a way to get more reliable results. His approach built on the brain's natural desire to reconcile information. You only had to expose people to enough counter-messaging until they accepted your message as truth. You did not have to go all mad scientist on people. They would expose themselves willingly if you wrapped the message up in videos, music, and games.

"I still want out," Callahan said finally.

Chapter 35

THROUGH THE GLASS WALLS of his office, Justin could see Alicia. She hadn't made it past his overzealous guardian yet, and Justin watched to see if he needed to rescue his fiancée. His heart sank. That was not the correct label anymore. Girlfriend? Prospective dating partner? He did not know what to call her. His secretary did. The matron of the office had already made it known to Justin a few choice names for his companion.

"Alicia?" Justin asked from his office door, opting to avoid the escalation of any office drama.

"Surprise!" Alicia made awkward hand gestures to punctuate her exclamation.

Justin returned the awkwardness with a silent stare. He did not know whether to believe his eyes. He did not know whether to believe the answer to his question.

"Well, I am. I'm surprised," Justin finally sputtered out something. "Why didn't you call me so I could pick you up?"

"And ruin the opportunity to see the surprised look on dear Mrs. Pluckette's face?"

The secretary stifled a manufactured yawn.

"Objective achieved," Justin said, frowning slightly with his piercing green eyes. He knew his disapproval would have no effect on her motherly advice.

"Are you able to get away? Lunch?" Alicia asked.

Justin looked toward Mrs. Pluckette. She returned his inquisitive stare without commenting until Justin upped their silent conversation with puppy-dog eyes. Alicia laughed.

"You do not need my permission. If you want to go do whatever, fine. You're the boss. I can reshuffle your calendar. It's what I seem to do around here," Mrs. Pluckette relented.

Justin shared a glance with Alicia and smiled.

"Only if it is no bother," Justin teased.

"Too late for that," Mrs. Pluckette said.

Justin motioned for Alicia to follow him into his office.

"Let's leave Mom to her work," he said.

"I told you not to call me that," Mrs. Pluckette said.

"Yes, Mom. I recall you saying that," Justin said as the newly reunited couple strolled into his office. He tapped the panel just inside the office door, and the glass walls turned opaque.

"That's a cool new trick," Alicia said. "The color. Is that jade?"

"Mrs. Pluckette picked the color. The windows go totally black."

"Why the change?"

"Your father."

Alicia pushed an awkward smile to her face and took a seat on the ornate sofa that her old self had manipulated Justin into buying. Justin stood where Frankie Zimmerman's antics set into motion a made-for-TV set of events that resulted in Justin being on trial for murder and, ultimately, landing her in jail.

"Well, you won't have to worry about him now," Alicia said.

She knew that obscuring the view into the office would have changed nothing about that day, but Alicia understood why he did it. She exposed Justin's vulnerabilities, too.

"I wouldn't count him out just yet," Justin said.

Justin did not want to hold back from sharing the truth. He wanted her to know how her father had manipulated federal prosecutors. He even wanted her to know that he might not have really been the horrible man she had always thought he was. But he knew it was not about what he wanted. His former mentor was right. It was safer for Alicia if she did not know.

"Oh. You know something I don't?"

"And if I did?"

"Then I would want you to tell me. Going forward, I want our lives together to be based on honesty."

"Then I honestly do not know what I'm talking about," Justin played off his doubts about his choice. "And to be honest, I haven't found you a place to live just yet. We can check out some places after lunch. Maybe something near your new art studio gig? Or are you wanting to be closer to the campus for classes?"

Chapter 36

EMILY WELCOMED the distraction of being on the annual street festival committee. Lana seemed less thrilled to tag along, but she did not want to be alone with that Candle character running around. Emily's job was to coordinate a handful of stages so drama and music students from the Academy could entertain audiences. Her friend, Pastor Dan, had the more difficult role. He co-chaired the committee responsible for corralling a dozen or so churches and community groups that funded the popular community event happening this weekend.

"Our caricature artist from last year is suddenly unavailable. Does anybody know someone who can fill in?" asked a woman at the far end of the table.

Pastor Dan smiled.

"Believe it or not, I was just talking to someone who became available this morning. I'll check to see if she will donate her time."

"Will that mean we can afford something better than stages made from several tables tied together with plywood on top?" Emily asked.

"You would think so, but you would be wrong," Pastor Dan replied, regretting the slightly dismissive tone of his words. "Besides, once the crew wraps them up in bunting, they will look great as usual."

"They wobbled last year. These poor kids are intimidated enough just to get up on stage in the first place, so we don't need anything else to unnerve them."

Emily held her ground.

"We can fix that with a few extra supports underneath. May cost an extra hundred bucks or so," a voice from across the room chimed in.

"Sounds like a suitable compromise," Pastor Dan offered.

"Fine, I guess. I'll just have to review the lineup to ensure there are no more than three people on the stage at a time," Emily relented.

"On to music. Are we set with musicians?" Pastor Dan asked.

Before anyone could answer, the doors to the small conference room opened. A flustered Gayle Maddox entered.

"I'm sorry I'm late, but it has been one of those days. Beyond anything you could imagine. It will take a busload of prayers to fix this day," Gayle lamented as she found a seat beside Emily.

"Glad you could make it, Gayle. We'll talk about your prayer needs after the meeting."

Gayle nodded in agreement.

"Back to the music?" Pastor Dan asked.

* * *

"So, what happened?" Emily asked Gayle as soon as the committee meeting ended.

"It was the strangest thing ever. Bobby and I were over at the Maldoons. You know Gloria, right?"

Emily nodded yes.

"We were checking in on them now that Joey has come back home."

"Thank God he's home safe," Emily said.

"That's the point. I'm not so sure he is home safely."

"What do you mean?"

"Somebody is stalking that poor boy, and he seems to want Joey to know it. He was all dressed up in a weird costume and dancing in the back of Bobby's pickup."

"Weird costume? Like one of those court jesters that run around at the festival?" Lana inserted into the conversation.

"Yes. How did you know that?" Gayle asked.

"Sounds like the same guy who roughed up Joey outside of the church yesterday, and he showed up outside my school this morning," Lana said.

"Joey mentioned that guy yesterday. He called him Candle, said he had stalked him before he left. Something Candle told Joey caused him to leave, but Joey wouldn't tell us anything about him," Emily said.

"I'll let Bobby know. I don't think Joey shared that with him."

A wave of emotions surged through Gayle as the reality of today's events overwhelmed her. She began to cry. Emily wrapped her arms around her, and tears welled up in her eyes as well.

"Gloria is beside herself. She seemed so happy to get Joey back. Then, she nearly lost it, had a panic attack or something, when she heard that court jester chanting. It was horrible. Something about tongues being slit and feeding them to dogs."

"Did he say tell tale tit, your tongue shall be slit, and all the dogs in the town shall have a little bit?" Pastor Dan asked.

"Yeah, I think that was it," Gayle confirmed. She looked at the pastor with a puzzled expression, conveying what everyone else was thinking about his knowledge of these disturbing words.

"As the literature teacher in the room, I'm impressed. Well, maybe more like a little scared that you knew that obscure rhyme," Emily said.

"I wouldn't be. I'm not even sure I know where I learned that little piece of trivia, but if I recall correctly, it is about tattletelling," Pastor Dan said.

"Yes, and it's not in support of it," Emily said.

"What does Joey know that he is not supposed to tattle?" Lana asked.

"Maybe Joey could have told us, but that guy probably scared him out of doing that," Pastor Dan consoled the group.

"Maybe, but something doesn't sound right," Emily said.

"What doesn't sound right?" Gayle asked.

"His running away. I was one of his teachers. Nobody said anything about why he just stopped coming to school. Nobody asked if I had an inkling that he might run. Not school officials, not the police. I didn't even know anything about it until yesterday," Emily said.

"Me neither," Lana said. "You would think the police would have at least asked a few questions of his closest friends."

"But the police investigated his disappearance and found no leads that could help them find Joey. Bobby has been keeping in touch with the lead detective in that investigation," Gayle rebutted.

"I'm pretty sure I know why they didn't find any leads," Lana complained.

"Be kind, Lana. We don't know what they did," Emily chided the frustrated teen.

"I know what they didn't do," Lana replied.

"I don't want to alarm anyone or pile on more gossip, but something else seems off. It just seems too unlikely that one family would have so many odd happenstances on the same day. It could be we are just a lot smaller world than we want to think. I don't know; it just feels too coincidental."

"Providence?" Emily sounded more serious than joking.

"Always. Even when someone manufactures coincidences."

"Okay. Not sure what you're talking about, Pastor, but don't leave us hanging," Gayle said.

"When I was there this morning, apparently before the clown escapade, I discovered Gloria's mother had been murdered," Pastor Dan explained.

"I knew that. It was tragic," Gayle said.

"The odd part was I knew the man who had killed her but never connected the dots to Gloria before. Other than the sharing of all the names, obviously, he was exceptionally forthcoming in confessing his past sins, including a lot of unnecessary gruesome details about that murder. Here's the weird part. He told me an odd character stalked him as well."

"Okay. Now you are scaring me," Emily said.

"Me, too," Gayle echoed.

"What about Joey?" Lana asked.

"Bobby took him into custody," Gayle said flatly.

"Why?" The forcefulness of Lana's voice startled everyone. Emily gently patted Lana's hand.

"I'm sorry. Why did they arrest Joey?" Lana asked.

"Oh sweetie, he's not arrested. Bobby took him downtown because he was not talking. Bobby thinks Joey knows a lot more than he's sharing. He's hoping the interrogation room might scare him into cooperation."

"This is just so terrible," Emily said. "Is Gloria with Joey?"

"Yes. I told Bobby he needed to bring someone in to talk to Joey. He is different now. I don't know what it is, but he's not the same sweet boy I knew a few months ago." Raw emotion still laced her voice.

"The fact Joey is acting differently is not a surprise," Pastor Dan said. "I would be more concerned if he didn't seem changed. But I think you are right. The police may not be the right people to get Joey to open up."

"What do we do?" Lana asked.

"To start with, let's pray," Pastor Dan said.

Chapter 37

A POLICE INTERROGATION ROOM is supposed to evoke a fear of potential consequences. Something hidden in the minimalist décor screams the commandment that thou shall not bear false witness. Most occupants of this room would not know this as the ninth commandment, just that it is somewhere on God's list of taboos. Mostly, they fear retribution from an earthly being now than any eternal consequence down the road. Detective Maddox never expected them not to lie. He understood that people have secrets that need to stay hidden. Rather, he tried to convince them that now was a good time to disclose enough truth for the detective to solve a crime. After forty-five minutes, the room was not working.

Joey was the exception. He knew the ninth and the fifth commandments—honor thy mother and father. The problem was, he could not fully obey both at the same time. If he told his Uncle Bobby everything he knew about Candle, he would have to expose an ugly truth about his mother. A truth he ran away to keep hidden. A truth that is forcing his hand to perform his little mission for Charlie. So, Joey remained silent. He ignored the badgering from the police detective and let his mind wander back to his ethics class in high school. He, like most of the students, pushed back against his teacher's wild claim that there is no such thing as a gray area in moral debates—all issues are black and white.

"A moral statement is either true, or it is not. It cannot be both," the teacher claimed.

A handful of students argued that would mean soldiers are murderers. Others argued that telling the whole truth could do more harm than good. Most expressed that what might be okay for one person might not be the right choice for another. The teacher did not budge. He held his ground.

"Let's put this idea to the test," the teacher said. He pivoted, took three steps to the right, and pivoted back to the class. "Should you murder another human being?"

Most responded no. A few said it might depend on the circumstances. The teacher then pivoted, took six paces to the left, and turned back toward the class.

"Should you have control over your body?" he asked a second and seemingly unrelated question.

This time, all the students said yes. The teacher pivoted one more time, returning to his position in the middle.

"What if the control over your body takes the life of another human being?" came a third question.

"See, that's what we are talking about. You can't answer that question without knowing the circumstances, and that's what makes it gray," one student boldly blurted out.

The teacher shook his head no.

"No, it's not gray. What we are talking about is the conflict between two value statements you believe to be true. In this scenario, these value statements are also group norms. Yes, it would be desirable to have more information. It would help us understand the circumstances better and might even affect our actions. But does our choice of actions change the truthfulness of either statement? Do our circumstances change whether murder is wrong, or our belief about the sanctity of our personal autonomy?"

A silent response.

"Or does our understanding of the circumstances force us to prioritize one value statement over another? Some would argue that control over your body takes precedence; others argue that the sanctity of the unborn child takes precedence. By now, I'm sure you all recognize this particular conundrum as the debate over abortion. What you may not grasp is that neither side seems willing to acknowledge that they are both choosing one value statement over another. Yet, each side has no problem disparaging the other side for not owning the consequences of their respective choice."

Joey understood the consequences. He had to protect his mother.

Chapter 38

LANA COULDN'T WAIT for her father to arrive. She paced around her aunt's small apartment on the third floor of a converted Victorian home instead of focusing on her homework as instructed. Auntie Em channeled her anxious energy into searching the internet.

"I can't believe this. There is no way Joey is mixed up in something like this," Lana ranted as she walked.

"And what do you suppose something like this is?" Emily countered.

She entered a dozen search phrases, like stalkers causing people to murder, but none of them had turned up anything useful. All the articles linked the stalker to the murder. None described the stalker as only the catalyst. She kept scrolling.

"You heard what Pastor Dan said, and I told you what Mom's Aunt Ruth said in those letters. It's definitely a freaky coincidence. I'll give you that. Really, what are the odds? Some uncle of mine commits a gruesome murder because of some weird stalker. And it just so happens that he killed Joey's grandmother. What am I supposed to take from that? We know Joey is getting stalked. Is he going to kill somebody? That freakazoid showed up at my school. Is he going to stalk me now, too? Does that mean I'm going to murder somebody?"

Lana worked herself into a tizzy. Emily did not play into her drama. She continued to plug away in her internet searches.

"Sounds like you have a lot of questions, but no answers," Emily said. Lana noticed her distracted tone.

"Thanks for stating the obvious. What are you looking for?"

"Answers."

"Answers to what?"

"Your questions."

"Did you find anything?"

"Yes and no, mostly no. There is one article here that may explain part of the mystery. Doctors think that these things called mirror neurons affect our ability to manage our cognitive control of situations. If you expose someone to enough negative influence, they will start acting based on that negative influence."

"That makes sense. Mom wouldn't let me watch certain TV shows because she didn't want me to pick up the character's bad habits unintentionally."

"Yeah, that's the basic premise. Just kick that up a few notches, put it on steroids, and you can have a murderer on your hands."

"Are they saying somebody can do it on purpose? That somebody could push Joey until he snaps and commits murder."

"Sort of. They kind of imply these people are victims of this negative influence, but the article does not want to come out and say it. Guess they don't want to give people an excuse to kill."

"Didn't Dad say Uncle Tory and those other murderers claimed they were trying to save their victims?"

"Yes, that's consistent with what this article is saying. If you bombard somebody with false information long enough, they will think wrong is right and right is wrong."

"That's weird stuff, but didn't we just read something like that in Bible study last week?"

"We most certainly did. Isaiah warned about it. So did Jesus, saying people will hide in the dark and call it light."

The doorbell rang. The two looked at each other and laughed.

"That must be your dad. He seems to have a knack for showing up in the middle of conversations like this."

Lana bounced across the room to let him in.

"Don't just open it. Check first," Emily warned.

Lana peeked and could see a distorted view of her father.

"You will not believe what happened today!" Lana exclaimed as she opened the door.

"Neither are you," said Detective Maddox and Pastor Dan in unison. They were standing off to the side—outside of Lana's peephole view. Pastor Dan held a couple of large pizza boxes out in front of him. Gayle Maddox peaked out from behind her husband.

Chapter 39

"I SEE YOU all got my texts," Emily said as the entourage strolled into the apartment. "Thanks, Gayle, for convincing your hubby to join us tonight."

Gayle nodded graciously and placed her hand on Detective Maddox's arm.

"I only had to tell this guy we were trading his normal salad for pizza tonight."

Lana stood with hands firmly on her hips and protested. "I thought you said you were scouring the internet?"

"No, I said I was searching for answers."

"But you implied."

"Grammar police," Detective Maddox punctuated his interruption with a siren sound. "Don't you mean you inferred?"

"Huh?" Lana tossed a dumbfounded look at the detective.

"Unless you can read minds, you can only infer what someone is saying. No matter how hard a speaker tries to imply a meaning, the listener can only infer a meaning based on their interpretation of the speaker's information. Having a shared language helps, but it is not a guarantee," Maddox explained.

"Kudos on the lesson. Maybe you should come teach the communication model to my students," Emily said.

"No thanks. I'm not brave enough to be a high school teacher these days," Maddox said.

"Don't let him confuse you, sweetie," Clark said. "He makes it his business to confuse people all the time, especially suspects."

"Don't make me look so nefarious, Clark. I never tell them anything that is not technically true. It is not my fault if they think I said something more advantageous to them than I really did," Maddox feigned innocence.

"Should we be concerned that you solve crimes by banking on linguistic confusion?" Pastor Dan joined the fray.

"Sadly, we generally don't catch the smart ones," Maddox said.

"And that's why we are all gathered here tonight," Emily said.

"But first, let's eat," Lana said as she grabbed the boxes of pizza.

After the first round of slices, Emily stood to explain the ground rules for the little gathering she had initiated.

"As you know, we are here to talk about what has happened over the last couple of days. I know you all have a variety of confidences that you must keep. Please keep them, but consider the bigger picture as well. There is a teenage boy caught up in something that is not likely going to end well."

"What do you mean, not end well?" asked Gayle.

"The best way to answer that question is to get all our bits and pieces of information on the table. Separately, they make little sense to any of us. Maybe together they will gel into something useful. Something we can do to help Joey."

Emily looked around the kitchen table to see somber faces nodding in agreement. Lana, who was sitting on the kitchen counter, piped in.

"I'll go first. There is a weird-looking dude dressed in a court jester costume who is stalking Joey."

"Not just Joey, but people connected to Joey, too," Maddox interjected.

"Joey called him Candle. He said Candle stalked him before, which caused Joey to run away in the first place?" Emily added.

"Why?" Lana asked.

"Why is Candle stalking him, or why did Joey run away?" Maddox asked.

"Both," Lana said.

"Well, Joey's not talking. So, you've tossed out the unanswerable $64,000 question."

After two hours of questioning Joey, the frustrated detective had to let the teenager go home with his mother. His gut told him that was not the safest thing to do, but the law did not give him a better option. The best he could do was to stop by patrol and ask them to keep tabs on the Maldoon home.

"There's an answer that dates you," Clark teased.

"Still before my time. I must have picked up the expression from my old man," Maddox rebuffed.

Lana looked at Emily and pleaded with her eyes for an explanation.

"Sweetie, they are talking about a popular game show from the 1950s that was kind of like *Who Wants to Be a Millionaire?*"

"Oh. I like that show," Lana said.

"I guess the stalking is my connection to this little tale," Pastor Dan said.

"Are you confessing something?" Detective Maddox prodded as he reached for his third slice.

"Bada boom," Pastor Dan said as he played air drums. "No. I am talking about the man who killed Joey's grandmother. I knew him, and he told me that someone had been stalking him in the days prior to the murder. He never said what the stalker did, but he only spoke of him with bitter words."

"Dad, that man was Mom's Uncle Tory," Lana said.

"Oh!" Clark's eyes got all big. "I was not expecting that little tidbit of information."

"When Pastor Dan told us that this afternoon, I knew we had to get together," Emily said.

"Then, I guess it's my turn to share," Clark said. "I received an email a few days ago with a list of old murder cases. Tory Avlah is on that list. The anonymous tipster says these murders are connected because they all used the same defense strategy. They all claimed they were trying to save the victim. While it is an interesting observation, it does not really mean anything unless there are more connections. They are not in the same town. The victim profile is all over the map. Yet, it captured my curiosity enough for me to dig into it more. I'm starting to think there is a second connection. It looks like each killer disappeared for a few months before the murder. When they returned, they were different somehow, but their friends can't quite figure out why."

"Joey is different, that's for sure," Gayle said. "And there's the problem with the police investigating Joey's disappearance."

"You mean, not investigating," Lana said.

"That has me concerned, too," Detective Maddox said. "I couldn't believe it when Gayle told me about this. I don't like this. I'm stuck with only two options. Either a fellow detective is doing shoddy work, or he outright lied to me."

"There's a third option. Maybe somebody made the detective lie to you," Clark said.

"You can't just make that big of a leap without some actual facts," Detective Maddox said. "Well, you reporters might, Clark, but the rest of us have to deal with facts and this cumbersome thing called the truth."

"Wow, you are on a roll tonight." Pastor Dan said.

"You mean jelly roll, right?" Emily said, prompting a round of groans. "Too much?"

Gayle patted the detective's belly, which covered up most of his belt when he sat down.

"More like too many," she said.

Laughter once again filled the room.

"I don't know if this is relevant, or just weird," Clark said. "I spoke with Marcus Delaney today, another name on the infamous list I received. This guy knows how to work the system. He has them convinced he is crazy, but I'm not so sure. He talks in riddles, so I'm not sure what this means."

"With that setup, you must share," Pastor Dan said.

"The doctor do not mind. He just makes candles, you see. Knock, knock on my door. See the mister, see me," Clark repeated Delaney's parting chant.

"Weird? Yes. Connected? I don't see it," Maddox said.

"Candles?" Clark weakly offered.

"That is what Joey said they called the court jester dude," Lana said.

"It was more than what he said, but how he said it. The guy was hot and cold. One moment very highbrow. The next primal," Clark explained.

"A Dr. Jekyll, Mr. Hyde kind of thing?" Emily asked.

"Exactly."

"You think somebody gave Joey some special serum that will turn him into an awful character?" Gayle asked. Worry and confusion infused her response.

"Are you saying Joey could be a killer?" Emily added to her question.

"Given the right circumstances, any of us could take someone's life," Clark said.

"That would be sheer speculation at this point," Maddox said as he placed a hand on his wife's arm to comfort her.

Clark pondered how Vernier would spin that idea into one of his patented wacky defenses. He did not share his musing with the group. The attorney's involvement was not something Clark could disclose just yet.

"By chance, Detective, does the name Archie Leach mean anything to you?" Clark asked.

"No. Why do you ask?"

"Delaney mentioned his name when I confronted him about faking his mental instability."

Emily laughed.

"That may be another old-school reference. Archie Leach is Cary Grant's real name."

"That's right. We sell a print at our street festival with a quote from him. I think it goes something like, I pretended to be somebody I wanted to be until finally I became that person or he became me."

"Archie Leach is also the name of the main character in the TV show *Leverage*. That guy leads a double life, too," Lana said.

"I guess that means Mr. Delaney was trying to give me some clues, but it is not helping. I still don't know what he is talking about," Clark said.

"You just need to find a doctor who makes candles that are like Dr. Jekyll and Mr. Hyde. How hard can that be?"

The sarcasm from Emily's observation hung in the room like a wet blanket, leaving each person to chase their inward thoughts about all that they had shared. Lana broke the silence.

"Detective Maddox?"

"Yes, ma'am."

"How do you make it so the inferred interpretation matches up with the implied meaning?"

"The answer to that $64,000 question, my dear, is called good old-fashioned detective work."

Chapter 40

"GOOD EVENING, Mr. Delaney."

The salutation came from a sixty-something man dressed in trendy business attire that seemed inconsistent with his age. The upscale look did not hide his identity. Marcus Delaney recognized him as soon as the guard guided him into the room.

"Guard. I do not want to see this man," Delaney said.

He tried to plant his feet so the guard could not take him any closer to Charlie. The guard ignored his attempt to retreat and pushed him forward.

"I'm sorry to hear that you aren't happy to see me," Charlie said.

The guard snickered. He could tell the visitor was playing with the inmate.

"Guard! Whatever he has told you about himself is a lie. He is not who he says he is. Take me back to my cell, please. Please!"

The guard continued to brush off the pleas as he secured Delaney to the table and the floor rings.

"Is there anything else you need, Director?" the guard asked.

"No, Officer, thank you. This will be fine," Charlie said as he pulled the chair out on his side of the table. The guard turned toward the exit, but Charlie paused him before he could take a step.

"Officer, there is something. Can you ensure no one disturbs us?"

"Understood, sir."

"Guard!" Delaney yelled. "I demand to be taken back to my cell."

"You are in no position to make demands, Mr. Delaney."

Delaney stared at his visitor. The smile on Charlie's face added to the creepiness of the encounter. Unlike earlier in the day when he toyed with Clark with his helter-skelter persona, he sat motionless. At least on the outside. His racing heart felt like it could drive right out of his chest. He tried to slow his breathing, but it was not working.

"You seem uncomfortable, my friend. I hope it isn't me making you uncomfortable."

Delaney remained silent.

"I see. You are the strong, silent type."

Delaney lifted his left eyebrow a smidge but refrained from uttering the screams trapped inside his head.

"That's good. I like the silent type. I hope you were that way when the newspaper reporter visited today."

Silence.

"I heard through the grapevine you were chatty today. They said you recited one of your silly little poems. Is that true?"

Charlie got up, walked around the table, and stood behind Delaney. The inmate bristled when he could feel the director's breath on the back of his neck.

"It is true, isn't it?"

Delaney kept looking straight ahead. His breathing became faster, and beads of sweat formed on his brow.

"I'm afraid you made a poor decision today, and that makes me feel sad, really sad. Do you want me to be sad, Mr. Delaney? Do you?"

Despite a desire not to respond, not to give in to the manipulations, Delaney shook his head back and forth.

"I didn't think so."

Delaney closed his eyes.

"I think you are a hero. A man of action who will do what it takes to save a person's life. Are you ready to save a life?"

Delaney forced himself to take a deep breath.

"You want to be that hero. You want to make me proud of you, don't you, Mr. Delaney?" Charlie punctuated his question by adding more volume to his otherwise calm voice.

Delaney took another deep breath.

"I know you are going to do the right thing. You are going to be a hero."

Charlie rapped on the door to get the guard's attention. As the door opened, Delaney began swaying and chanting.

"My life did not shine. It was too stark, not right. So, I sat in my cell all that time, lost in sight. I sat there with folly. I sat there; I did. And I said, when can I be dead if God forbids?"

Charlie chuckled at the rhyme and turned to face Delaney. He did not understand what the doctor did or how it worked to collapse the spirit, but Charlie could see that the good doctor really did a number on this man. There was no relighting this candle.

"I do not forbid," Charlie said as he walked out the door.

Chapter 41

WAITING IN THE SOLITUDE of commuter traffic, Greg Vernier let his mind wander to when this recent chain of events began. Experience taught him that genuine coincidences are like miracles. They don't happen as often as people would like to believe. Maybe it was because people misuse words. They say miraculous when they really mean unexplainable. Yet if they follow the breadcrumbs back far enough, most of the time they will find someone who put into motion the circumstances leading to the apparent coincidence. Bumping into Doctor Ambrose Callahan was no accident.

A woman facing driving under the influence charges came into his office about two months ago. A junior associate usually handled this type of case, but the defendant's unusual sobriety claims elevated the matter to his attention. Police had pulled her over on claims of a faulty taillight, but the stop quickly escalated to possible drunk driving. She knew she had not been drinking and thought the officer was out of line, so she declined the field test. Her resistance caved when they arrested her. She took a blood test to prove her innocence. The petite woman's blood alcohol content came back at 2.7, more than three times the legal limit.

"That's just not possible," Teri Marcos adamantly asserted during her conversation with Vernier. "I kept telling the officers I had had nothing to drink. They wouldn't listen."

"Had you been around anybody who had been drinking? Did you smell of alcohol? Possibly somebody spilled some on you?" Vernier asked.

"In that crowded club, you're always getting bumped by somebody."

"If they could smell alcohol on you, then the police had probable cause. Is it possible somebody switched drinks on you?"

"Doubt it. I can't walk a straight line after just a couple of sips of wine. I googled how much I would have to drink to have that much alcohol in my system. Couldn't happen. If I drank even half that amount, I'd be passed out somewhere in a coma."

"We could get an expert witness to testify to your intolerance, but that kind of defense is going to be expensive."

"The doctor who performed the test said you might say that. He told me to tell you he could prove I hadn't been drinking."

"That's odd. You say a doctor did the blood test?"

"Yes."

"Are you sure it wasn't a male nurse?"

"No, he said his name was Doctor Callahan."

"Which hospital?"

"Mercy."

"And this doctor said to tell your lawyer that he could prove you hadn't been drinking?"

"Yes, and no. He didn't say to tell my lawyer. He said to tell *you*. He said to talk to you specifically. He slipped me this card."

Vernier examined the business card. It was his. Scrawled on the back was the name Callahan and a telephone number.

"Did he say why he didn't just go to the police?" he asked.

"I asked him that. He said talking to you would be better."

The indirect communication with the doctor bothered Vernier. He clearly had something to hide from the police. Why else would he send a patient to a lawyer instead of just telling the police what he knows? Vernier needed more information. He tried culling intel on the doctor from a friend in the records section of the hospital.

"Patty, I've sent you a records request for a Teri Marcos," he lobbed the obligatory opening remark.

"No problem. When I get the paperwork, I'll track it down and send it right over," Patty said. She knew this was not his only request if the criminal defense lawyer was tracking down records personally. "Is there something else you need?"

"Why do you ask?" He feigned innocence.

"Do you really want me to answer that question?"

"Guess not," he said with a laugh.

"Then what is it?"

"Can you give me some intel on her doctor that night, a Doctor Callahan?"

"Let me see," she said. "Doctor Ambrose Callahan, nickname Brody. That's an interesting pairing. It looks like he's an ER doc with another specialty in psychosomatic medicine. We don't seem to use him much. He works a few nights a month as a fill-in doc."

"Part-time? Does his file give a day job?"

"That is probably more than I can tell."

"Come on. This isn't about the hospital in any way."

"Well, in that case, let me give you his social security account number, too." Her voice dripped with sarcasm.

"That doesn't sound like my sweet Patty."

"Speaking of which. Sounds like I'm going to be eating one of those decadent desserts with my dinner at the Mark real soon."

"I'm sure you are. Where else does he work?"

"It doesn't say."

"Aren't you sly?"

"Learned from the best."

"Well, can you tell me if he's a good doctor?"

"Nothing in the file suggests otherwise."

"Thanks, my dear. Enjoy your dessert."

A couple of days later, Vernier met Callahan at a trendy diner in the financial district. The doctor's disheveled appearance surprised him. Not that he had a preset image in mind, but Callahan's graying red hair, stocky build and frumpy plaid suit conveyed a shyster, not a doctor.

"Doctor Callahan, please tell me how you can prove my client had not been drinking that night?" Vernier asked after the waiter took their order.

The doctor started to respond, then pulled back. Vernier seemed perplexed that the doctor did not respond directly.

"Sir, didn't you tell Ms. Marcos that you could prove she had not been drinking?" Vernier rephrased his question.

"Before I answer your question, can you answer one of mine first?"

"Okay."

"Is it true that anything I say as a witness you are obligated to share with the prosecution?"

"The correct legal answer is it depends. More importantly, why wouldn't I want to share information that exonerates my client?"

"And I would have to testify in court?"

"Possibly, if they don't drop the charges."

The doctor reached into the breast pocket of his jacket and pulled out a silver money clip. He thumbed through it, peeled off a ten-dollar bill, and slapped it on the table.

"If you take this, it makes you my lawyer, and everything we say is now protected by attorney-client privilege, right?"

The doctor slid the money until it rested in front of the criminal defense attorney.

"You have the mechanics right, but my fee is a lot more than that."

Vernier studied this man sitting before him. This is not the typical behavior of witnesses unless they are afraid that something they say will upset a less-than-legal scheme or expose a relationship they preferred to keep hidden. Yet, this man directed Marcos to him with specific instructions. He wanted to tell him something.

"Before I go any further, I have to know if accepting you as a client creates a conflict of interest with my existing client."

The doctor shrugged.

"That's not for me to say. What I know I can only tell my lawyer, but it will prove she didn't have alcohol in her system."

"I don't doubt that. My concern is that I'll know she is innocent but will have no way of proving it without violating privilege with you."

"You will be free to use the information I share, but you cannot let anyone know I gave you the information."

"Will I be able to corroborate the information?"

"Probably, if you are astute enough."

Vernier reached across the table and picked up the money.

"Now spill your guts," Vernier directed.

The doctor smiled.

"It's quite simple, you know. It never happened."

"It never happened? Why didn't I think of that? I don't know how I could have missed that defense strategy in all my career. And I am supposed to believe I'm imagining all this?"

Vernier slapped his hand on the client folder sitting in front of him.

"Oh, she was arrested, and some blood was tested, but the crime never happened," Doctor Callahan explained. "I manipulated the situation so I could talk to you without anyone getting suspicious."

"And she is in on your little scheme?"

"In a manner of speaking."

"What does that mean? She either knows she is involved, or she doesn't."

"Precisely."

"You are not making any sense."

"Not true. You've figured it out already, but don't want to accept it."

"She doesn't know she is involved?"

"Correct."

"The police officer?"

"Just doing his job."

Vernier rubbed his fingers across his face. The doctor's revelation confused him.

"Let's go a bit further down what I'm afraid is a rabbit hole. You said you manipulated the situation to avoid anyone getting suspicious. Suspicious about what?"

"My confession."

Chapter 42

THE NERVOUS CHATTER from Gloria as she drove home from the police station made Joey feel even more sullen. He wanted to tell her the truth about Candle, the whole story about why he ran away. That was not an option. The irony of the situation smacked Joey in the face. Trying to hide the truth, probably under the guise of protecting somebody, set all this chaos in motion.

"Joey," Gloria said as they rounded the corner to their street. The conversation switched to a more serious tone. "I need you to tell me the truth about what's going on. Don't hold anything back. I'm sure you have some chivalrous notion that your silence is protecting somebody, but it is misguided."

Joey sighed before setting his eyes on the woman who raised him. He did not let her see him flinch at any slap of irony.

"We all keep secrets. Don't we?" he said.

Gloria did not respond to what seemed like teenage drama.

"Most people fib on their taxes too, but that doesn't make it the right thing to do."

"Wouldn't know anything about that."

"I guess you wouldn't. Just the same, you are lying to me, to Uncle Bobby and your friend."

"I never lied."

"Oh, the words coming out of your mouth may be technically true, yet you deceive us with the words you hold back. I believe Pastor Dan would tell you that's a sin of omission."

"I can't control what other people think."

"Then stop trying to. Tell the whole truth and let the chips fall where they may."

Joey could not handle it anymore. He let his emotions burst into words.

"Do you have any idea how hypocritical you sound?"

Gloria looked at Joey. She could not believe what her child had said. She wanted to scold him for being rude, but he seemed too sincere.

"What do you mean?" she asked.

"You are chastising me for omitting details. Details that change the truth into a lie. Or, maybe in your case, a lie into the truth because you have told the lie for so long you don't recognize the lie anymore."

Now he had crossed the line, and it was her turn to react. Anger boiled up inside her until it almost spat from her mouth. She swallowed and replied more calmly than she thought she could.

"I do not know what you are talking about."

"That's not what my brother said."

"Brother?"

Gloria blurted out the question as she slammed on the brakes. Turning toward her son, she repeated her question in a softer tone.

"Brother?"

"Yes, you heard it right. I know about my brother. I know my dad didn't leave because he got you pregnant. He left because he thought you had gotten pregnant. You didn't tell him the truth either."

"That's no way to talk to your mother!" she scolded.

"Mother? You are the master of irony. You raised me, but you did not birth me."

"Where are you getting all this nonsense from?"

"Can ...," Joey caught himself. He had let his pity party go on too long. He almost violated Charlie's first rule: We do not reveal what happens here to the outside.

"Can what?"

"Nothing."

Joey retreated into his hoodie shell. Gloria pushed on the gas. The two rode the rest of the way home muzzled by the revelation. As the garage door noisily lumbered its way open, she turned toward Joey.

"You know I don't accept nothing as an answer."

"Yes, I do."

"Then, where did you get the idea that I'm not your birth mother?"

Joey peeked out of his shell. He recognized the look on his mother's face. The teen could have continued to argue, but it would not have changed the outcome. Resistance was futile.

"Candle. Candle was the one who told me about my brother. He threatened to expose your little secret, saying the police would take you away and put you in prison unless I went with him."

"And you believed him?"

"Not at first, but he showed me proof. I had to do something. I couldn't let them take you away."

"You ran away to keep me from going to prison?"

"Yes."

"I did nothing that could send me to prison."

"Are you my mother?"

"Absolutely."

"Did you give birth to me?"

"Is that really all that important?"

"I'll take that as a no."

"I'm your mother, Joey. It does not take DNA to make me your mother."

"No, it doesn't. The truth is, I've always thought you were the best mom ever. Still do."

"Thank you, sweetie. I couldn't have asked for a better son."

"That does not change the fact that you lied to me."

"Nor that you are lying to me."

A text notification banner lit up Joey's cellphone resting on his leg. He did not recognize the number, but he knew it was Charlie reaching out from a new burner phone.

"Your brother sends his love."

Joey grabbed the phone, hoping his mother's eagle eyes did not see the text. He shifted in his seat so that he could respond privately.

"You promised."

"Have you broken your promise?" Charlie replied.

"No."

Gloria noticed Joey had left their heated conversation for a silent one.

"Who's that?"

"Nobody."

"Uhm. Weren't we just talking about your lack of truth problem?"

"Okay. Nobody I can tell you about."

"While you may think so, it is still not true."

"Oh, it's true whether or not you want to believe it."

Gloria pulled into the garage, lowered the door and opened the floodgates. Tears streamed down her face as an ache pounded in her chest.

"I can't help you if you don't let me," she said through the sobs.

"You can't, Mom. You are just going to have to trust that I'm doing the right thing."

She pulled a tissue from her purse and wiped tears from her cheeks. Joey felt perplexed. His emotions were in a quandary. He wanted to reach out and comfort his mother. He needed to see Charlie's response. He chose blood.

"I haven't either," Charlie texted. "Not yet. Understand?"

The second line conveyed an impatience with the delayed response.

"Yes," Joey texted back.

"Good. Now, bring your mom inside."

Chapter 43

SITTING ALONE in her hotel room, Alicia let her doubts surface. Not just about Justin, about everything. She was not sure she really could be the new person she envisioned. Could she really hack it in the real world as a poor art student working at a local gallery? This new persona could not just disappear whenever she lost control of a situation.

Yet she persisted.

Yet she resisted.

In some ways, her afternoon with Justin rekindled their romance. They laughed over silly things and made plans for future weekend getaways. She forgot how the simple act of holding hands or touching somebody's arm when talking could feel so exhilarating. It was the Justin she longed to be with.

In other ways, it exposed some of their innermost fears. Gloria forgot how easily she could be swept away by the allure of luxurious living.

Her meager salary at the art studio would not afford her the first apartment Justin showed her. She struggled to be content with her new incarnation.

"I can't afford to live here," Alicia told Justin as she stepped out onto the balcony. "Not with that view of the Bay."

"The landlord said he could make it affordable for you."

Justin's smile told her the truth. He owned the building.

"I know what you are doing, and thank you for trying, but I need to learn how to live on my own."

"You would be. I will still keep my place."

"Really? Truly on my own? Do you really think I'm on my own if you are paying most of my rent?"

Her questions hurt Justin. They assaulted the vulnerable side of his manhood. Being truly on her own meant she did not want him anymore. At least, that's how those words felt. He would normally have swallowed those feelings, but she wanted nothing but honesty going forward in their relationship now. He gave her what she wanted.

"I'm confused. You seem okay for your newfound father of the year to get you a job and pay for art school."

"I get it. It doesn't make sense, but that's different."

"Only conveniently different. Sounds more like you are telling me you don't need me anymore?"

"No, don't go putting words into my mouth. Being on my own is about me, not you."

"It doesn't feel that way to me."

"Probably not, which is why I could do what I did for so long."

"Huh?"

"Are you going to make me say it?"

"I'm not making you do anything. That makes no sense."

"Fine. I exploited men, men like you who needed to feel needed."

"So, it's the man's fault that you conned them?"

"No. I said I exploited their weaknesses."

"You are not making me feel any better. Now I am weak, and you don't want me."

"You don't get it."

"That would seem obvious."

"I want to want you, not need you. If our relationship is based on needing what you can offer, then what happens if my needs change?"

"Your wants can change, too, you know."

"Not wants, as in things, but want. A feeling of love and desire that is rooted in who you are, not what I can get from you."

"You mean, you would still love me if I were dirt poor?"

"Yes."

"I could give all this away. None of this really matters anyway. I would give it all away if it would make you happy."

"Now, let's not do anything rash here."

Alicia ran her index finger from his lips, down his cheek, and resting on his chest. She played with a shirt button for a second before continuing.

"I want to want you, but that doesn't mean I don't want to enjoy the benefits of what your money offers along the way."

"Then why can't you let me help you with the apartment?"

"Because it is important to me. I want to know that I can make it on my own."

"So, I can spend all the money I want while we are on a date, as long as I pick you up in some dump apartment you can afford."

"Exactly!"

Justin stared at Alicia.

"I'm not sure I get this new you. At least I knew where I stood and what to expect from the old Alicia."

This time, it was Justin's words that hurt. Her greatest fear surfaced. The person he fell in love with was her false persona. She tried to convince herself that the Alicia character she created was most like the person she wanted to be, but that may just be ego pandering. She was not Annie either. She did not know who she was.

A church bell chime interrupted her pity party over the afternoon's romantic missteps. The ringtone belonged to Pastor Dan. Alicia tapped the green phone button.

"Hello."

"Sorry to call so late, but I have a favor to ask."

"Will I regret saying yes?"

"Of course not."

"Then how can I help?"

"Our caricature artist bailed, and we need a last-minute replacement."

"Are you wanting me to step in or give you recommendations on who to call?"

"We want you."

"You sure you don't just need me?"

"Can't both be true?" Pastor Dan seemed confused by her questions. He did not know he had just played into her conversation with Justin.

"Not necessarily. I can need something I do not want and want something I do not need." Alicia dug deeper into the little rabbit hole she had created.

"Yes, that is true, I guess," his confusion persisted.

"You know that's pretty easy to understand with things, but a lot harder to figure out with people."

Pastor Dan closed his eyes for a second, took a deep breath and switched to counselor mode.

"Yes, I suppose that could be equally true. It sounds like there's more to your esoteric remarks than whether you can draw cute pictures of people at the street festival tomorrow."

Alicia smiled through her own deep breath.

"I'm sure I'm going to regret this, but I can use one of your silly sermons."

Chapter 44

THE CLANG OF THE DOORBELL set Lexi into a barking frenzy. Clark did not respond. His mind had not yet caught up with his body. The conversation last night at Emily's apartment left his brain working while his body wanted to crash. Those roles reversed when the alarm insulted his slumber too early on a Saturday morning. He stood there staring at the empty coffeepot. Lana had already dashed away to help Emily at the street carnival.

The doorbell clanged again.

"Alright. I'm coming," Clark hollered at the noise.

He scooped up Lexi and peered through the peephole to see a man in a courier uniform and a stack of boxes on a dolly. The man checked his clipboard and pushed the doorbell again. Clark checked his robe and pulled the door open a few inches.

"Can I help you?" Clark asked.

"Are you Clark Solo?"

"Yes."

"I have a delivery for you from the law office of Vernier and Associates."

"What?"

Clark's brain still yearned for his caffeine fix.

"They said you might be a little confused," the courier said as he pushed the clipboard toward Clark. "If you sign for these, I'll go get the rest of the boxes."

"There's more?" Clark asked as he let the door swing open and struggled to sign with a squirming poodle in his arms.

The courier laughed.

"Yes, sirree, Bob. There are eighteen boxes in all."

Clark stood there, staring at the boxes. A cool morning breeze fluffed his robe about the time the courier returned with the second stack. He laughed again.

"Sir, would you like me to wheel these into the house?"

A stunned Clark responded with a slow up and down nod. He stepped aside and pointed the man toward the middle of the living room. The distant ring of Clark's cellphone added to the commotion.

"I bet that's somebody from the lawyer's office," the courier said.

"Hope so."

Clark disappeared down the hallway, locked Lexi in the bathroom, and grabbed his phone. The screen scrolled Greg Vernier.

"Eighteen boxes?" Clark answered the phone with more exclamation than question.

"You get right to the point, Clark."

"There's no point in tiptoeing around the elephant in the room. Actually, it would be easier to get around an elephant."

Clark returned to see a wall of boxes. The courier had taken the liberty of pushing the coffee table to one side to make room for the boxes.

"I figured I'd save you the trip of coming down to my office this morning," Vernier explained.

"What's in all those boxes?"

"Just everything you need to know about the cases you asked me about."

"Everything I need to know?" Clark's voice went up an octave on the word need. "Odd choice of words. I'm staring at a lot of information for somebody who arguably just became aware of these cases less than twenty-four hours ago."

"What can I say? My staff is efficient."

"Don't be sly with me, Greg. It's obvious you've been playing me on this. I've let it slide so far because I figured there was still a legit story here. But all this says you've been working on this for weeks, maybe even months. Come clean with me. Tell me what's really going on here."

"All I've done, Clark, is respond to your request for information. What you do with that information is entirely up to you."

"I don't buy that."

"That's okay. I'm not selling anything. By the way, you will have more time than you think to read over those files. My client is still feeling quite ill. It appears to be some kind of virus. The judge has granted a continuance until Wednesday."

"How convenient for me."

"There is no reason for such sarcasm."

"Sorry to be so lowbrow."

"Well, I'll leave you to it. I am at your convenience if you have any further questions."

"Oh, I'm sure I'll be calling you."

※ ※ ※

Vernier smiled. He imagined Clark's dumbfounded expression growing in contortion as the delivery guy dropped box after box of case histories. The act may have been a little dramatic, but Clark could not expect any less flair. Could he? The reporter's pushback met his expectations and filled Vernier with more confidence in his choice of reporters to leak this story. Clark clearly knew the defense attorney was up to something. Yet, Vernier knew the reporter hadn't pieced the picture together, but he was hopeful Clark could figure it out before the end of the Kuzmin trial. Hence, the need for the massive info dump on an otherwise boring Saturday morning.

Confidentiality rules prevented Vernier from openly sharing Doctor Callahan's confession. The rules, however, did not say he had to go out of his way to prevent others from being diligent and discovering the fruit of that confession. Those case histories had all the necessary details— assuming a lot of *ifs* play out on the parts of the people doing the digging. If Clark viewed the crimes collectively, as the acts of a single mastermind, and if he could report how the cases are connected correctly and dramatically enough to force the district attorney's office to pay attention and act on the information. In the right hands, Vernier knew a prosecutor could expose the secrets of the confession. If handled incorrectly, the truth would continue to be expunged.

Vernier feared he might need to nudge Clark more and cross a line that even the famed rule bender had ethical qualms tiptoeing around. He had to give the reporter clarity, to focus his attention so all the shades of gray in the case files emerged into a crisp black-and-white picture. He could not push Clark too far or too fast. The reporter could break ranks in this little drama of deception the two were sharing. Yet, he could not just ignore the warning from Doctor Callahan. He underestimated him before, and Teri Marcos became murder victim number eighteen.

The criminal defense attorney could not fault the police he had blamed countless times before. They had no reason to suspect that a murder was about to happen. He also could not fault them for a quick investigation afterwards. They had no compelling reason to delve into why Kuzmin had killed Marcos. They found him holding the dripping murder weapon and covered in her blood. That was enough to wrap up the case for them. Besides, she lacked the pedigree that brought squeaky wheels into the investigation process. No one had a reason to connect this murder with the victim's drunk driving arrest only a few months earlier. Nor did anyone have a reason to connect the assailant's mental state to his disappearance at about the same time as the victim's brush with the law. Vernier knew, at least he kept telling himself, enough that he should have known but did not.

Doctor Callahan's confession failed to surprise Vernier, despite vindicating several conspiracy theories on government mind-control efforts and big pharma's manipulation of the masses. The socially inept man did not come forward with any delusions of grandeur that his whistle-blowing confession would right a horrible injustice. Vernier could tell he had an ax to grind with somebody, which was why he hesitated to act on his information.

Chapter 45

ALICIA STRETCHED and snuggled in the soft queen-size bed. She reached for the edge and giggled when she could not find it. The hotel linens weren't quite the luxurious comfort her former self knew, but it was a far cry from the pillow-topped cement block she endured in jail. Such gyrations there would have landed her on the floor.

Today was her first full day of freedom, yet others had already scheduled her movements. A breakfast meeting with a lawyer representing Zimmerman Holdings, Inc., presumably her father's more legit interests, started her day. Pastor Dan owned most of her day with drawing caricatures at the street festival. Justin wrapped up the evening with plans for a romantic dinner cruise that promises to sail under the Golden Gate Bridge at sunset.

The latter intimidated her the most. Her reunion yesterday with Justin was not as magical as she had hoped. Alicia feared another romantic blunder might dash all prospects of the relationship they once had. She could not worry about Justin now. Those tears fell last night. If it weren't for the late-night call from Pastor Dan, her head would ache from a drained minibar.

"You are made in the image of God. We all possess this: *Imago Dei*," she recalled his words as she let the hot water from the rainwater showerhead stream over her.

"I'm not saying that to puff you up, that you are some kind of god or anything. Reality is far from that. Being an image bearer comes with the responsibility to act mentally, morally, and socially like the image creator. We have the capacity to reason and choose, but as a reflection, we often do this badly. We come with a moral compass, yet we can ignore it. We are designed for fellowship—with each other and our creator—but we can mess that up, too."

"You are so encouraging," her voice tinged with regret for inviting one of his little sermonettes.

"There is encouragement in there, tons of it. Notice I said, we mess it up. I didn't say God messed it up. When we act as if the reflection is the original, everything gets distorted. Life as an image bearer only works when we stay close to the image creator, so our actions are truly a mirror image."

"So, God made me a total screw-up unless I do it his way?"

"He didn't make you a screw-up; you did that. Think of it this way. Toddlers have the capacity to choose right from wrong, but they don't always get it right. The best way for them to learn is to model their parent's behavior."

"I'm pretty sure I did."

"I know. There is a flaw in that analogy. Parents. Parents are flawed, but God isn't. And our society is the culmination of thousands of years of distorted copies producing more flawed copies. The remedy is to remake your image to reflect the original, thus breaking the cycle of imperfect copies."

Alicia was still ruminating on the good pastor's words when she found her way to the restaurant in the hotel lobby. She could still hear their echoes as the lawyer explained how her father had set up a company—Zimmerman Holdings—to provide for her. She would simply be its benefactor and pursue her passions in the arts.

"What if I want more?" Alicia asked.

"What do you mean? This should provide you with a very generous stipend each month."

The lawyer seemed befuddled by her question. His furrowed brow punctuated the excessiveness of his receding hairline, which at this point was nothing more than a rim of short gray hair.

"What if I want more of a say in the company?" she corrected herself.

"Your father didn't think you would be interested in day-to-day operations. He set you up only to be a major shareholder."

"He's probably right, but then again, I don't really know what Zimmerman Holdings does."

"I would not say it *does* anything. It holds assets on behalf of your father's other business interests."

"I'm sure that was supposed to mean something, but it didn't."

"Most of the time, your father acquired properties and turned them over quickly for a nice profit. Zimmerman Holdings manages assets that need time for the market conditions to become more favorable."

"So, it is a bunch of old buildings?"

"Yes, and no. There is a substantial inventory of old buildings, as you describe them, but there are a few operational factories, warehouses, and even a few retail shops in the mix, too."

"All back in Chicago?"

"No, there are properties locally, mostly industrial buildings up in the northern part of the Bay Area," he explained as he reviewed his notes. "Again, you will not have to deal with any of the day-to-day operations. He just wanted you to benefit from the earnings they generate."

"Okay. I guess being a benefactor is best for now. I'll talk about it with my dad down the road."

"Ma'am, that's going to be difficult."

"Well, yeah, it's inconvenient getting to his prison and submitting myself to their visitor screening process, but I can deal with that."

"It's more complicated than that."

"Don't tell me he's gotten himself locked up in solitary."

The lawyer pushed down his glasses and offered a look of condolence to Alicia.

"No, Ms. Bauer. Clearly, nobody has informed you yet, and I regret being the one to tell you that your father is dead. I'm sorry. I shouldn't have assumed that the police had already told you. As I understand it, an inmate stabbed him repeatedly with some sort of knife made from an old toothbrush."

"I don't believe you."

Her words were terse but fell short of yelling. She wanted to say people don't just die and nobody knows about it. The lawyer did not respond. He sat there waiting for her to run through her emotions. A few moments later, she asked a practical question.

"When did it happen?"

"I understand it was Thursday evening."

Alicia bowed her head. She was still in jail. Outside information takes time to make its way to inmates. Besides, she had made it abundantly clear to staff that she did not want to talk to her father. They must have assumed that news of his death was not important to her as well.

"Once again, let me apologize. Given the timing and all, I just assumed you understood the purpose of this meeting was to go over your father's estate," he explained.

Alicia nodded her head, showing she understood his dilemma.

"I still don't believe you. He can't be dead."

Chapter 46

LANA LOOKED AROUND the street festival. It was a low-budget version of the Renaissance fairs she visited on one of the weekend adventures her dad instituted after her mom died. Booths stretched up and down the street in front of the church, with dozens of vendors selling the interesting, the crafty and the totally unnecessary. The festivalgoers themselves added to the event's appeal. Many came dressed in various shades of Elizabethan-era attire. They filled the street with overly cinched corsets, gaudy fabrics, and nostalgic delusions of an era far harsher than costume sellers wanted them to understand.

If truth be told, most people came to the festival for their indulgences. They stood in long lines for sweet, salty, and fried delicacies that made enduring the almost-talent gracing the stages bearable. The growl in Lana's stomach directed her attention across the cluster of tables to a somberly dressed peasant maiden selling monkey tails. Suddenly, her tastebuds yearned for one of those chocolate-covered frozen banana delights.

The teen had already logged her mandatory time—the hours necessary to meet her school's requirement for community service. She had moved on to helping her godmother keep the stages filled with skits, musicians, and singers. She admired their courage to get on stage, in putting themselves out there for others to judge. Lana thought they had to know their mediocre talent only attracted crowds looking for a laugh. In the middle of the cluster of food trucks, an image startled Lana. She saw the court jester—her stalker.

"Auntie Em," she hollered in a whisper. With her hand behind her back, she waved frantically to garner her attention but not his. "It's him. He's here."

Emily did not hear the almost inaudible scream. The chaos of little girls dressed up as fairies resisting her efforts to corral them backstage absorbed her attention. Lana stood motionless, staring at the court jester. He did not seem to pay any attention to her. The colorfully dressed character seemed singularly interested in a young woman dressed up as an underclad barmaid.

"Auntie Em!" Her words searched blindly for her godmother.

Lana did not know whether to be relieved or embarrassed when a small child came up to the court jester and tugged on one of the bells dangling from his wrist.

"Daddy!" she heard the child proclaim.

The court jester reached down and hoisted her into his arms. Then he walked over and shared a family moment with the barmaid.

"You are just being paranoid," Lana told herself and looked the other direction to cleanse her mind of her self-initiated fear. And what to her wandering eyes should appear but a parade of eight tiny jesters marching past the main stage down the block.

"Lana! Quit standing around and help me keep these little fairies in line," Emily admonished.

* * *

Joey could see Lana towering over the herd of pink, green, and purple fairies. A smile broke through his veil of seriousness. A part of him wanted to stroll down the street toward her as if nothing had changed. He could not. Charlie made sure of that. Only a call from one of his spies confirming Joey had completed his mission would interfere with the natural proclivities of the man standing guard over his mother.

His little mission. Everybody back at the mansion had little missions. Charlie talked about them as if they were a calling from God. Nobody questioned Charlie, even when what he asked meant someone might get hurt. Nobody broached the subject of right and wrong. Only Charlie's truth mattered. Instead, they gushed about the tasks he doled out with overwhelming devotion and enthusiasm. The group deemed any attempts at understanding their purpose as heretical.

Joey got caught up in this blind faith in Charlie at first, but that feeling wore off like a numbing shot at the dentist. The pain of reality eventually set in. Only for Joey, though. The others remained spellbound in Charlie's web. To avoid the consequences of disloyalty by the crowd, Joey had to pretend his loyalty. The pain of this loneliness eventually crushed Joey into compliance—to accept his task in hopes of escape. Like an insect caught in a spider's web, Joey feared giving in to its trappings had only one conclusion.

At the moment, Joey had only one task in mind. He must save his mom from her mistakes and his. To do so, he needed to get into position and wait. Turning his back on Lana, he now faced the big stage. His feet straddled the blue-and-black duffel bag that he had stowed at the luggage storage facility when he got back into town.

Joey looked around. He half expected someone walking down the street to complain about how loud his heart was beating. They had to hear it. Nobody paid him any attention, other than noticing that his urban attire—baggy blue jeans and an oversized hoodie—did not share in the day's frivolity.

Chapter 47

AS A CO-CHAIR of the street festival, Pastor Dan had the unenviable task of entertaining the stream of VIPs who used the popular charity event to be seen. Somehow the former rough-and-tumble neighborhood had garnered high marks in political schmooze appeal, which drew even more media coverage. Every now and then, the public learned how the street festival raised funds for the community center and its before-and-after-school programs, which are credited with pushing out gang activity on this street.

Pastor Dan normally shied away from the world of politics, at least the messy kind that is on public display in the months leading up to an election. He understood, however, that sometimes you must play the game or the game will play you. Today was one of those times. A local state senator with a hat tossed into the race for governor wanted a feel-good story to warm the public prior to the next televised debate. His tough stand on crime needed a soft touch to appease a small but vocal opposition.

"We need more good people like yourself to take back their neighborhoods," Senator Buster Campbell lauded Pastor Dan with ambiguous platitudes as they strolled around the festival.

"I get your sentiment, but I wouldn't use the term take back. It is more like we tried to give people a way to feel more invested in their neighborhood, more of a sense of ownership. That's a tough thing to do when most folks around here rent and can barely do that."

"I like that phrase. Take ownership." The senator nodded toward his aide, who promptly started clicking away on her phone. "And that's why I wanted to recognize your efforts today. People need to know, especially your people. They need to know that their efforts are being noticed. I'd like to showcase your efforts as a model for other neighborhoods across the state to imitate."

"We'd be glad to share our journey away from being one of the roughest neighborhoods in the city. However, I don't think you can boil down what happened here into a simple neighborhood DIY project."

"You have a good way with words." He nodded to his aide again. "Neighborhood DIY project. I like that. I think that could catch on."

Pastor Dan smiled and nodded, hoping the senator would not notice him swallowing a more animated vocal response. He knew there was no point in correcting him. The dimness of his prospects for the governorship should be sufficient.

"We thought you could make your presentation on this stage here," Pastor Dan shifted the focus of the conversation. "And over there, where that little gang of cute court jesters is walking by, you can see where your staff has roped off an area for the TV cameras and reporters. Do you really think they will come out for this? We appreciate you taking the time out of your busy schedule to honor our team, but I'm not sure it's that big of a story."

"They respond when they are told to," Campbell responded in a matter-of-fact tone.

"Wow! You have got more pull than I realized."

The senator studied Pastor Dan's face and smiled. The uncomfortableness of the exchange caused Pastor Dan to look away. Across the street, he could see Joey standing alone. Something was not right. Joey just stared blankly in his direction and kept fidgeting.

"Please excuse me for a few moments," Pastor Dan said. "I have another matter to attend to."

The senator's staff swooped in, filling the void made by Pastor Dan's absence, and ushered him to his staging area. A couple of television reporters wandered into their huddle, hoping to get details to promo his upcoming speech.

"What can our viewers expect from your remarks today?" a reporter asked.

Pastor Dan only heard blah, blah, blah in response. Joey had captured his attention. His face looked pasty, and perspiration dotted his brow.

"Joey, are you alright?" Pastor Dan asked.

"Yeah, why do you ask?" Joey downplayed his fears that the youth pastor could hear the pounding drumbeat of his heart.

"You seem distracted."

"No," Joey choked out as he cleared his throat.

Pastor Dan looked down to see the bulky duffel bag, and the instructions from Detective Maddox last night echoed in his ears. "Take notice if something seems out of place or out of character."

"Is that your bag?"

Joey looked down and sputtered a few unrecognizable sounds.

"Should I be concerned about what's in the bag?" Pastor Dan pushed.

The panic in Joey's eyes gave him his answer. Pastor Dan pulled out his cell phone with his right hand, grabbed Joey with his left, and commanded the phone to call Detective Maddox.

"Detective, Joey needs his Uncle Bobby."

Chapter 48

ALICIA SLIPPED BACK into her old skill sets. She feigned being a happy-go-lucky artist who made festivalgoers believe she was delighted to transfer a comical likeness of them onto her sketch pad. She masked the real her and hid the argument raging inside over the unbelievable bombshell dropped by her father's lawyer.

"Here you go, sweetie."

The artist handed the young girl a caricature of her dangling from the iconic spire dominating the city skyline.

"Mommy, is that me?"

"It sure looks like you."

"But, Mommy, I can't climb that high."

Alicia shared a laugh with the young mother. Not necessarily at the unknowing wit of the four-year-old, but at the emerging thought of impaling the lawyer on that spire.

"Sweetie, always remember, you can always climb higher than you think. The trick is knowing when you've climbed too high."

The overly retrospective comment caught the mother off guard. An awkward silence hung in the air for an eternity of a second before the mother clumsily tucked the drawing into her bag and grabbed her daughter's hand.

"Olivia, we've taken up enough of this nice lady's time. Tell her thank you."

"Thank you, nice lady."

"You are welcome, sweetie."

Alicia needed a shoulder to cry on, but her Justin was in the middle of something complicated at work. He declared yesterday he would be dark today, which was code for "do not call me until I call you." She glanced toward the main stage and noticed the familiar outline of her jovial counselor. His body language described him differently. A rigid posture replaced his more amiable pose. His patented patience seemed set aside, as it looked like he had an unusually firm grip on a teenage boy.

Alicia felt alone. People had always surrounded her, but she never let them into her life once she put her unpleasant childhood in the rear-view mirror. To her, they were only unwitting actors in a contrived life she staged for the latest big score. That was until Justin. The mark who became her love. The man who abandoned his own fears and recklessly pursued her, even when the truth of her sins slammed him right in the face. And then there was Pastor Dan and her estranged father. Circumstances wove them into her life, but she had only let them in on her terms. Or so she thought; her loneliness told her maybe she hadn't.

Those pangs amplified her contempt for the lawyer. In an appalling disdain for compassion, he disclosed a thug had murdered her birth father. It was the same matter-of-fact tone he used to reveal a complex business arrangement designed to provide her with a windfall. She could not understand why he hadn't told her about the death first. Why did not he come to her hotel room and allow her to absorb the news in private? Instead, he chose to unveil the scheme her father cooked up in jail to provide financially for her. Not as an inheritance, but as a matter of normal day-to-day business. She had run enough cons to know that you cannot leave details like that hanging out there. People latch on to the little inconsistencies until any chance of pulling off the con disappears. Her father would have known that. So should have his lawyer. His actions were so overwhelmingly inconsistent, Alicia had to believe they were intentional. Even down to his deafening silence when she denounced his death proclamation as a lie.

"Ma'am. Ma'am. Oh, ma'am." A woman dressed as a barmaid waved her hand back and forth to get attention.

Alicia did not react. She kept staring at Pastor Dan and the teenage boy. Neither moved. Both bodies were rigid. She could not make out what the good pastor was saying to the boy, but she could tell his words came slowly. He never loosened his grip, not even when another man joined them. She recognized him. He was the detective who ended her old career. Something was wrong. Something did not make sense.

"I'm on break," Alicia mumbled.

"But I've been standing here," exclaimed the barmaid.

"That's nice. You'll be first up then when I get back."

She brushed past the woman and took a few steps toward the inconsistency in front of her before a buccaneer grabbed her arm.

"Hey lady, watch where you're going."

Alicia looked at the man. The disdain in her eyes made him cower. He lifted both hands up by his head.

"Fine, next time I'll let you get knocked over," he surrendered.

"Don't you know you are supposed to make way for a lady?" Alicia spoke more to the air than to the disgruntled man.

"I will when I see one," he retorted as he walked off.

The commotion caught the eye of Pastor Dan. His facial expression abandoned its normal, calm demeanor. Alicia could see the panic in his eyes as he shook his head back and forth.

Chapter 49

DETECTIVE MADDOX TURNED to his wife, lifted his phone, and waved. Her heart sank. Once again, duty called, and she had to press on without him. She hated that contraption. It had left her abandoned more times than she cared to count. Instead, she counted the days until his retirement—one thousand nine hundred and sixty-seven. They laughed about that number this morning at breakfast.

He weaved his way through the little court jesters and walked toward Pastor Dan, whose tight angular face was already visible over the frivolity. The detective did not understand the call. The pastor's words said Joey needed his Uncle Bobby, but his tone pinged the detective's radar. As he got closer, Maddox could see the rigid postures and the firm grip on Joey's arm. He surveyed everything around the two, trying to fill in details as he approached.

"Is that why you called?"

Maddox pointed to the clunky bag underfoot.

"Yep."

"What's in the bag, Joey?"

Silence.

"He's not talking to me either," informed Pastor Dan.

"Okay, Joey. I'm going to reach down and open the bag."

"I wouldn't do that if I were you."

"Why?"

Silence.

Maddox deflated. He knew this could mean only one thing.

"Damn it, Joey! No!"

The detective took a few steps back and called dispatch.

"This is Detective Maddox. Request EOD at the corner of Guerrero and 22nd. We have a possible explosive device. Be advised, this is the site of a street festival. Need backup to clear the area."

Maddox moved back in close to Joey.

"Pastor, you can let go now. I can hold on to Joey from here."

"I'll stay."

"No. I can't let you. It's not part of your job description."

"I wouldn't be so sure. The top line says to go save lost souls. Well, right now, Joey's a lost soul. Besides, it doesn't take much skill to hold on to him tight. I don't have the authority to clear all these folks out of here."

As Maddox conceded, Pastor Dan barked out a polite command.

"Now is not a good time, Alicia."

"You look like you could use a hand," she said as she took a couple more steps forward.

"No," his voice became more adamant, but calm. "We can talk about our ski adventure another time."

She looked at him. Her confusion wrinkled her forehead.

"You remember? Our ski adventure," he said slowly, placing extra emphasis on adventure.

Alicia's eyes got very wide. She did not know exactly what was going on, but it had danger written all over it. Their accidental introduction on the way to his ski trip ended up leading the police to an insane murderer. That boy could not be the problem, could he? Alicia took a few steps backward before turning around and darting toward her booth.

Maddox stepped back and shifted into on-scene commander mode.

"Ladies and gentlemen. I'm Detective Maddox with the San Francisco Police Department. I need you to exit the area calmly and quietly."

He walked over to the folks gathered at the main stage and started shooing them down the street. Alicia did the same on her side of the intersection.

"Hey! You!" shouted Senator Campbell from the stage. "These people came here to hear me speak."

"That's nice, but now they are in the middle of a crime scene and need to be evacuated. Get off the stage now!"

"Do you know who you are talking to?" hollered back the senator.

"A man violating a direct order from an officer of the law. Now, get off the stage now."

Reporters rushed to Maddox. Whatever he was doing had to be more exciting than another political speech.

"What's going on?" asked a reporter as she stuffed a microphone in his face. Another cameraman focused on Joey and Pastor Dan.

Maddox hated talking to the media. No matter how well you explained the facts to them, he found they always seemed to focus on the wrong details and confuse the public with a feigned sense of accuracy.

"The situation is unclear at this time. We are clearing the area out of an abundance of caution," he parroted his media training.

"But you clearly think it is something. Tell us what you think," the reporter prodded for a more sensational answer.

"I think it is prudent for you to leave the area as ordered."

Two uniformed officers arrived on the scene. Maddox pointed to the media intrusion with his right hand and threw his extended thumb over his shoulder like a referee ejecting a player. The detective then returned his attention to Joey.

"You've got to tell me what's going on here. Your mom has already seen enough hurt already."

"I know. That's why I'm here," Joey confessed.

"Let me help. Talk to me."

"I can't talk, not to you. Not to anybody. They told me the only thing I could tell you was that Marcus Delaney regrets speaking out of turn."

"Who are they?" Maddox asked.

Silence.

"Dispatch," Maddox barked into his cell phone. "Call the state and get the status on a one Marcus Delaney. He is at CMF in Vacaville."

"What do you mean, status?"

Maddox looked back at Joey, who was standing over what he had to assume was an improvised explosive device.

"Is the man dead or alive?"

He continued to stare at the teen whom he had watched grow up. His running away did not make sense. Whatever he was doing right now did not make any sense either. What he was seeing seemed so out of character. Joey was the kind of kid every parent wished they had. He was polite, good at school and picked his friends well. He was not much of an athlete himself, but he could hold his own when talking about football or baseball. He was just the all-around responsible kid who you could count on to do what needed done, especially when it came to taking care of his mother.

"Dispatch." Maddox's voice became very intentional as he gave instructions to send a patrol unit over to the Maldoon's house. He watched Joey's body stiffen. Joey shook his head abruptly.

"No! Don't do that!" Joey begged. "Uncle Bobby, no!"

Chapter 50

LANA DID NOT UNDERSTAND what was going on. The stream of revelers going by had suddenly changed from a casual stroll to a nervous stampede. She climbed onto a bench and looked upstream from the panicked crowd. As the hole in front of the main stage widened, Pastor Dan and Joey came into view. Something did not look right. Their bodies were rigid, not moving with the crowd.

"I can't tell what, but there's something going on with Joey and Pastor Dan," Lana hollered to Emily, who was still on the stage with an abandoned fairy.

"Ma'am, you need to get down and clear the area," a uniformed officer instructed Lana.

"What's going on? Those are my friends up there. They're not going anywhere."

Lana did not budge from her perch.

"That doesn't matter right now. The only thing you should be concerned about is getting yourself to safety," the uniformed officer instructed.

"What about their safety?" Lana's voice trembled.

"Ma'am, all I know is we are here to clear the area. I can tell you they do not bring us in just so somebody can plant flowers. Now, get down and get moving."

Lana could clearly see Joey now. The crowds had pushed their way up the street, past the food court at the end of the street festival. Joey was not moving because Pastor Dan was not letting him leave. That made little sense, she told herself. Why would they be standing there while everybody else abandoned the ship? Her eyes kept looking for something, any clues to reconcile this dissonance. Then, she spied a bulky duffel bag at Joey's feet. She thought that seemed like a rather clunky bag to bring to an event like this.

"Oh, my God! No!" Lana screamed. "Joey. No!"

"Lana!"

Emily tugged on Lana's shirt. The teen looked down to see a matching expression of anguish and pointed toward Joey.

"Lana, whatever is going on down there, we can't do anything about it. Right now, I need to get you to safety."

"But, Joey," Lana protested.

"I know. Let's go."

Lana took Emily's hand, stepped down and numbly followed in stride as her godmother led the two down the street. Behind the barricade, Lana turned around. Joey was no longer in sight; the food trucks were blocking her view. She reached into her back pocket and snagged her cell phone.

"Dad!" a breathless Lana yelled. "I think Joey has done something really stupid."

Chapter 51

A PATROL UNIT PULLED UP to the Maldoon house with lights flashing and sirens blaring. Before getting out of the vehicle, the officers visually scoured the area around the home. Nothing seemed out of the ordinary. They looked up and down the street of well-maintained modest homes. Faces emerged from behind curtains and blinds, which they would expect on a Saturday morning. One older man stepped out onto his stoop to see the commotion.

"Look," Sergeant Ugalde pointed to the only faceless home.

Drawn curtains filled the large picture window that dominated the front of the gray-and-charcoal house. Light poured through the ornate steel-and-glass front door.

"Something isn't right," he declared. "Look at the big window there. You don't pull the curtains closed like that and then turn on all the lights. Definitely not at this time of day in a quiet neighborhood like this."

"Bet you a dollar that we are going to find a dead body in there," his colleague responded as the backup unit arrived. "Parents of stupid kids with bombs do not fare so well."

Sergeant Ugalde took the lead, approaching the front door. His partner held back, watching the front of the house. The other two officers circled around the back of the house. He rapped on the door. No response. He rang the doorbell. No response.

"There's no way we can bust through this front door," Ugalde declared over the radio.

"Easy access back here," came the reply from the backyard. "The door is open."

"Proceed with caution," Ugalde directed.

The officer pushed open the French doors with his foot, revealing a knocked-over chair and other debris strewn over the floor. The officers shared a glance, affirming the obvious signs of a struggle. They entered the home in standard police fashion, each officer leapfrogging his movements past the other. One inspected the room, the other provided cover with their firearms drawn, until they cleared the upper level. They let in Ugalde, who was waiting at the front door, and silently signaled toward the stairwell.

Ugalde regained the lead role, slowly edging his way down the left side of the stairs as another officer mirrored his stance on the right. At the bottom of the stairs, the officers fanned out, clearing each of the rooms uneventfully. Ugalde noticed the undisturbed bedding and a little sports car in the one-car garage.

Back upstairs, Ugalde shook his head as he took in the scene and noted the discrepancies.

"Nothing about this feels right. The lights were left on. The door was left open. And look at that chair." He pointed to a Queen Anne chair with its legs aimed at a spindly legged side table.

"Yeah, somebody knocked it over in a struggle," the junior officer seemed unaware of any discrepancies.

"Possibly, but why isn't the table knocked over, or the drink spilled? At least one of the chair legs would have had to have hit it in a struggle."

"Random luck?"

"Once, maybe? Not this much. Look around. This is the cleanest home struggle I've ever seen. It looks like somebody staged it."

Ugalde's partner entered the room with the neighbor from the stoop in tow.

"Sergeant. I think you'll want to hear what this guy has to say."

The sergeant stepped forward with his hand extended to the seventy-something man with white-streaked red hair. His hand felt rough, and his grip felt strong.

"Good morning, sir," he said. "What is it you think I should know?"

"As I was telling this officer here. Gloria left with her ex-husband about an hour before you guys stormed the place."

"Do you know the Maldoons well?"

"As well as you can know neighbors. We moved in at about the same time. Oh my, must have been back in Reagan's first term."

"That's been a few years, sir."

"Nobody has even come close to him since either."

Ugalde chuckled but avoided the trap of that conversation.

"Have you seen anything unusual over the past few days?"

"As I was telling this officer, I hadn't seen Joey for a long while. Then, maybe a couple of days ago, he just showed up again. I guess he must have been visiting his dad."

"Is that typical?"

"That he visits his dad? I don't know. I was more of Miles's friend. Well, I was until he up and disappeared without so much as a goodbye shortly before Joey was born."

"Thank you, sir. Your information was very helpful. The officer will get your information, and we will contact you if we have any further questions."

Chapter 52

THE HUMAN BODY can only hold its arms extended for a few minutes before fatigue sets in. An ache forms in the shoulders and burns its way down the arms. Pastor Dan hadn't thought about this human limitation when he grabbed Joey. He also hadn't thought about how adrenaline speeds up body processes so we can get away from danger. His adrenaline understood danger lay only inches away.

"Oh, Detective?" he queried quietly.

"Yes, Pastor?"

"Is this going to take much longer?"

"The Bomb Squad should be here in a couple of hours."

Pastor Dan could see the glimmer in the detective's eyes that told him they were getting here as fast as possible. Joey could not.

"Are you serious?" Joey asked.

"Dead serious. We could end this a lot faster if you started talking."

"I can't."

"You can't, or you won't."

"I won't because I can't. I'm supposed to stay silent."

The clang of an old school telephone interrupted the conversation.

"Maddox."

The detective tried to slip on his poker face as dispatch updated him on the status of Marcus Delaney. The operator then patched him through to Sergeant Ugalde, who shared his observations at the Maldoon home. Pastor Dan could tell the person on the other end of the call had not dealt the detective a good hand.

"Was that the Mrs. calling to bring home some milk?" Pastor Dan joked.

"If only," Maddox replied as he studied Joey. "How do you know Marcus Delaney?"

"I don't," Joey answered.

"Then how did you know he hanged himself?"

"I didn't. I told you only what they told me to tell you."

"Okay. Did your mom have to leave on another business trip?"

"No."

"Is she off doing errands?"

"No."

"A friend picked her up?"

"No."

"Are you asking Joey if he knows where his mother is?" interrupted Pastor Dan.

"And who is she with?" Maddox added.

"I can't say."

"Why? Is it a big secret that she went off with your dad?"

"My dad?" Joey asked.

"Excuse me, detective," interrupted the lead tech from Bomb Squad. "Is that your little package that's causing all the ruckus?"

"Yep."

"Well, let's see if Rico here can tell us if there is anything that will go boom," the officer said as he nodded toward his canine partner.

"Let's not go boom. Okay?" Pastor Dan said.

"We'll try."

"Try real hard."

"I am pretty good at what I do, so don't worry. Nobody alive has yet to complain about how I do my job."

"And how many did not live long enough to complain?"

The bomb tech smiled. During the chatter, Rico sniffed the backpack but did not react. The tech did a wider search with the explosive detection dog and still had no response.

"I don't think we have any explosives here," the bomb tech declared.

"That's good?" Pastor Dan asked.

"You would like to think so," the bomb tech said. "There are other bad things to rule out. First, let me take a peek inside."

"Won't that trip some wires?" Detective Maddox asked.

The tech shrugged his shoulders. The tech clearly liked to toy with people in these incidences.

"Young man," the bomb tech addressed Joey. "What were your instructions today?"

Joey looked at his Uncle Bobby.

"Answer him, Joey. Whatever your plans were, they are not going to happen that way, so telling us now will not make any difference to them," the detective directed.

"I was told to set the backpack here, wait until the speech started and walk away," Joey explained after considering his limited options.

"Do you know what was going to happen?" the bomb tech asked.

"No."

"Did they tell you to get far away?" interjected the detective.

"No. Just walk away and wait for a call."

"What would the call be about?"

"My mom."

"Who has your mom?"

"Charlie."

"If Charlie has her, then why did she leave with your dad?"

"I don't know what you are talking about."

"Gentlemen, you can figure that out later," interrupted the bomb tech. He turned to his colleague and motioned for her to proceed with the robotic unit. "That little guy there is going to get as close as he can and take some pictures of the bag."

"Souvenir photos?" Pastor Dan continued to joke.

"Yep. The kind that glows in the dark. It's going to send pictures to that guy way over there, where it's safe. We hope it will give us a better idea of what we can do next."

"Not sure why you had to point out that he is where it's safe," Pastor Dan said.

"Clear to open the bag," hollered the tech monitoring the pictures.

"Okay, boys. We have only a couple of things more to do until it's all over."

"You mean this is over?"

"Okay, I can go with that." The tech operated smoothly despite the macabre humor. He gently unzipped the gym bag and peeled it open to discover another bag inside.

"Young man, did you know what's inside this bag?"

"Not really. They told me not to look inside that bag."

"You need to pick better friends."

"I didn't pick them. They picked me."

He continued his delicate approach of slowly unzipping the inner bag and peeling it open. When he had exposed the inside of the second bag, the bomb tech started laughing.

"Detective, it's safe to take him into custody. This hunk of plastic has already done all the harm to the environment it's going to do."

Maddox rushed in and hugged Joey. Pastor Dan released his grip on Joey and began massaging his arms.

Chapter 53

"WHAT DO YOU MEAN?" Clark asked his distraught daughter.

"I don't know, but Pastor Dan and your detective friend are keeping Joey in the middle of the street, and everybody else is being pushed back," Lana explained.

"Are you okay?"

"Yes, I'm fine. I'm a couple of blocks away."

"Where's Emily?"

"I'm not sure, but she's safe, too."

Lana took a deep breath.

"Joey looked really scared. Is he going to do something bad like those other people we talked about last night? The ones who went missing?"

"I don't know, sweetie."

Clark wanted to say something more comforting, but he could not. The same thought was running through his mind as well.

"You look for Emily, and I'll get down there as quickly as possible. I'll call you when I'm nearby."

"Okay, Dad."

At times like these, Clark wished he had a car that could get him where he wanted fast. However, the only thing fast about owning a car in the city was debt. The frustration of traffic jams, the fear of theft, and the struggle to find a parking spot added insult to the injury of high car payments, insurance premiums, and parking fees.

Clark tapped his phone to get a ride to the festival, then switched from dad mode to reporter.

"Hey, Maureen. It's Clark. Can you tell me who's working the cop beat today?" Clark asked the news desk.

"Shaunda. Why?"

"Something is happening over on Guerrero Street."

"Yeah, we know. The political reporter was already on scene when the bomb squad got called in."

"Did you say bomb squad?"

"Yep. We don't have any details yet, but it appears some teen-aged idiot came out of his basement all angry at the world."

"Wow! Then who's working the story?"

"Andy."

"I may know the idiot."

"Hook up with Andy. I'm sure he wouldn't mind the assist."

"Will do. Thanks."

Clark stepped out onto the street just as his ride pulled up. He slid into the back seat and gave the driver his destination.

"There's a lot of commotion going on over there," the driver said, looking at Clark via the rearview mirror.

"I know. Get me as close as you can."

The driver acknowledged with a shrug. Clark settled into his seat. He did not have enough information to figure out what to do next. Only enough to make his heart race. His phone rang. Clark did not recognize the number.

"This is Clark."

"Mr. Solo. This was only a trial run."

"What's a trial run? Who is this?"

"Who I am does not matter. All you need to know is we could have made this a very bad day for Mr. Maldoon."

"I don't think it is a good day for him."

"Depends on your perspective. He's still alive, isn't he?"

"So, I hear. If this is the trial run, when is the real thing?"

"Oh, I don't know. Ask the senator."

"Senator who? That title fits forty-two folks in this state, you know."

"You'll be able to figure it out."

"Thanks for the confidence. Will I figure out why you are doing this?"

"I think so. If not, then you could lose a few hundred subscribers."

"Why are telling me all this?"

"I like your reporting style. You seem to enjoy getting up close and personal with your news coverage."

"Thank you, I guess. It would help if I knew who you are and why you think setting off a bomb is a good thing."

"Oh no. I don't think bombs are a good thing. A necessary thing? That's different. The senator knows how to save the day."

"So perceptive of the senator. How will I know he is telling me the truth?"

"That will be a dilemma, won't it?"

"Could be."

"You'll figure it out and make Lana proud."

"Excuse me!"

"Mr. Solo, you don't think I didn't do my homework, do you?"

"You are not making friends by threatening me."

"Good thing I'm not trying to make friends."

The driver pulled over to the curb on Mission Street, a few blocks down from his destination.

"This is as close as I can get," the driver said.

Clark slipped out of the car and looked up 22nd Street. The chaos added to the bad feeling in his gut.

"You are so close. The action is only a few blocks away, Mr. Solo."

"I guess that means you are nearby."

"I'm where I need to be."

"And you need me to be where?"

"Such a cooperative question. Just go see how Mr. Maldoon is doing. I'll keep an eye on Lana for you."

The phone went dead.

Chapter 54

UNCLE BOBBY HELD JOEY tight. He knew it was a false hope to believe that such a simple human gesture could stave off the inevitable. Yet, he tried.

"Umm," a uniformed officer cleared his throat. "Detective?"

Pastor Dan shook his head back and forth.

"Let him be family for a little bit longer."

The officer shrugged and waited.

"What's going to happen now?" Joey whispered.

"You are going to keep your mouth shut until you speak to a lawyer," Uncle Bobby whispered back. He closed his eyes, took a deep breath, and broke their embrace.

"Officer," Detective Maddox directed with a hand gesture. The teen's body deflated. Joey hung his head as the officer pulled one arm, then another, behind his back to place the cold metal cuffs on his wrists.

"It's probably best that I stay with him until you can find his mom," Pastor Dan said.

The officer looked at the detective for guidance. Maddox nodded his head in agreement.

"That may be awhile, Pastor," Maddox quietly confessed.

"What does that mean?" Joey perked up. "Uncle Bobby, what does that mean?"

"It means we do not know where your mother is, who she is with, or how to get in touch with her."

"Something tells me I may be able to help with that," Clark said as he walked up to the conversation.

"How?" chimed in Detective Maddox and Pastor Dan.

"Whoever just called me made it pretty clear he was calling the shots in this little fiasco," Clark said.

"What makes you think that?" Maddox asked.

"He told me to see how Mr. Maldoon is doing while he kept an eye on my Lana. I've tried calling her. She doesn't pick up."

Chapter 55

LANA HELD EMILY'S HAND and stared down the street. She could not see past the food trucks, but looked intently in the direction of Joey, anyway. Her thoughts bounced between the bulky duffel bag at her friend's feet and the horrific images of the Boston Marathon bombing. She was only ten when a couple of backpacks went unnoticed near the finish line of the race. Was that Joey's plan? Was he supposed to drop the duffel bag, disappear into the crowd, and wait for a bomb to fill the air with thousands of sharp metal objects? That did not make sense. Not Joey. That did not sound like the boy she knew. Something must have happened while Joey was away. But what? What could cause him to get mixed up with something that hurts people?

"Do you think he has a bomb?" Lana asked.

"I don't know what to think," Emily replied, echoing Lana's blank, forward gaze.

"I know it ain't good."

"No, it isn't good."

"Really? This isn't the time to be correcting my grammar," Lana said in a tone that conveyed she rolled her eyes as well.

"I wasn't ..." Emily stopped her defense when Lana turned and exposed a smile she could not hold back. Emily wagged her index finger at Lana. "You are a mean one, Miss Solo."

The two laughed. The gaiety felt wrong somehow, but Lana set aside those feelings and enjoyed the break.

"You can still laugh, I'm glad to see," came an exaggerated voice imitating a children's puppet character from behind the two.

"We're sorry," Emily said, letting go of Lana's hand as she turned around to see who was joining in on their laugh fest. "Sometimes you just ..." Her words froze in her mouth. The strange-sounding man was not a stranger.

"Have to what, Ms. Geoffrey?" He unsuccessfully added a serious tone to his cartoon falsetto. His eyes did not mask his amusement at her reaction.

"Laugh," Lana proclaimed without turning around and lifted her right arm in a salute to the sky. "Mister, sometimes you just have to ... Ouch!"

An elbow from Emily interrupted her sentence.

"What was that for?" Lana asked, her eyes still transfixed toward Joey.

"For me, methinks, Miss Lana."

His stilted language reinforced the arrogance of his hands fanning in his face.

"How do you know my ..." The man's image as she turned around stopped her words.

"Words all gone. Did they go bye-bye?"

"Get away from us!" Lana yelled at the strange little court jester, ignoring the wave of fear pulsating through her. This time, she was positive it was the same man who had been stalking her and Joey. She grabbed Emily's hand once again.

"Me sad. You no like me?" he asked.

"No!" the two replied in unison.

"Why?"

"Seriously? You have to ask?" A frumpled forehead punctuated Lana's confusion.

"Me a little sad. Me bring flowers. Me like Lana."

Lana turned to her godmother. Each read the facial twitches of the other. Silently, they screamed that the character in front of them had reached a new level of scary. Emily squeezed Lana's hand and cleared her throat.

"Sir, umm, we don't know you." Her words, barely audible, struggled to leave her lips.

"Me know you. That's enough."

"No, it's not." Her volume returned, along with that tone of authority she used to manage teenage boys who towered over her in the classroom.

"Why?"

Emily gave him the scolding-teacher look, but it failed to achieve the desired results. He mirrored her gaze with a cocked head and wide puppy-dog eyes.

"May we go?" asked an exasperated Emily.

"Yes!"

The jester sprang into full animation, arms and legs flowing up and down as if a puppeteer was tugging on his strings. Lana and Emily could only watch the spectacle. He danced in a circle around them and sang in his childlike voice.

"Ring around the rosie, pocket full of posies, ashes, ashes, we all fall down!" During his third orbit and as he sang the final stanza, he inserted himself between the two. With Lana in his left hand, Emily in his right, the jester pranced forward. His swift movements surprised them, and they lunged forward like cars on a train.

"New song," he proclaimed. "The goats came marching one by one. Hurrah! Hurrah!"

The jester's fast pace and exaggerated arm movements as he marched about prevented Lana and Emily from slowing him down or escaping his grip, which was far stronger than his less-than-impressive stature suggested.

"Let go of us!" Emily shouted as she and Lana smacked in the direction of their abductor. Most of their attempts failed due to his limber and animated movements.

The jester ignored their flailing attempts. He kept singing his marching song and pulling them through the crowd without hesitation. Nobody seemed to pay attention to the commotion. The chaos of the morning had already tainted their perspective of normal. On the edge of the crowd, the jester spoke.

"You meet my friend," he said with enthusiasm.

"I don't want to," Lana proclaimed.

She ran forward and threw herself to the ground, hoping her impromptu actions would cause the jester to tumble as well. It did not. Not even after his sudden stop caused Emily to rear-end their captor.

"That bad idea. You get hurt," the jester said as he pulled on Lana's arm. "Now get up. Get up now."

"I'm not taking orders from you," Lana said defiantly.

"You can't meet my friend here. Must go over there."

The jester pointed with his head to the windowless white van conspicuously out of place. It was stretched across four angled parking spaces.

"I'm not getting in that van," Lana yelled. "Nothing good ever comes from something that looks like that."

"Not true. My friend nice." Hurt tinged the jester's voice. Emily noticed the change in tone.

"We're sorry," Emily said as she moved so Lana could see her.

"We are?" Lana asked.

"Yes, Lana. We shouldn't fight our friend here but play a fun game."

"Me like games," the jester weighed in.

"We all like games," Emily said. "Lana, let's play a game of musical chairs."

"We cannot play that game. We don't have any chairs or music," the jester said.

"That's okay," Lana said, catching on to what Emily was proposing. "I'll sing and you can pretend you are the chair."

Lana jumped up and darted left around the jester; Emily followed in chase. The jester spun, but he did not loosen his grip on the two.

"Go wider," Emily hollered.

Lana went as wide as his grip allowed. Emily ducked under the arm holding Lana and passed her up.

"Stop," Emily hollered a second command.

Lana stopped, and Emily continued to pull the jester into a pretzel, but he did not let go. Emily pulled and pulled until Lana interrupted.

"Auntie Em. We are not going to break his grip."

"Me not play musical chairs like that before," the jester said. "That fun. Again?"

"No, Jonah. No more games," said Doctor Callahan from the open door of the van.

Chapter 56

FROM HER VANTAGE POINT on the edge of the barricade, Alicia could only see the outline of Pastor Dan intertwined with that teenage boy. Her brain could not process what was happening to her friend. The panicked look in his eyes and his cryptic warning of danger kept flashing through her mind like a bad music video. It was making her brain hurt, but it was the ache in her chest that had her more concerned.

Somehow, this annoying man had permeated her defenses. During her stay in jail, he had moved past being a convenient acquaintance who could help her pass the time. He had become more than just a counselor willing to put up with her antics. He had become her friend. The person she called first when she got out of jail. The person who had her worried, and she could do nothing about it.

Alicia tried pushing her way back up the street when she saw the bomb squad move back and Pastor Dan unclench his death grip.

"Look, it's over. I need to get back in there," she pleaded, but the uniformed officer held her back without considering if she might be telling the truth.

"Ma'am, I can't let you in until I'm given the order," the officer explained. "The best thing you can do to help the situation is to go home."

"I can't go home, not with my friend in trouble up there. So, I order you to let me in."

The officer smiled.

"Nice try."

Through all her verbal tussles with the human dam, Alicia kept her eyes on the events unfolding in front of the main stage of the little street festival. Her heart sank when she saw something unimaginable—a police officer guiding Pastor Dan's head into the back seat of a patrol car. She knew what that meant. Her mind exploded with confusion.

"Was I seeing this all backwards?" she thought.

Deflated, Alicia made her way through the onlookers. She plodded down the street and turned right at the corner. Her mind was not on her amble, but on the dissonance she had witnessed. Her heart, let alone her brain, could not absorb her friend being the bad guy. Yet, her eyes saw Pastor Dan restrain the boy. They saw the police take him away. They also saw her friend's eyes begging her to stay away.

Alicia pulled out her cell phone and did the only thing she could think of doing. As she tapped on Pastor Dan's name, she looked up to see three street performers dressed in the regalia of the now abandoned street festival. The sight of a nun and a peasant woman wrapping up a court jester like a pretzel made her laugh. His limber body parts seemed to ignore all precepts of human anatomy. It took her a bit to realize she was the only person watching the performance. That was until the van door opened and two trench coats popped out of a white van and pushed the trio inside. The van pulled forward and made its way into traffic.

"Oh my! They just kidnapped them!" Alicia blurted.

"What?"

Alicia looked down. The voice was coming from her phone.

"How are you answering the phone?"

"Like everybody else does," Pastor Dan said with a laugh.

"But you shouldn't be able to talk on the phone," she replied, transferring her confusion to her friend.

"Alicia, you are not making any sense. Are you okay?"

"Didn't they arrest you?"

"No. Why would they arrest me?"

"I don't know. I just know that's what they're doing when they put you in the back seat of a black-and-white car with lights flashing on top of it."

Pastor Dan laughed again.

"What's so funny?"

"You. They didn't arrest me. I'm helping them."

"Oh."

"So, what did you mean by they kidnapped them?"

"I just saw two thugs push three people into a van and take off."

"Did you get a look at who they took?"

"They were all dressed up for the festival. A nun, a peasant girl, and a court jester."

Chapter 57

"ARE YOU SURE LANA didn't just decide to go home?" Detective Maddox asked Clark.

"Positive. I told her to look for Emily and that I would be down here as quickly as possible. With everything going on, she wouldn't leave without telling me."

Clark tried calling his daughter again. Still no answer. He tried Emily for the fourth time. No answer. Neither of his calls went straight to voicemail, either.

"Something is wrong," Clark told Maddox.

"We've got a BOLO for them, so they'll turn up soon."

"Unless ..." Clark stopped. He could not bring himself to say the words.

"There's no point going there just yet," Maddox said.

"Do you think the man on the phone is blocking her phone signal?"

"No. Somebody jamming the signals down here would cause quite the ruckus."

"Maybe he has some kind of technology that blocks specific numbers." Clark knew he sounded desperate.

"Not even the feds have toys like that," Maddox said. He was relatively sure of what he was saying.

"I don't know about that." Clark picked up on the detective's lack of certainty.

Detective Maddox placed his hand on Clark's shoulder. He wanted to say something comforting but could not find words that did not sound hollow. He did what men like him do when they want to express their feelings.

"Clark, I need a favor," Maddox said.

"I'm not sure what good I am to do favors right now."

"Probably better than you think. Can you track down info on Joey's dad, a Miles Maldoon?"

"If he wants to be found, probably."

Clark knew what the detective was trying to do. He appreciated the gesture, even though it was not likely to distract him.

"While you do that, I'll find out more about Marcus Delaney. I'm sure it isn't a coincidence that he turned up dead shortly after you visited him."

"You suggesting I had something to do with his death?" Clark asked abruptly. A little too abrupt; the reporter in him knew it made him sound guilty of something.

Maddox snickered.

"You were one of his last visitors. I guess I should ask you where you were last night."

"I spent the evening with you, then took my daughter home and crashed until Vernier sent over a way too enthusiastic courier to wake me up around 7 a.m."

"Any witnesses?"

"Lexi."

"Lexi? I thought you and Emily were a thing."

"We are."

"Then who's Lexi?"

"My dog."

Maddox shook his head. Even in these circumstances, Clark knew how to play him. It made the detective feel better about his friend.

"Cute."

"Are you going to tell me who else visited Delaney?" Clark redirected the conversation.

"That's where I've hit a stumbling block. The system says Delaney was taken to the visitors' area, but there is no record of a visitor."

"Did the visitor bail?"

"Not likely. If Delaney had a visitor, he would have to jump through all sorts of hoops to get in and would be stuck inside the prison until the visit was over. The guards don't get the prisoner until all the visitors' clearances are done. Whoever came to see him knew how to work around the system."

"Like somebody in law enforcement?"

"That's a possibility."

The thought ran chills through Detective Maddox. He did not want to believe that one of his own could be connected to the death of a prison inmate.

Clark could not be still any longer. Emily and Lana were out there somewhere, and he knew someone was keeping them from him.

"I'll get someone at the paper to investigate Joey's dad. In the meantime, I've got to go find them," Clark said.

Maddox knew there was no point in telling him no. If he were in Clark's shoes, he would feel like doing something and failing was better than doing nothing. Besides, he might just stumble across them.

"Okay," the detective said. "You go up this side of the street, and I'll take the other side."

Clark smiled and nodded quietly.

214

Chapter 58

PASTOR DAN FROZE. Emily had dressed in a nun costume; she did every year for the festival. All her student helpers dressed up as peasants. It was her idea of a joke—a terrible pun about an order. The self-amusing humor flew over the heads of her students, but it enabled her to recycle the costumes from year to year. And the jester. He seemed to be the culprit behind Joey's disappearance.

"Do you remember that family we helped rescue from Rudy?" he asked Alicia, referencing their own drama a few months ago where her half-brother terrorized Clark and his family.

"Yeah. How could I ever forget that? Why?"

"Do you think the nun and peasant girl could be them?"

"Maybe. They were about the right age and body types."

"Where are you?"

"In the alley near 24th and Mission, I think."

"Go to where they abducted her. I'll give Detective Maddox a call to meet you there," Pastor Dan ordered.

He did not wait for her to answer. He tapped the red button and searched his contacts to find the detective.

"Maddox," the detective answered.

"Bobby, I think somebody has taken Emily and Lana," Pastor Dan blurted out.

"What?" Joey and Detective Maddox questioned in unison.

Pastor Dan motioned for Joey to be quiet.

"Alicia saw two thugs push a nun, a peasant girl and a court jester into a van."

"If I didn't know better, that sounds more like a setup for a joke."

"It's no joke. Emily was wearing a nun outfit. That's not a common costume," Pastor Dan explained.

"Wait a second," the detective interrupted. "Clark. We got a tip."

He tried to get the reporter's attention, but Clark was engaged in a phone call of his own.

"Where is Alicia?" Detective Maddox continued.

"She is at the site of where they took them. An alley by 24th and Mission."

"Thanks for calling. Take care of Joey. Remind him to keep his mouth shut and let the lawyer do the talking."

"I will."

Pastor Dan turned to Joey and studied the teen at the center of so much drama recently. Whatever he got himself into has pulled several others into his quagmire.

"Are Lana and Ms. Geoffrey okay?" Joey asked.

"We don't know," was all the answer that Pastor Dan could muster. "You know, your uncle cares a lot about you and wants to protect you. He reminded me that it's best if you keep quiet until after you meet with your lawyer."

"He didn't seem to think I should keep quiet yesterday." Joey did not intend for his comment to sound sarcastic, but he found the irony a little too convenient.

"If you talked yesterday, maybe, just maybe, Lana and Ms. Geoffrey would be okay," a slight scolding tinged his voice. "Not to mention that the festival would still be going on and raising the money we need to operate the community center."

"I didn't think about that."

"Didn't think so. What were you thinking about?"

"My mom," Joey mumbled. He looked down for a second and then turned back toward Pastor Dan. His eyes consumed his face. "The same people who have my mom, probably have Lana and Ms. Geoffrey!"

"Probably so."

"That ain't good."

"No, it's not."

Pastor Dan looked out the window and watched the nameless people on the street disappear as they made their way through city traffic. The makeup of the faces streaming by changed as they approached the freeway overpass. Sleek, modern attire made way for grunge and tattered. Makeshift homes, nothing more than a collection of meager possessions, dotted the landscape. He could see the Hall of Justice approaching.

"We are almost there," he told Joey.

The turnoff to the intake center slid past.

"Isn't that where you were supposed to take us?" Pastor Dan asked.

The officer did not reply.

"Officer. Detective Maddox is meeting us here."

No reply. The officer kept his eyes forward, oblivious to the confusion in the cage behind him. He proceeded down Bryant Street until he took the Interstate 80 on-ramp toward Oakland.

"Where are you taking us?" Pastor Dan yelled as he fumbled with his phone to call Detective Maddox.

The phone kept promising it was calling, but the familiar ring of the phone remained elusive. The officer held up a small electronic device and shook his head. Shadows filled the car as they entered the lower deck of the Bay Bridge.

"Joey, don't worry. Everything is going to be okay." The soothing comments were as much for him as they were for his charge.

Chapter 59

CLARK FELT HELPLESS as he walked up the street. His daughter was in danger. So was his girlfriend. And the only person who seemed to know where they were was an anonymous caller that he feared might hurt them. Clark tried something desperate.

"Answer, damn it!" Clark demanded of his phone.

He did not really believe the caller would leave such an easy trail, but Clark had to try. The phone rang a fourth time, then a fifth. Then silence.

"Hello," Clark spoke cautiously.

No answer. Clark wanted to shake the phone, but he knew it would accomplish nothing. The call had fallen into a cellular limbo—a world where connected calls roam in dreaded silence while a nefarious computer hacks your phone. Clark quickly hung up and stared at his failed attempt.

"Where are you, Lana? Tell Daddy where you are," Clark whispered, almost prayer-like.

Suddenly, the phone rang, and his heart nearly burst from his chest.

"Hello," Clark pushed out as he tried to catch his breath.

"I'm disappointed in you, Mr. Solo."

"I'm not happy with you either, but I guess we are stuck with each other."

"In a manner of speaking, I guess you are right. Why did you let them take Mr. Maldoon away?"

"Like I had a choice. Remember, I'm a lowly reporter, not a cop."

"Let's not disparage yourself so quickly, Mr. Solo. Let's wait to do that after you explain why you didn't ask about the senator?"

"I don't care about some corrupt political hack. I just want to find my family!"

A chuckle rolled through the phone, a maniacal little laugh that made Clark's skin crawl.

"Oh, Mr. Solo. I believe you have the order of things all wrong."

"What did you do?" Clark demanded.

"I told you I would keep an eye on Lana for you. And we've got Miss Emily here to keep her company, too."

Clark did not know whether to collapse from sheer terror or to explode into a wild-man rage because a lunatic had abducted his family. He opted for something in the middle.

"What do I have to do to get my family back?"

"Solve the mystery."

Clark tried to focus. What did this guy say already about the senator? Something about the bomb scare being a trial run.

"Can you give me some more clues? I don't know where to start."

"I told you, talk to the senator."

"And ask him what? Do you know why somebody would want to blow up a crowd of innocent people?"

"You might be surprised by what he says. Then again, you might want to figure that out before you ask the question to see if he knows how to tell the truth."

Clark closed his eyes to process the data he had received so far. The fate of his daughter and girlfriend rests in the hands of an unknown senator. Does this person have skeletons to keep hidden? Or is he a good guy pushing back against a heavy-handed political interest that wants an illegal return on its investment?

"What's the endgame here?" Clark asked.

"You make it sound like I am up to something nefarious."

"Pardon me. I guess I was just misinterpreting the bomb thing and the kidnapping thing."

"You are far more clever than sarcasm, Mr. Solo."

"Not really. Nor am I clever enough to do your bidding without more information."

"Tell him about Marcus Delaney, and he'll come around."

"That's supposed to help me?"

"It better."

"Or what?" Clark screamed at the phone, but it did not matter. He had already ended the call.

"Are you okay, Clark?" Detective Maddox asked as he stepped up onto the sidewalk.

"No, nothing is okay."

"Well, I'm not going to make your day any better."

"Let me guess. You have confirmation that somebody abducted Lana and Emily."

"Yes. How did you know?"

"I was just talking to the kidnapper."

Chapter 60

FROM HER SEAT opposite him, Gloria studied the man who had invaded her home. Joey called him Charlie. Other than some graying at the temples, he looked the same as he did when he disappeared from her life fourteen years ago. Their lives were different then. Much of it she regretted, but not his bringing Joey into her life.

"Good evening, Gloria."

He paused on her name in such a way that it sounded more like a question than a statement. She knew what he meant. He was really checking to see if she still went by Gloria. It was not her birth name; nor was he using his. She never really knew what his parents called him. The agency preferred you to keep information like that to yourself. She knew him as Miles. Everyone else knew him as her husband. The agency knew him as her partner in an undercover operation designed to root out a rogue element inside the Central Intelligence Agency.

Technically, their mission was a success. After a couple of years, they penetrated the rogue cell. In reality, their mission was an utter failure. Miles lost sight of their objective to reign the rogue players in. He stopped seeing them as the bad guys. Gloria never quite figured out whether their complex manifesto justifying the need to control certain kinds of people swayed him, or if he became intoxicated with the power that comes with the ability to control people. Either way, the man she once knew was no more.

"Charlie, I presume?"

Her response was as coy as his. He shook his head.

"You know my new name. Guess that means my little project failed his first test."

"How is the truth a failure?"

"What do you know about the truth?" he laughed through his mocking words.

Gloria knew he was not speaking in any grand existential way. He was never that deep. This was just one of his tactics to lower her threshold for resistance, to create self-doubt by manipulating half-truths. He knew her secret. He knew her lie.

"I know it exists, or more accurately, I know He exists."

He snorted. Then he studied her.

"You're still playing the role of a churchgoing woman, aren't you?"

"It's not a role."

"It's always a role. Everybody is playing a role, pretending to be something to get ahead."

"Only liars have to play roles."

"I'd say you've made my point, but I doubt you would concede. I guess there comes a point when the lie has been told long enough, it just becomes the truth. Wouldn't you agree, my dear Gloria?"

"That's clever, for you anyway. You always thought you were cleverer than I did. That's probably why you got snookered."

"No. You were the one who got snookered. You bought the Agency line that we had to shut them down. You accepted the lie that the Agency wanted out of this line of operations. That wasn't true. It never was, and you knew it deep down. They just wanted back in charge, to own us like the puppets we make."

"You are saying that's why the operation had the silly codename of Pinocchio?"

"Always thought that moniker was a little on the nose."

"Why are you back?"

"Back? I never left the agency. You did," Miles said.

Gloria recalled making that tough decision. If she stayed and outed Miles for the turncoat that he was, she would have to give up Joey. Removing Miles would have only destroyed the operation, and the rogue agents would have gone even deeper underground. She naively hoped her departure at a critical point would force the Agency to regroup and insert a new team. It was a false hope.

"Okay. Then riddle me this, bad man. Why did your operation target Joey? I can't imagine he has any strategic value. And what is this thing you've put into Joey's head about introducing him to his brother? I'm assuming that's just another one of your clever tactics for control."

"Oh, Joey just happened to be the right person to cast for the role. And no, it was not a tactic, good theater, but not a tactic. And yes, he has a brother. I just never told you about him."

"Why?"

"Pragmatism mostly. It's not like you could fake a pregnancy and hatch a 4-year-old."

"We could have figured something out. What did you do with him?"

"He's been useful."

"What does that mean?"

Miles smiled. Gloria closed her eyes and rolled them upward. Her brain screamed a prayer. "Help me, Lord!"

"It's a ruse. There is no brother."

"I'm impressed. You still have that amazing talent for reading people, but your divining rod is a little bent. It's only a partial ruse. Joey and his brother have met; they just don't know it."

"Why the diversion?"

"Let's just say I didn't want any unnecessary distractions."

Gloria rolled her eyes. Her former partner never liked giving straight answers. Miles reveled in the illusion that it made him sound more intelligent. In all their time together, she never quite narrowed down which of the laundry list of psychological inadequacies plagued him. His actions only told her of his desperate need to compensate.

"You coerced Joey into all this. You threatened to hurt me. You threatened to hurt his brother, and you needed someone expendable to ensure Joey complied."

"Once again, kudos to you for your deductive skills. The agency could use someone with your talent again."

"Only if that meant putting you behind bars."

"You could have pursued it back then."

"As you say, I had reasons to be distracted. And you knew that when you brought Joey to me."

Miles smiled and placed a finger on his lips as he brought the phone up to his ear.

"I'm disappointed in you, Mr. Solo."

Chapter 61

THE POLICE CAR BARRELED down the crowded interstate. Pastor Dan took note of each familiar landmark as they strolled by—the Yerba Buena Island tunnel, the dreaded interchange cluster of the MacArthur Maze, and now the horseracing track at Golden Gate Fields. He still did not know where they were going.

The silence from the front seat frustrated and confused him. Part of him wanted to believe this officer was legit and doing Detective Maddox a favor. Nothing good for Joey would come out of him getting plugged into the system. Maybe the detective was part of the deception. The rest of him knew it was a false hope. The whole wishful notion ran inconsistent with the man he had come to know. Such clandestine actions would have more than pushed the limits of the detective's integrity. They would have pummeled them to the point where Detective Maddox had changed roles with the bad guys. That did not make any sense.

He glanced over at Joey. A scrunched face pulled the teen's cheeks up into his closed eyes. His lips moved fervently, yet no sound escaped. The pastor readily knew what Joey was doing.

"You know you can say it out loud," Pastor Dan said as he touched Joey's knee.

"But he might hear me?"

"Isn't that the objective?"

"Not God!"

Joey opened his eyes and tossed Pastor Dan a perplexed look. He started flicking his eyes toward the front. His awkward attempts at being coy brought a smile to Pastor Dan's face.

"Is there something wrong with your eyes?"

"No," he whispered. Now, his entire head jerked toward the front.

"That twitch. It's moved to your neck. Do you need to see a doctor?" Pastor Dan put his hand to his face to conceal his amusement.

"No!" Joey pushed out with an exacerbated breath. "I don't want whoever that is up there to hear what I'm praying."

A quiet laugh let Joey know he had once again fallen for the youth pastor's twisted sense of humor.

"Maybe he should hear you pray. Looks like he needs to have the fear of God put into him."

"It's not his fear I'm worried about. It's mine." Joey paused and looked out the window. The last split in the freeway slid out of his view, and they continued north on Interstate 80.

"I think I know where he is taking us," Joey whispered. "You are not going to like it."

Chapter 62

CLARK AND MADDOX RACED over to the alley where Alicia saw the costumed trio pushed into a white van. Two uniformed officers were in tow. She was standing in the street, returning insults to the honking horns and angry cries for her to move out of the street.

"Where was the van?" Maddox asked, skipping any polite formalities.

Alicia pointed straight down.

"I figured you didn't want other cars parking here." Then she looked around and added, "You know, people can be rude."

"Officers, set up a perimeter and let's see if these idiots were stupid enough to leave any evidence," Maddox ordered.

He returned his attention to Alicia.

"Miss Bauer, I never thought I would be glad to see a criminal like you," the detective said.

"I'm assuming there is a compliment in there."

"Only if you can use your powers of observation for good."

"Then there isn't much of a compliment in there."

"There might be more good hidden in there than you realize. What kind of van was it?"

"I don't know. Long and white. The kind you see delivery people use."

"Notice any logos on it that might help us figure out the make and model?"

"No. It happened really fast."

"Okay. Anything distinguishing about it?"

"It was clean and shiny."

"Okay. Did it have windows?"

"No."

"Did it have the extra headroom?"

"No, it was short and really long." Alicia realized how stupid that sounded.

"You said they pushed them into the van. Where was the door?"

"On the side."

"Driver's side?"

"No, he pulled away going right, so it had to be the passenger side."

"Okay. One or two doors?"

"Two."

"Did you get the license plate number?"

"Seriously. Does anyone ever have that for you?"

"Not generally. This should get me enough info to get a BOLO."

As Maddox stepped away to call dispatch, Clark started his own interrogation.

"Miss Bauer. I don't know if you remember me, but I'm the reporter who covered Justin's trial."

"Yeah, I remember."

"Well, that's my daughter and my girlfriend in that van."

"Somebody's kidnapped them again?"

"Unfortunately, yes."

"Could you see if they were okay?"

"Probably. They didn't look hurt, but I can't say for sure."

Alicia paused for a moment. Then, she opted to tell him everything she could. It could mean something to him.

"They were playing with this funky little dude in a court jester outfit when the van doors opened up; two guys came out and snatched them."

"What do you mean, playing?" Maddox asked, rejoining the group.

"He was holding on to them, and they were going in circles around him. The jester never lost his grip on them."

"Did you get a look at the two men who grabbed them?"

"No, but they wore white lab coats and moved fast."

"Could you see inside the van?"

"Not really. There was a man standing at the entrance. He was kind of stocky with graying red hair. Yes, graying red hair. I thought you don't see that often."

"Was he wearing a lab coat as well?"

"No, he was wearing some awful-looking plaid suit that even thrift stores would reject."

Maddox laughed. It never ceased to amaze him how people could remember certain specific details even though they thought they did not really see anything.

"Well, Miss Bauer, it seems like there was a compliment in there after all."

Maddox turned to Clark.

"Maybe Joey might know this guy with no fashion taste."

Maddox stepped away again to make another call.

"This is Detective Maddox. I need you to bring Joey Maldoon to a phone."

The color faded from the detective's face. Clark started to ask what had happened when Maddox whispered, call Pastor Dan.

"What do you mean, you can't find Joey? He should have been there already. Have dispatch ping the car."

Clark scrolled through his contacts for Pastor Dan. Alicia tapped him on the arm and showed him her phone.

"He's not answering," she said. "Maybe he's just ignoring me?"

Clark called. The phone did not ring; it went straight to voicemail. He looked back toward Maddox and shook his head.

"Then somebody call the officer's personal cell!" Maddox yelled. Panic and frustration had taken over.

"He doesn't answer either?"

Maddox paused and took a deep breath.

"Well, I guess we need to put out another BOLO."

A dejected Maddox put his phone back in his front pocket.

"What just happened?" Alicia asked.

"I'm stupid. That's what happened. I put Joey in a police car with an officer I didn't know."

"You can't be expected to know every officer," Clark comforted.

"Yeah, that's okay for run-of-the-mill crooks, but not Joey."

"What are you doing about it?" Alicia asked.

"Not much we can do."

"You have four, maybe five people, kidnapped and you say you can't do anything? No wonder Justin took matters into his own hands."

"There's no point in kicking a man while he's down," Clark said. "I guess that means the man on the phone is our only real lead."

"Looks like it," Maddox affirmed.

"He told me to visit some senator and tell him today was just a dry run. He didn't say which one, but that I could figure it out."

"Probably the pompous one who was going to make a speech today at the festival," Alicia interjected.

"That would be a good start, Clark. But what do I do?"

"I would check on Mikhail. Maybe he can shed some light," Clark suggested. "There's also Delaney. Who killed him, or caused him to be killed?"

"What do I do?" Alicia asked. "My friend is one of those kidnapped, you know."

"Go home," Maddox ordered. "And don't do anything stupid."

"I guess I have to leave that up to you," Alicia said as she stormed off.

Chapter 63

A MILD PITY PARTY enveloped Senator Buster Campbell. He always knew his chances of becoming governor were slim at best, but there was a theoretical shot. Today's failed media grab was supposed to give him a little boost to get the momentum of his campaign going, but the interference of that gallant preacher messed everything up. A generous donor, a self-proclaimed political action committee of one, said he could create a little disturbance that was not likely to hurt anybody, at least not too badly—but it would plunge the relatively unknown state senator into the middle of a media circus. He confidently claimed reporters would not be able to resist the irony of the tough-on-crime candidate being attacked at an event praising a neighborhood celebrating its rebirth from a crime-ridden past. A few news cycles of this storyline and voter sympathy would push him up in the polls, which always translates into the swelling of the campaign coffers. All he had to do was once again hold his nose a bit and take a gamble on the shadier side of politics. He rolled the dice, and it came up snake eyes.

"Senator, there is a Clark Solo here to see you. He is a reporter with ..." His aide did not get to finish his sentence.

"I don't care who is, I'm not talking to any more reporters today."

The thought of giving that obstructionist preacher even a little nauseous praise was more than he could handle today.

"He told me to tell you it was in reference to Marcus Delaney."

"Say that name again." His voice sounded somewhere between shocked and confused.

"Clark Solo."

"Not the reporter. The other name."

"Marcus Delaney."

The senator could feel his day going from bad to worse.

"Okay. Send him in."

"Yes, sir." His aide stepped back out of the office. "Mr. Solo, the senator can see you now."

A flurry of thoughts ran through Campbell's head as Clark entered the room. Why does this reporter want to talk to him about this old case? As far as the public knew, Delaney was a disgruntled client who killed his lawyer when the trial went south. There was no way he knew about anything else.

"Mr. Solo. How can I help you today?" The senator turned on his congenial voice—the kind of tone you need in a political campaign to feign sincerity. After all, he would never get elected if he just said what his mind wanted. "Hey guy, whoever you are, can you try not to screw me over because you don't have a clue what you are talking about."

"Your name was given to me as a person who would know more about today's bomb scare," Clark started.

"Pardon me. Bomb scare? I thought this was about Marcus Delaney." He let a little irritation slip into his tone.

"Well, yes, and no. This call isn't about Delaney per se, but an apparent mutual acquaintance said to bring up his name to ensure you would talk to me."

"Who is this mutual acquaintance?"

"Actually, I was hoping you could tell me."

"How on earth could I know who your friends are?" Irritation morphed into a condescending annoyance.

"Oh, he is not my friend, but he has my attention."

"Sorry, Mr. Solo. I don't think I can help you."

The senator stood.

"He said to tell you that Marcus Delaney is dead. The poor guy apparently killed himself last night. It is not clear whether he had help in the suicide."

Campbell sat back down in his chair. The ambiguity surrounding Delaney's death piqued his interest.

"Did he tell you that?"

"No, our acquaintance was a little light on details. But I'm a reporter, so I did some digging and figured out who Delaney is—make that was. All your friend said was, and I quote, tell him about Marcus Delaney and he'll come around."

"Come around to what?"

"Apparently, according to your friend, today's bomb scare was just a trial run."

"A trial run?" the senator asked. Campbell almost missed a heartbeat. All may not be lost after all.

"He didn't share anything else. To be honest, I thought it sounded like he was using me to convey a threat."

"Oh, it's a threat all right. You know, in my bid for governor, I've taken a pretty hard line on crime and those who make it easy for criminals to walk the streets. I guess my message has upset some folks who would like this state to stay on the namby-pamby approach."

"Who do you think you upset?"

Campbell laughed.

"In this business, even your enemies act like friends, so I'm not sure."

"So why connect the bombing to Delaney?"

Campbell grinned. This is just too easy. He could not have set this up better if he had tried.

"I'm not sure. I was the district attorney over his case, but I didn't handle it directly."

"Which murder case? His lawyer or your employee?"

"Both."

"It doesn't add up," Clark puzzled out loud. "This person made it sound like these questions should rattle you."

"I don't know why he would think that. The fact that I'm not rattled only goes to show I am the right guy for the governorship. I can't be bullied."

"Are we talking about extremist groups? Drug cartels?"

"I can't be certain."

"Well, which one of your enemies would go to the extreme of kidnapping my daughter and my girlfriend just to ensure I wrote a story on you?"

Ouch. Campbell hadn't expected his donor to take such drastic measures to get the media attention. As if setting off a bomb at a public event in San Francisco was not radical enough.

"Kidnapped? Oh my!" The full-on congenial voice had returned.

"Our mutual friend also told me to do some research so I could tell if you were lying or not."

Campbell looked at the clock. The bomb scare fizzle was only two hours ago. How much could he have dug up in that amount of time?

"I don't mean to be flippant, but did you?"

"Yes."

"Yes, that you did the research? Or yes, that you think I am lying?"

"Yes."

"Well, clearly you have some sort of ax to grind. I am sorry about your situation, but I am not your whipping boy." A condescending annoyance returned to his voice.

Clark mused about the senator's roller-coaster ride of voice inflections—a clear indication that this conversation was not going where the senator felt comfortable. Things were about to go from annoying to hostile, thanks to a loose net of cynical reporter connections Clark developed over the years. They all have their stash of dirt on political figures that never quite makes into print. Clark was not sure if their mutual acquaintance anticipated this type of research or was banking on it.

"I wouldn't be so sure about that, Senator. I understand you kind of had a slight disappearance problem back when you were a district attorney. The headlines questioned whether you had abandoned your post."

"I didn't disappear. I took a little time off to address a personal family matter."

"Yeah, I heard that was the spin after the fact."

"No, Mr. Solo. That's just the facts."

"But for a couple of weeks, you were gone without a trace."

"That was just a misunderstanding. In my rush to attend to my family, the paperwork got misplaced in the system somehow."

"So, you said. I find it curious, though, that you just happened to disappear at the same time as Marcus Delaney disappeared."

"Pure coincidence."

"I figured you would say as much. Is it a coincidence too that Molly Milton was Delaney's first murder victim? The same Molly Milton who had a sexual harassment complaint against you. A case that just disappeared when she got murdered."

"You seem to be grasping at straws, Mr. Solo. All of that ancient history is just that—history."

"Well, there is no story about good old Senator Campbell being attacked for his tough-on-crime stance until you answer my questions."

Campbell stared at Clark, trying to size him up like he would a defendant. This man has too much to lose. That kind of pressure makes a man either meek and compliant or bold and defiant. He did not see meek before him. Maybe he needed just a little more pressure.

"I don't think that's a good idea. As you called him, our mutual acquaintance—whoever that is—seems to be calling the shots here, not you. Didn't I hear you say he was securing your compliance by holding your dear ones captive?"

"He didn't tell me what kind of story to write. He just told me to come and talk to you. He said you would know how to save the day, how to prevent the real bombing. I don't know what all that means, but

Senator, I'm inclined to believe you were behind the attempted bombing today, or at the least, it did not surprise you. I'm also inclined to believe our acquaintance is going to throw you under the bus just to show you he can. If I'm right, he is also going to create a plausible cover story to divert the negative attention from you. In this dirty little process, you might just get the governorship after all. And when you do, our little friend is going to remind you how much you owe him, time and time again. You'll hate it, but you will continue selling your soul one piece at a time until there is nothing left. So, have I got the story figured out?"

"Only if you are writing fiction."

"I'm not interested in writing this story, or any story for that matter. I am just looking for answers to get my little world back. If you want me to keep my mouth shut, then give me the answers I need. Who is our mutual friend?"

Campbell felt deflated. Clark had given a compelling closing argument in the trial of his donor's loyalty. The lawyer in him would have told his client that it was time to consider a plea deal. He did not know what to do. Trust the reporter and kiss his political future goodbye or continue to gamble with his donor.

Chapter 64

JONAH SEEMED TO TRANSFORM before their eyes. The quirky mannerisms Lana saw over the last couple of days faded as quickly as he brushed the pointed hat from his head and plunged his face into his cell phone.

"Hey Doctor C. I didn't know you were going to be part of the fun today," Jonah proclaimed in the most normal teenage voice Lana had ever heard. "I don't see anything from Charlie saying there was a change of plans."

"Not everything goes according to plan, Jonah. We just have to adapt and overcome. Isn't that one of Charlie's famous quotes?"

Lana and Emily exchanged glances. It was as if each could read the thoughts of the other: the normalcy of the conversation added to the weirdness of the court jester who had taunted them. Emily shrugged her shoulders in return.

"Sure is. So, where does Charlie want us to meet up?" Jonah asked as he continued to scroll through his phone for some guidance.

The doctor did not answer. He let the question linger in the air and turned his attention to his compelled guests.

"I hope you are comfortable, given the somewhat unusual circumstances," he said.

"I guess so. If I can have my phone, I could look up what the proper etiquette is for kidnapping," Emily retorted.

"I'm sure it says that these bindings are not proper." Lana could not resist adding a little jibe.

"You two are too funny. Joey said he missed how much you guys made him laugh."

"So, you and Joey are friends?" Lana asked.

"More than that."

"That's not what Joey told us."

"He's just joshing with you. He can't stay mad at me; he's ..."

"Jonah," Doctor Callahan interjected while shaking his head back and forth. "This is not the time."

"I was just going to ..."

"No."

"But?"

"No."

Jonah finally relented. His enthusiasm collapsed with an audible sigh, and he retreated into a virtual world on his phone. The sound of whatever game he was playing was barely audible, but it caught Emily's ear. She knew the tune of sorts sounded familiar but could not recall why. The doctor interrupted her distraction.

"Jonah, my boy. Let me have your cell phone." Doctor Callahan extended his hand.

"Why?" Jonah asked as he complied.

Without answering, the doctor passed the phone up to the driver, who tossed the device out of the window. Jonah's eyes fell toward his chin. Soon his shoulders collapsed as the jovial character struggled to hold back tears.

"Charlie just gave me that phone. He said it was a reward for doing a good job. I guess this means you don't think I did as good of a job as he did," Jonah mumbled.

Doctor Callahan wanted to comfort Jonah and explain why he had to get rid of the phone and the tracking device Charlie had installed. He could not. Not here. He feared how it would agitate the teen if he introduced ideas contrary to his conditioning. Instead, the doctor directed his attention to his other captives.

"This isn't really a kidnapping," Doctor Callahan asserted.

"Oh, really?" Emily said, almost laughing. "What do you call it, then?"

"A rescue."

"A rescue?" Emily and Lana said practically at the same time.

"Maybe that isn't the best word. It's more like a preemptive strike than a rescue."

Jonah glanced at the doctor. He wanted to say that he did not know what the doctor meant either but thought better of it. Instead, he looked past Callahan, over his shoulder and through the only view of the outside from the van. On the hillside, he spotted a long row of massive cream-colored tanks connected with a labyrinth of pipes that seemed wider around than he was tall. Jonah figured the doctor must be taking them to the mansion.

"In my experience, when somebody takes you against your will, that's considered kidnapping," Emily said.

"If the police arrest you, is that kidnapping?"

"No, that's different. They only arrest people when they think they have done something wrong," Lana said.

"Ever hear of a thing called protective custody?"

"Yeah, but you are not a cop."

"True, but you all need protection."

"Protection from what? Jonah was the one who was bothering us."

The doctor smiled.

"Jonah is a sweet boy. Maybe a little too loyal for his own good."

"What's wrong with loyalty?" Jonah piped in.

"Nothing, if what you are loyal to is worthy. Otherwise, it can be a heavy burden when you finally realize your mistakes."

"Sounds like a confession to me," Emily said. "Letting us go would go a long way toward showing your repentance."

"I'm sure this is not the best place to drop you off."

Jonah looked beyond the doctor again. They hadn't veered left to go up along the Napa River as he expected.

"Where are we going? I thought we were going back to the mansion," Jonah asked.

"I never said where we are going," the doctor replied.

"Charlie will not like this," Jonah said. His voice trembled slightly.

"You don't have to worry about Charlie anymore."

"No, he has to worry about you now," Lana said.

Chapter 65

DETECTIVE MADDOX STUDIED Mikhail Kuzmin through the observation glass in the interrogation room. He hadn't snagged this case originally, so he listened to the assigned detective rattle off its details as he read over the file of Marcus Delaney. The narrative sounded eerily similar, yet there were no clues to suggest that the cases were connected.

"Do you think this guy is legit?" the detective asked as he finished his case report.

"Do I think he killed her? Absolutely. Do I think he was in his right mind when he did it? Not as confident. Do I think someone else might be involved in this? I'm thinking so," Maddox replied.

His response seemed more directed at his ears than at his colleague. Somehow, he hoped, saying his thoughts out loud might give him clarity. It did not. He put the file down and looked squarely at the other detective.

"When I'm done, Kuzmin needs to go into protective custody."

"Why? Who are we scared of?"

"The biggest why is I can't answer your second question."

"Well, that cleared everything up."

"I know. If this case is connected to Delaney, then Kuzmin is at risk. I already know we have one dirty cop on our hands, and I'm afraid there are more."

There was deep sadness in his voice. Maddox knew his police department was not perfect, but he had been fortunate that all the officers he had worked with put the law first—in both the spirit and the letter of the law.

"I heard about the kidnapping of the bombing suspect. That's just bizarre. Was he kin to you?"

"My godson."

"Any ideas about the others?"

"No. For all I know, it could be you."

"Well, you are safe on that front. I'm not smart enough to get away with being dirty."

"That's a good thing, my friend. That's a good thing." His voice trailed as he walked off to see his guest on the other side of the glass. He carried an extra coffee from the shop next door

"Mr. Kuzmin. I hope this won't take too long. I just had a few questions on a different case that I hoped you might shed some light on," Maddox said in his cheery, performance voice.

"Not sure how," Kuzmin replied.

"You might be surprised. I brought you a coffee—one of those fancy double latte espresso mocha cappuccino something or other that your generation seems to like."

Maddox feigned confusion, though he did not truly understand why people drank those liquid candy bars.

"Thanks."

"You're welcome. I wanted to talk to you about where you went away to a few weeks before the death of Miss Marcos."

"You mean before I killed her?"

"That's not my case. I'm only interested in where you went."

Kuzmin took a swig of his sweet concoction and shrugged.

"I'm not sure where it was?"

"Then how did you get there?"

"I don't know."

"Are you saying somebody took you there against your will?"

"I guess so. I was at my apartment, and the next thing I knew, I'm waking up in a room much like this."

"A police station?"

"I don't know. I never left the room."

"Not even to eat or go to the bathroom?"

"No. The facilities were right there."

"How quaint. Did it have a big window like this one?"

Maddox pointed to the observation window.

"Yeah."

"Do you remember anything else about the room? Like, what color the walls were?"

"Battleship gray. Everything was painted battleship gray. There was a table like this, one chair and a cot. On the wall over there was a big TV. That's it."

"What about the people?"

"What people? Nobody ever came into the room. Some man kept talking to me over the intercom, but no real people ever came in. I felt like a monkey in a zoo."

"Do you know how long you were there?"

"After a while, I lost track of how many days. My friends said I had been missing for at least a couple of weeks."

"Why didn't anyone report you missing?"

"I don't know. Work thought I was just another flake. My friends thought I had gone on a trip or something. My life is not that rigid—well, it didn't used to be."

"Did your friends think your behavior changed after you got back?"

"No. They pretty much let me be me."

"Let's go back to that voice. Was it a man or a woman?"

"A man, I think."

"What did he say?"

"He didn't say much; he just kept repeating it."

"Like what?"

"That's the funny thing. I don't know. I know I heard the voice, and I know he kept repeating things. I just can't remember what he said."

"Does anything ...," the detective paused and switched gears. "Was it a sound or a phrase?"

"Are you suggesting somebody hypnotized me?" Kuzmin interrupted.

"I'm not suggesting anything."

"Can you hypnotize somebody into killing someone?"

"Not that I know of. Unless, they say, you already wanted to do it."

"I didn't want to kill her. I wanted to save her."

"You said there was a big TV. What did you watch?"

"I can't really say. The images went by so fast. I'm not sure I ever saw anything."

"Did the images get you excited? Make you angry? Sad?"

Kuzmin pondered the question. He hadn't really thought about how the images made him feel. He remembered thinking the speed of the images had made him anxious at first. After a while, he started feeling good after a round of images. He even started looking forward to them.

"I know this is going to sound weird, but I felt like I had a sense of duty to do something. I just didn't know what."

"There might have been a time when I would have said that sounds weird, but not anymore. Have you had that feeling since?"

"Once."

Maddox was almost afraid to ask the next obvious question.

"When?"

"When I was trying to save Teri Marcos."

Chapter 66

ALICIA AMBLED HER WAY back to the festival. Workers had already started the teardown process. Her tent was gone. The fanfare that once filled the street evolved into a clang of tools and the occasional barking of commands as vendors picked up stakes. They were moving on to their next event. Alicia was not. She seemed stuck. Everybody seemed to have a purpose except her.

She kept walking down Guerrero Street and made a right onto Market. Her mind did not know where her feet were going. It was focused on Pastor Dan; somebody had kidnapped him. Not just anybody, but a cop. The old Alicia avoided the badge-wearing crowd. The new Alicia was starting to think maybe it would be wise to continue that practice. Detective Maddox seemed okay, a far cry from her sheriff back in Oklahoma. Alicia had used her time in forced captivity to speculate on how life might have turned out differently. What kind of person would she have been if her mom had married that young deputy instead of tricking Frankie Zimmerman into matrimony? There would have been no Rudy Johnson, no running away, no Justin in her life and none of the drama of the last few months. Then again, there is no guarantee that the unfaithful deputy would not have sired outside his vows. Frankie could have been the one to break up the marriage. Rudy could still have been the spurned high school sweetheart. Justin could still have been the one to capture her heart. And her friend would still be in harm's way.

"It's almost as if someone is in control of all this chaos," Alicia thought. A tear ran down her cheek when she longed to know what little sermonette he would have given in response to her comment.

Soon Alicia found herself in the neighborhood of Justin's office. She checked her phone. In all the excitement of the day, she missed his text alerting her that his work distraction was over.

"Still at the office?" she texted.

"Yes."

"I need a hug." The phrase came with an animated image of a couple clinched in a desperate hug.

"Where are you?"

"Almost to your office."

"On my way."

By the time Justin emerged from his building, Alicia had him in her sights. Her right arm swung high in the air to capture his attention. His eyes were already scanning the horizon. He spotted her and made his way toward her. When they met, the two mirrored the animated image.

"I guess today didn't go all that well," Justin said, trying to comfort her.

"That's an understatement."

Alicia relayed the events of the day as the two strolled down the street toward Fisherman's Wharf.

"On top of that, I found out this morning that some prisoner shanked Frankie. He's dead, Justin. He's dead."

"Are you sure?"

Justin regretted the words as soon as they came out of his mouth.

"I didn't see the body, but I can't imagine the guy was making it up. He was an insensitive jerk in how he told me, but he wasn't outright horrible."

"That didn't come out the way I wanted. That sounded totally different in my head."

"I get it."

Justin felt relieved. He could not tell her he was not being insensitive. He only wanted to know if this was part of Frankie's scheme to avoid going to jail.

"By the way, he set me up as the owner of a holding company he created that will give me a nice stipend to stay out of their business."

"So, you might be able to afford one of my nicer properties."

Justin tried to inject a more jovial tone into the conversation. It was short-lived.

"Maybe. I can't think about that right now. I just need to figure out how to help Pastor Dan."

"I don't want to sound cold, but why is this a big deal to you? It's not like you go to his church or anything."

It was not his intention to sound petty and jealous. He just did not understand why this man of the cloth meant so much to her.

"I don't know. You're right. I haven't been going to his church, but if you knew him, really knew him, you would understand that he has been churching me anyway. He's one of the good guys. He's not like you and me. The streets did not toughen him. He's strong in spirit, though, and he's definitely as stubborn as it gets. Still, I don't know if he has what it takes to survive."

Her worried tone touched Justin. In all the time he had known her, he had never seen her show genuine compassion for another person. Of course, it bothered him that this newfound emotion was for another man—a man with whom the old Alicia shared a special bond of tragedy. He told himself that his fears rested with a different Alicia. He hadn't completely sold himself on the idea yet.

"Do I need to round up the guys for another commando mission?" he half-heartedly joked.

Alicia laughed. The infectiousness of her amusement drew Justin into the moment as well.

"I know you were probably just kidding, but that might be exactly what we need to do," Alicia said.

Excitement exuded from Alicia for the first time today. She had a purpose, and it was not focused on her own woes. Once again, she was about to take on risks with no concern for a potential reward. She had changed.

Chapter 67

THE SOUND OF THE DETECTIVE'S VOICE echoed through the pulsating throbs in Clark's head. His brain was pushing back, crying uncle at the myriad of details whirling in his mind like a dust storm. It craved action—doing something to get Lana and Emily back. It craved results—holding them in his arms once again. His cravings were not being met; his brain was starving for what it needed.

The detective was only feeding it more of these seemingly unrelated tangents that made it difficult to focus on what he learned from Mikhail Kuzmin. Under normal circumstances, his reporter instincts would have told him to doubt this report. Things seemed just a little too convenient, like Kuzmin was trying hard to put random pieces together for a slick defense. Then again, his exchange with Senator Campbell was not any less over the top.

"What do you make of all this?" Clark asked.

"Honestly, nothing. I make nothing of all this because nothing makes sense."

The detective resorted to pacing. He paced. It was his thing. Some detectives stroked their beards or twiddled pens. It was a mindless thing detectives do as their brains process disjointed information.

"That's our only consistency. Nothing. Nothing is what it seems."

The comment stopped Maddox.

"You're right."

"Woo-hoo! Do I win a prize?" Clark's flippant answer mirrored his confusion over the detective's aha moment.

"Do you not see, my dear Watson? We are busting our brains trying to fit the extremely weird into something that approaches normal. It does not fit and never will. What if we do the opposite; embrace all the bizarreness as normal and see where it takes us?"

"Well, Sherlock. I guess we have exhausted all the possible explanations and have only the impossible left," Clark said in a British accent.

"Indubitably."

The detective allowed himself a brief smile before resuming his pacing. The revelation hadn't exactly produced the answers they were hoping to find. Clark rattled off the random pieces of the puzzle they had. An anonymous tip clues them into the fact that a couple dozen murders are connected. Not by the victims, not by the perpetrators, but by the defense that claimed they were trying to save the victims. Kuzmin said he felt like he was doing his duty. Joey disappears and reappears just in time to set off a bomb scare that a seedy politician may have helped orchestrate. An odd court jester fellow fits in here somehow, along with Joey's parents being connected with Clark's anonymous caller. And, lastly, two sets of kidnappings within minutes of each other are somehow linked to this dubious politician and the murder of a crazy inmate after Clark spoke to him in prison.

"If we assume some sort of mind control is happening, where does that put us?" Detective Maddox postulated at the end of the reporter's tally of events.

"In some pretty scary territory."

Clark thought about how understated those words were. Of course, it is scary. How could it not be? Some strangers in a white van kidnapped Lana and Emily. A rogue cop kidnapped Joey and Pastor Dan. Nothing made sense as to why kidnap any of them. They had no strategic value, no power, no influence. They certainly did not have connections to someone with money. This could not be part of an elaborate ruse to manipulate Clark into abusing his bully pulpit. Something must have gone wrong. Somebody is punting and making random innocents pay the price.

Clark's phone rang, almost on cue with his thoughts. He looked at the caller ID. It showed an anonymous caller, but, unfortunately, he knew who it was.

"Clark here."

"Good day, Mr. Solo," Charlie offered.

Clark put the phone on speaker and motioned to the detective to keep quiet.

"Not as long as you have my daughter and my girlfriend."

"Oh, it could still be a good day."

"Sounds promising."

"That's much better. More pleasant, don't you think?"

"I'm not concerned about how pleasant you feel."

"Oh, don't be like that. Hostility doesn't become you. Like the hostility you showed the good senator."

"You ain't seen hostile. I was direct. If he can't handle being asked direct questions about his actions, he does not belong in public office."

"Did it work? Did you get the answers you had hoped for?" Charlie teased Clark.

"Aren't you really asking if I got the answers you were looking for?"

"Is there a difference?"

Clark tired of the caller's coy answers. He pushed forward with some more of his directness.

"There is if you are scrambling to figure out who has taken control away from you. I don't think you have my daughter or my girlfriend. Somebody else got to them before you could. That's why you co-opted that patrol officer to get your little minion back. He's our link to your agenda. I guess you figured getting the pastor was just the cost of doing business. How am I doing for getting the answers I was looking for?"

"My, my, Mr. Solo. You got all that from the senator?"

"Not from him. He's just a bumbling idiot who seems easily outmaneuvered, which is why you are trying to get him elected. I got all those answers from you."

"I guess I should be more careful with my words."

"Guess so."

"All that cleverness does not answer our mutual problem," Charlie said, letting a tinge of defensiveness slip into his voice.

"No, it doesn't."

Clark did the unthinkable in this situation. He hung up on Charlie. Detective Maddox did not allow himself to be shocked by Clark's actions.

"What are you doing?" he yelled.

"He doesn't have Lana and Emily, so I wasn't wasting my time with him."

"Uh, what about my Joey? Pastor Dan?"

"I can't worry about them right now."

"Excuse me?"

"I'm not writing them off. If we find my girls, I think it will lead us to Joey."

"That's a pretty big gamble you are taking."

"Yeah, I know."

"I pray it wasn't a gamble."

"I guess I should do that, too."

Chapter 68

CLARK CAPITALIZED ON THE CLARITY of the moment and rushed off to the law offices of Greg Vernier. The detective wanted in on the questioning, but the reporter declined the invitation.

"There are things he can say to me that he can't or won't say to you," Clark explained.

"True, but that doesn't mean I can't still be listening," Detective Maddox said with a smile.

Clark conceded, although it probably went against every grain of his journalism ethics. Then again, he was not really concerned about writing a story. He was primarily a father seeking answers. His journalism training was also pointing him back to the wisdom of one of his old professors. "If a story has you spinning like a top, just stop and start walking things backwards. It will either fall over from a lack of momentum, or it will start going the other direction where you are in control."

Clark did not wait for the normal pleasantries with the receptionist. Her presence on a Saturday surprised him. He expected Vernier to be alone.

"I don't have an appointment, but that doesn't matter."

He stormed past her desk and made his way down the corridor. The receptionist was not fast enough to block his path, but had time to buzz her boss's office and tuck away into the secure room behind her desk.

"You've been holding back," Clark yelled as he pounded on the locked mahogany door. He looked down the hall and saw the empty reception desk. She must have tripped some security measures. He forced himself to calm down and proceeded with a less forceful tone.

"I knew it from the beginning but thought I would hold my tongue to see where this story played out. Greg, I never imagined you would be involved with a kidnapper."

Clark could hear an audible click and opened the door. Vernier stood with his back facing him, apparently studying the afternoon skyline.

"Good afternoon to you too, Clark."

Vernier continued to stare out the window. The lawyer did not want Clark to know he was more shocked by what the reporter had just said than by his bursting into his office.

"Do not play lawyer nice with me. Where are they?" Clark shouted as he pounded on the desk. He knocked over an ornately framed photograph on the desk and clumsily righted it.

"You are going to have to slow down and catch me up," Vernier said as he turned around. Looking deep into the eyes of his accuser, he proclaimed, "I don't know what you are talking about."

"Somebody kidnapped my family. Somebody in a white van, who I suspect, double-crossed whoever was behind the bomb scare this morning. Then a rogue cop, presumably on the take of the angry person who just got double-crossed, kidnapped the kid being used as a stooge for the bombing and a local youth pastor. And you are involved somehow. That pretty much catches you up, so where are they?"

"Clark, if I could tell you something to get them back, I'd do it in a heartbeat."

"Don't hide behind attorney-client privilege. Your client is involved in a new crime, so that privilege crap is out the window."

"Only if he told me was going to commit a crime."

"Or you had reason to believe he was." Clark had just double-checked how that law worked.

"True, but I didn't have that either."

Clark collapsed into one of the red leather chairs in front of the lawyer's ornate wooden executive desk. The whoosh of his body tipped over a picture frame again.

"That was not the answer I was hoping for," he muttered as he righted the frame.

"We both knew this was going to be messy and involve some obviously dangerous people. I never imagined they would resort to kidnapping," Vernier consoled as he took his place behind his desk.

"How could you not? People going missing is all part of their modus operandi."

"They all seemed to have disappeared voluntarily, not kidnapped."

"Apparently, your client hasn't been forthcoming with you."

"What do you mean?"

"Kuzmin said he doesn't know how he disappeared. He was in his apartment and woke up in some kind of secured facility."

"Clark, I didn't know. You have to believe me. I didn't know."

"I believe you, but that does not help me much. What do I do now to get my family back?"

"I don't know what to say. I gave you everything my client allowed me to share."

"Well, can you tell me at least who your client is?"

"No, I'm afraid I can't."

"Then, I'm still stuck."

"Let me double-check something."

Vernier pushed a button on his desk phone console.

"Nora. Everything is okay. Can you come into my office, please?"

Clark could hear a door open and the click of heels coming down the hall. When silence returned, Vernier cleared his throat.

"Nora, did you get everything we talked about over to Mr. Solo's house?"

"Yes, Mr. Vernier. The courier said he had delivered everything this morning."

"Including all the redacted medical records?"

Nora did not answer. Her body language conveyed her unwillingness to answer the question with Clark in the room.

"It's okay. Go ahead and answer my question."

Nora looked at her employer with puzzled eyes. She could not under why he wanted her to admit that they may have exposed to the media the name of their client, who wished to remain anonymous.

"You didn't tell me to redact the medical records," she confessed. Nora wanted to add that Vernier had made it sound like the copies were being sent to a civil lawyer to determine if there was a possible class-action lawsuit.

"Oh my! That was a terrible oversight on my part. I can't believe I could have made a mistake like that. Clark, I know it is a lot to ask, but I need you to refrain from examining the medical records in those files until Nora has time to correct my mistake."

"Sure, Greg. I'll do that."

Chapter 69

PASTOR DAN LOOKED UP. He did not recognize his surroundings. It appeared he was in some sort of open building. Someone had bound his feet, wrapped his arms around a metal column and cuffed his hands together. The cold cement floor reminded his aging body that he was not as young as he tried to act. The paint-covered windows kept most of the light out, except where streaks of sunshine peered through curls in the dark brown paint.

He looked around. He did not see Joey. It was difficult for Pastor Dan to remember what had happened. His groggy head vaguely recalled the police car exiting the interstate and traveling north along a river, the Napa River, if his geography was right. They drove past the ferry preparing to dock and made their way over a high bridge that took them to a more industrial area with bulky, old buildings. There was something distinctive about them, but he could not bring it to mind. The movie scrolling in his head showed only flashes of scenes. The last scene was of the police officer who had abducted them exiting the car and tossing something back in as he closed the door. White smoke filled the vehicle. He and Joey started coughing just before everything went black.

In the distance, he could see a small portal open, and a man stepped through the opening in the large bolt-studded door. Pastor Dan thought about calling out but changed his mind. He stared in the man's direction. He could make out a gun in the man's right hand. His heart pounded faster with each step the man took.

"I don't suppose you are here to rescue me," Pastor Dan said when the man stood before him.

"Maybe. What do you think you need rescued from?"

The man let a smug smile push up the corners of his mouth. His eyes remained cold, staring directly at his captive on the floor.

"Well, for starters, I don't normally wear this kind of jewelry."

The man laughed.

"That's just to keep you from wandering off accidentally. There are some places around here where you can get hurt if you are not careful."

"That seems like a polite lie."

"I prefer structured truth."

"Truth? I'm not sure the truth is all that important to you."

The man took a step back and eyed the pastor.

"You know, you are kind of cocky for someone in such a precarious position."

"Believe it or not, I've been in worse positions before."

"You know. I believe you. That would have been about six, seven years ago, if I recall correctly. It was a shame what happened to Tory. The little mishap with your girlfriend. I have to confess, it wasn't supposed to happen that way."

His response shocked Pastor Dan. Was this man responsible for Rebecca's death? He had always assumed they were just a couple of random addicts who thought she was an easy score for drugs. It sounds like this was the man who tormented Tory Avlah. Anger swelled up inside him. Pastor Dan could feel the color of his face deepen to mirror the dark rage pulsating through him. He pulled on his chains in a feeble attempt to lunge toward the man. When gravity took its hold, Pastor Dan could feel something else take hold of him. Whispers into his ear brought a calm that belied his situation.

"You seem to know something about me, and yet, I know nothing of you. Let's start with something simple. What is your name?"

"Today?"

The response puzzled the youth pastor.

"Okay, I guess I'm asking, what is your name today?"

"You can call me Charlie."

"What was your name back then?"

"Some folks were calling me Miles, too."

"I guess that answers my earlier question. Truth isn't all that important to you."

"I wouldn't say that. Truth is important to me when it serves my purpose. If not, I create my own truth."

"You know the proper name for creating your own truth is a lie."

"So judgmental, Pastor. No wonder people these days are abandoning your church. You make everything enjoyable and beneficial sound like a sin."

"Only a liar would turn evil into good and good into evil."

"I don't know much about the things of which you speak. I just know that I do what I do because I need what I want," Charlie said.

"So good or bad doesn't matter to you?"

"I only do things that are good for me."

"That's not the same thing as doing good."

"Says who? Is your good better than my good?"

"If it were my good, then no. My good is no better than your good. But I do not define good; God does."

"I don't believe in your god, so his definitions don't matter."

"I did not realize you were so powerful that your beliefs determined whether God exists."

"In my world, that is a correct statement, and right now, you are in my world."

"I guess now is not a good time to point out that you are in God's world, not yours, so what's true is not up to you."

Charlie laughed. He liked how this man stuck to his convictions, seemingly unfazed by his circumstances. Pastor Dan either had a reason to be confident, or he was too stupid to understand the gravity of his situation. The latter did not seem to be the case, but only time will tell.

"Okay, Pastor, let me ask you this. You know when Eve put that so-called forbidden fruit to her lips? Do you think God could have shown her everything that would go wrong?"

"Is it possible? With God, all things are possible as long as they don't contradict his perfect character. The more salient point is not what God could have done, but what Eve did, or more accurately, didn't do. She didn't trust God," Pastor Dan explained.

"Okay, if you say so. But in that instant between the fruit touching her lips and her teeth biting into it, God could have revealed all the death and destruction to follow."

"Okay. I get what you are describing, but what is your point?"

"Do you think if she had had that information, Eve would still have eaten the fruit?"

"You know what if questions are often pointless, but I'll play along. Not just because you have that gun pointed in my direction."

Charlie lowered the gun slightly.

"Thank you. I think the first thing you must do is ask yourself, why didn't she believe God in the first place? He had already said if you eat of the fruit from the tree of good and evil, you will surely die."

"So, eating the fruit was not the first sin?"

"Let's just say it was a multitude of sins occurring almost all at once that resulted in man abandoning God. Coveting and pride, mostly pride. Don't forget, Adam failed before his first bite, too. He never rebuked the serpent or Eve for their actions. Some have suggested that his sin trumps hers."

"Interesting. Then, Eve would still have eaten the fruit?"

"Yes, I think she would have."

"You don't think knowing the outcome changes behavior?"

Pastor Dan just stared at Charlie. He felt his eyes shooting the look of disbelief his mother used to scold him with as a child.

"We can see it hasn't affected your behavior," Pastor Dan said.

"You are assuming the police want to do anything about me."

"That's not the outcome I'm talking about. I was thinking a little bit more eternal."

"I told you I do not believe in your god."

"You keep saying that, but it does not change reality. If I tell you I don't believe in your gun, does that mean those bullets can't kill me?"

"Do you want to find out?"

"No, do you?"

"That's pretty slick the way you did that," Charlie said with a laugh.

"It's not slick. It's the plain, simple truth."

"You keep saying that too, but you could be wrong."

Pastor Dan paused again. He knew he needed to speak from a heart not his own and set aside the thoughts rampaging through his head.

"Well, Charlie, if I am wrong, it will only be for a few more years. Eternity will be a long time for you to be wrong."

"You seem pretty confident about the few more years."

Chapter 70

WHEN THE VAN DOOR rolled back, Emily could not believe her eyes. It looked like they had parked in front of the childhood home of her best friend's aunt. She looked at Lana. Her eyes must have shared the question racing through her mind.

"I think it is," Emily whispered as they both looked back at the Victorian farmhouse.

"Is Charlie going to meet us way out here in the middle of nowhere?" Jonah asked as he jumped out of the van.

"No, Jonah."

"It's not nowhere. It's my family's house," Lana proclaimed.

"So, it is," Doctor Callahan said. "So, it is."

The driver shuffled Emily and Lana toward the house where Lois grew up. Doctor Callahan called Jonah to him and motioned for him to walk with him toward the barn.

"Jonah, my boy, I need to talk to you about your friend, Charlie."

"Okay." The words reluctantly emerged. He battered a rock between his feet before slowly lifting his head and staring at the man he called Doctor C. "Charlie doesn't know we are here, does he?"

"No Jonah. He doesn't."

"Why?"

"It's the only way to keep you safe, to keep Joey's friends safe."

"Nobody was going to hurt them. Charlie promised."

"He's made that promise before. He's never kept it."

"Really?"

"I'm ashamed to admit I know so, because on some of those occasions, I was the one who helped him break that promise."

"I don't get it. Charlie said we must take care of each other. Outsiders are the evil ones."

"Outside of what? It took me a long time to realize what that really meant. Anyone outside of him is expendable."

"That's not true."

"I know it's hard for you to understand. That's my fault, too. You know all those training sessions you had with me."

"The ones with all the flashing lights and weird music."

"Yes, those. I was training you. I was conditioning you so you would be susceptible to control, so Charlie could control you."

"He doesn't control me. I do things for him because I want to."

"Because you want to make him happy? Because you want his approval? Did you ever think that maybe what you were doing was not okay?"

"Charlie wouldn't have us do anything wrong."

"True, if you let Charlie define what is right or wrong. But he doesn't get to do that; that's only something God can do. And no matter what Charlie told you, he is not on par with God. Satan maybe, but not God."

"He never said he was a god."

"Maybe not in so many words. Did he ever tell you where he got his authority from?"

"No, he's Charlie."

"That alone should tell you something. Good people in positions of power don't act on their own authority, but on the authority vested in them. They don't just assume it because that would be tantamount to stealing from the person they are lauding power over." Doctor Callahan paused for a second or two, then continued. "I don't suppose he ever mentioned that he works for the CIA either?"

"No, but so. He doesn't have to tell us everything about himself."

"True, he doesn't. This little tidbit, however, would have been important to know before you pledged your loyalty to him."

"Okay, he works for the CIA. That's not a bad thing."

"No, it is not. In fact, I must admit there was a time when he was one of the good guys. He was even trying to clean up the agency of the very kind of person he has become. But once he tasted the power they possessed, he only ousted them so he could take over."

"You are making this all up."

"Jonah, I wish I were. I've been part of his scheming for a long time. If I'm honest, I have to admit my hands weren't all that clean when I got into this so-called business, maybe just a little naïve about where my ego had led me. That said, he has gone too far. What he has done to kids like you and Joey; it's just wrong."

"He did nothing to us," Jonah said confidently. When his words faded into silence, so did his certainty. "Did he?"

"Yes. Your mom was so desperate when she came to us all those years ago, and he knew it. Life had been hard on your mom, and she had made a few bad choices along the way. She knew it. She wanted something better for the two of you, something she could never have imagined doing herself. She didn't want your lives tainted by her circumstances. He knew it and sold her on promises to fulfill all her motherly dreams for you two. He never intended to do anything he promised, and somehow, in that Charlie way, she didn't live long enough to hold him to his word."

"Are you saying Charlie killed my mom?"

"Not with his own hands, but still just as guilty. Me, too. In some roundabout way, I'm guilty in her death as well."

Jonah's eyes exploded with that revelation. Before the doctor could explain further, the familiar sound of his phone interrupted them. He could not avoid this conversation any longer. He motioned for Jonah to remain quiet.

"Hello Charlie?"

"Well, Doctor Callahan. I guess you are not so meek and mild after all. What plans do you have for your guests?"

"Nothing that concerns you."

"Everything about them concerns me. I'm concerned about you, too."

"I'm touched, but don't expect me to shed any tears."

"It's not tears you should expect to shed."

"Resorting to threats, are we?"

"No, keeping promises."

Then, Jonah snatched the phone out of the doctor's hand and raced up the driveway.

"He has brought us to an old farmhouse. Lana said it is her family's house."

The phone flew from Jonah's hand as someone tackled him from behind. Jonah hadn't seen one of Callahan's henchmen following them from a discreet distance. Doctor Callahan recovered the phone.

"Charlie?"

"Yes, good doctor. I'm still here. I'm glad to hear your magic touch doesn't just rub off."

"I wish it did. Just leave us alone."

"You know I can't stop caring about you and the boys."

Chapter 71

THE CONFRONTATION WITH CLARK irritated Vernier. Not that he blamed the newspaper reporter for his emotional invasion of his office. He could hardly blame him for that. No, he was irritated at Doctor Callahan for inserting him into his scheme of redemption, as he called it. Vernier was not sure it was all that redemptive, more like purging his soul by way of revenge.

He also did not like the cloak-and-dagger mystique. Why couldn't he just reach out to his client through normal means and not send out a bat signal of sorts and wait? It had been nearly thirty minutes and still no response. Vernier reached for his phone to send another cryptic text message but was startled as it buzzed in his hand.

"Tell that newspaper reporter I'm sorry. I really was trying to keep his family safe." The words spewed from Doctor Callahan before Vernier could even acknowledge his call. They came so quickly. He did not know how to react to the doctor's despondent tone—an odd mixture of genuine remorse and utter failure.

"Why are you apologizing? Did something bad happen?"

"Yes, someone compromised my location."

"What do you mean, someone has compromised your location?"

"Charlie knows."

"Charlie knows what?"

"He knows I have Jonah and Clark's family."

"Kidnapping. You are telling me you kidnapped them?"

"No. I just got them to a safe place before Charlie could hurt them."

Vernier paused as he stared at the photograph of him fishing with his father. It was out of place on his desk. A vintage wooden pen peeked out from its side. Clark must have left his pen, he thought. He smiled and tapped the speaker button on his phone.

"I don't understand. You took Emily, Lana and Jonah to a safe place, but you didn't kidnap them? Is that right?"

"Yes. It's not that hard of a concept if you know what Charlie does to people."

"Okay. Where is this safe place you say is no longer safe because of Charlie?"

"It doesn't matter. I won't be there."

"What do you mean you won't be there? What are you going to do with Clark's family? Take them with you?"

"That's the idea."

"You can't keep running—not with three people in tow. The police or Charlie will catch up with you, eventually."

"Right now, I can't tell the difference."

"You mean you think the police are working for Charlie?"

"For. With. I'm not sure which is more correct, but Charlie clearly owns a few of them."

"That means there are a few he doesn't own. Doctor Callahan, where are you? Where can I send some folks I trust your way?"

Doctor Callahan paused. His plan was not to surrender himself for his part in Charlie's scheme. He hoped Clark's reporting skills would do what he did not have the courage to do. He hoped to put enough crumbs out there so that they focused on Charlie alone. He could not rely on that hope now.

"You're right. There is no point in running."

The doctor could hear the ping of an incoming text. "Two black SUVs coming your way."

"Then where are you?"

"I'm in a world of hurt, that's where I am."

The sudden sense of urgency in his voice startled Vernier.

"What's wrong? What's happened?" the lawyer exclaimed, mirroring his tone.

"Tell Clark to go where it all started. The old Victorian farmhouse. Its secrets will be staring him in the face."

"What does that mean?"

Doctor Callahan did not respond. The screen on Vernier's cell phone gave him the answer why. He thought for a second and continued the conversation anyway.

"Are you telling me that Clark will find his family at some old Victorian farmhouse? Are you sure they will be safe from Charlie? What do you want him to do with Jonah?"

Vernier paused long enough for a phantom response.

"I guess you are done talking, Doctor Callahan. I pray Clark can unravel your cryptic message better than I can."

Chapter 72

ALICIA SAT BACK and marveled at Justin. His black hair slightly ruffled from trying to put into action an off-the-cuff remark he had made a couple of hours earlier about rounding up the boys for another commando mission. Joining them at the dining room table to map out the possibilities was the private eye, who tracked an out-of-place character at Justin's trial to an old Victorian farmhouse and stumbled onto the place where Rudy Johnson had stashed Alicia and her father.

"The biggest problem, as I see it, is we don't know where to look," explained Tim Martin. "It took a lucky happenstance to find Alicia. It could be weeks before we catch a break like that, if at all."

Justin shrugged in agreement and stared for a moment out the picture window at his Russian Hill home. He could see the Golden Gate Bridge in the distance. He recalled that, too, was considered an impossible task. Justin thought if they could persevere and get it done, so could he.

"We still have to do something. I kind of owe this guy everything. He did more to save Alicia from that psycho than I did."

Martin recognized the calm, resolute tone of his friend. Once again, his commitment to this idea showed he needed to act, even if it was foolhardy.

"I get it. But you've gotta face the facts. We just don't have the kind of resources it takes to track down this Pastor Dan," Martin said, trying to insert a little bit of reality into the conversation.

"Don't worry about the money."

"It ain't about money. Tracking a person who is trying to hide is tough enough. You know them, so you can see the clues they leave behind. But we are talking about a person who has been kidnapped, and we don't even know who or why. That's next to impossible. Remember, Rudy essentially came to us. We didn't find him."

Justin looked toward Alicia. He could see how Martin's comments had burst her enthusiastic bubble. He felt uneasy about her emotional attachment to someone who was supposed to be nothing more than a counselor to her.

"What do you think?" Justin asked her.

"I think I'm going to be sick," Alicia said as she dashed away. She failed to hold back the tears long enough to shut the bedroom door.

"I guess that tells you our answer," Justin told Martin.

"Okay," he said, throwing his hands up to show he would no longer push back on the idea. "What do you want me to do?"

"Nothing. I think we should let Frankie take care of this?"

"Frankie? I thought Alicia said some guy shanked him in prison."

"Maybe. Maybe not. Frankie is like throwing trash into the ocean. It may disappear for a while, but it will wash ashore again somewhere."

"Rather philosophical of you, I think. But I don't get it."

Justin smiled as he pulled out his cell phone and selected one of his favorites.

"Randy. Can you get me access to a safe deposit box tonight?"

"Why?"

"It's too complicated to explain, but it's important. Can you do it?"

* * *

Alicia could not bear the thought of doing nothing. Pastor Dan had become more than just a counselor to her. He seemed more like family. At first, she would have placed him in the weird-uncle category. Now, she considered him more like a big brother who picked on her but would let nobody else do the same. Ironically, he was now the one she would go to in a situation like this.

"What would the good padre do?" Alicia asked herself as she paced about the room. "What would he tell me to do if I dropped this ugly mess on his lap?"

She looked down. A flokati rug lay along Justin's bed. She remembered getting it for him because she did not enjoy getting out of a comfy bed and placing her delicate feet on the hard, wood floor. Justin had joked that the pile was so long he could sleep on it without a blanket. She almost looked away, but something compelled her to look back at the wool rug. She suddenly knew what he would do.

"But Padre, I don't know how to pray. At least, not the way you do."

She said the words out loud as if he were in the room with her. Then, she filled in the blanks of what she knew he would say.

"So what! It's not about you anyway."

Alicia laughed at her friend's candor and could not wait to tell him about this little conversation. She collapsed her body on the edge of the bed and slid to her knees on the rug. With her eyes closed and hands clasped together, she spoke to the person who Pastor Dan said gave him great comfort.

"Heavenly Father ..."

Chapter 73

GLORIA LOOKED AROUND, slowly rising from a chemically in-duced slumber. Miles was not even subtle about imposing it on her, tell-ing her she knew the drill and why he was going to give her a little blackout time. She was in a jail cell of sorts. She stood and could see it was a row of old prison cells. Each adorned with two metal bunks stacked on one side and a solitary white porcelain commode on the other. Everything about the place felt familiar, not that she had been on the wrong side of the bars before. Yet, her eyes were experiencing déjà vu. She could see Joey a couple of cells down the row.

"Where are we, sweetie?" Gloria called out.

"The brig." His matter-of-fact tone surprised her.

"Oh, when did you learn to speak Navy?"

"I guess when in Rome, do as the Romans do."

"We are on a Navy base?"

"Used to be," Joey continued in his sober tone. He did not even stir from his position on the upper bunk. "I guess they used to build ships and submarines here."

"Is this where you stayed while you were gone?"

"Not the whole time. These are pretty nice digs compared to the place we called home."

"Why did you come here?"

"Well, for me, the idea of being in the movies lured me here. Other guys didn't come here as willingly as I did."

"Why did you stay?"

Joey sat up and looked toward his mother's cell. He just stared at her.

"Sorry, I guess that was a dumb question." Gloria realized it was not his option when he got to leave.

"Don't suppose anybody has ever escaped?"

"A few, but the word is at a severe cost to someone they cared about."

"Oh."

A heavy metal door opened, creaking under its weight and age. The slow pace of thuds told Gloria a large, ungraceful man was coming their way. She looked toward Joey. He had disappeared from the top rack. She followed his lead and tucked herself into the lower rack. As the threatening sound lumbered past, Gloria held back a chuckle. Whoever he was, he was only an oversized teenager. He did not even look into the cell. He kept his eyes looking forward and plunged ahead until he made his way back to the door. Gloria waited until she heard the door close.

"What was that?" she asked.

Joey laughed.

"We called him the cuckoo. He does a walk-through like that at the top of every hour."

"It doesn't look like he's any threat to stopping us from getting out of here," Gloria pondered out loud.

"He isn't. There are more guards on the other side of the door."

"Oh."

Gloria felt slightly embarrassed about her off-the-mark observations. They betrayed her CIA training. It did not really matter that she was rusty, having walked away shortly after Joey entered her world. She should have expected such Machiavellian tactics from Miles.

"Obviously, I am just guessing about what's going on out there, but you would think somebody would have noticed all of this activity and gotten suspicious."

"Not really, Mom. All people see is a bunch of people hanging around on movie sets. Weird is normal in that world."

"Still."

"Don't you get it? People see only what helps them survive, and then they misinterpret half of what they see. It's like they walk through life all drugged up."

"Most people, though, are not on drugs."

"More than you might think. No, the drug I'm talking about is ignorance. They would rather wallow in the familiar pain of their ignorance than take a chance on experiencing actual truth."

"Wow. That's some heavy stuff there. Is that your thinking, or somebody else's?"

"Mine, I think. Maybe Charlie's. I can't tell anymore."

As her son continued to talk, Gloria realized that even their conversation echoed something she had experienced before. Then the light bulb illuminated; she was figuring out Miles' setup here.

"You said the movie sets lured you in?"

"Yes."

"Then, I have probably seen all this in a movie."

"Probably."

Gloria laughed. She just let it spill out of her in waves, opting not to subdue herself to her usual proper decorum.

"What's so funny?" Joey called out.

"That it all makes sense. Of course, Miles—Charlie as you call him—would be attracted to a movie set, if for no other reason than to feed his own ego."

Her laughter faded, and her voice became serious again.

"What I don't get is why."

"Why what?"

"Why is all this so sloppy? None of this is the way Miles operates. It's not his M.O. Yes, he has an ego a mile long, but he is a thoughtful, long-game kind of player. Putting himself in such a high-exposure environment isn't the way he does things."

"Maybe he wants to get caught. Maybe he's just getting old."

"Hey, don't go down that old-people thing. I'm only a couple of years behind him. But you may be on to something."

Gloria started ticking off questions. Joey knew to ignore them. It was her way of thinking through a problem.

"What would be his advantage in getting exposed? He would gain notoriety but would lose the power position. He would not do that. Then who would expose this operation? Somebody who has already lost the power position and resents Miles. Who did Miles usurp in this process? Who lost their claim to fame because of Miles?"

She looked toward Joey. He had resumed playing his air drums.

"Sweetie."

"Yes, Mom."

"What kind of command structure does Charlie have? Who's in charge when Charlie is not around?"

"Nobody."

"Nobody?"

"By the time you get through all the stuff with Doctor C, most people aren't really able to do anything that strays from what Charlie wants."

"What did this doctor do? Wait!" Gloria shuddered. "I don't think I want to know that right now. Just tell me, was the doctor's name Callahan?"

"Yeah."

"Oh, no!" Tears formed in Gloria's eyes. "I'm sorry, Joey. I'm so sorry."

Chapter 74

CLARK SHOT A LOOK of disbelief at Detective Maddox as they strained to hear the conversation between Vernier and his client. Clark's reporter instinct sensed Vernier was more involved in today's events than he could share, but he did not really believe the lawyer was this heavily involved.

As they continued to listen, Clark's heart nearly leaped from his chest. Vernier was talking to the man who kidnapped Emily and Lana. He was not all that comforted by his claim that he was protecting them from being hurt by somebody else. Especially since this call was his confession of failure.

"The old Victorian farmhouse? Its secrets staring you in the face? Where it all started? Obviously, it was some kind of coded message, but do you have a clue what this guy is talking about?" asked Detective Maddox.

"Not completely, maybe not at all," Clark said. His voice and demeanor echoed his lack of confidence. "If that's supposed to mean something to me, then the farmhouse must be a reference to Aunt Ruth's place. It's where Lois grew up outside of Rio Vista. Beyond that, it's pure speculation."

"Speculate away."

"Remember those letters Lana was reading, the ones between her mom and Aunt Ruth?"

"Vaguely, but yeah," the detective affirmed.

"Somewhere in there is a comment that makes me think this guy is talking about her husband, Vic, and his brother, Tory. He regretted letting him get involved in something. Aunt Ruth was always vague about him. Given how he was involved in the death of Lois's parents, I thought nothing about it. I didn't even know his last name wasn't Emigh until I read the letters a few days ago. Everything I thought I knew about her aunt was based on the assumption that this was just the way it was with her generation, not knowing and all, but now I'm not so sure."

Detective Maddox could see the wheels spinning in Clark's brain. He opted not to go on a rant about the brothers' names. Vic and Tory. Why do parents do such cruel things to their children? It's not cute. It's just creating fertile ground for future criminals.

"Then what about the secrets staring you in the face?"

"I don't have a clue," Clark said, more flippant than confessional. "I guess we will have to figure that out when we get there."

"The other unanswered question is, can we get somebody to that house before Charlie gets there?"

"I'm not holding my breath," Clark said.

"Me neither," the detective said as he placed a call to the sheriff's office. He knew they knew the place. They had been there just a few short months before when a different band of degenerates held hostages there.

Clark ruffled through his notes to find what he wrote about Aunt Ruth's comment on Vic's regret. Before he could find this tidbit, his phone rang. It was Vernier.

"Clark here."

"Mr. Solo, did my father get you all the details about where your family is?" Vernier asked without his normal pleasantries.

"Excuse me?"

"I said, did my father get you all the details to locate your family?"

Clark cringed. He fumbled in placing the listening device behind a photo on the lawyer's desk. He hoped the lawyer thought he was just clumsy. The man fishing with Vernier must have been his father.

"Oh," Clark eked out. He cleared his throat. "Yes, as much as he could."

"Good. Do you have any questions?"

"Yeah. Who is Charlie?"

"I don't know, but you've seen boxes of his work."

"And Doctor Callahan's role?"

"I don't think you need me to answer that question."

"You are being a lawyer again, aren't you?"

"Always. Good luck, Clark."

"Thanks."

Clark stared at Detective Maddox as he wrapped up his conversation with the sheriff's office.

"Something tells me that look means something bad has happened," Maddox said.

"Maybe. Maybe not. Vernier knew we were listening in on his conversation. Apparently, I was not subtle enough."

Maddox laughed. He thought it was strange Vernier switched his phone to speaker mode in the middle of the conversation and made it a point to repeat key things that Doctor Callahan was saying.

"Was he upset?" Maddox asked.

"Not really, but he clearly wanted me to know he knew."

"Then let's not worry about it. I suspect he would not want us to think too hard about it. We might just figure out that he just used us to work around attorney-client privilege."

"Do you really think so?"

"It's what I would have done if the roles were reversed."

Chapter 74

JUSTIN STARED at the contents of the safe deposit box Frankie had left in his care. His so-called insurance policy was nothing more than an unusual-looking business card. It was not the typical piece of precisely trimmed white card stock with a person's name and contact information embossed in black lettering. Gold-leaf artwork covered the front and back of the smoky red fold-over card. Justin thought it was a little too artsy for what he figured was a hired gun. Two lines with arrows on both ends intersecting off center with an incomplete circle around where they crossed. A larger incomplete circle was under that circle, with two arcs crossing upwards from the edges of the bigger circle. Inside, in more gold leaf, was an international telephone number and the phrase "Cousin of Babylon."

The second article in the box was a plain white envelope with Annie Zimmerman printed on it. Justin could only guess this was a beyond-the-grave letter from Frankie to his little girl. Part of him wanted to trash the letter, but he left it in the safe deposit box. That was a disaster for another day. He handed the box back to the clerk and gave a nod to the security guard to escort him out of the bank.

"I guess it pays to have friends in high places," Martin joked as Justin jumped into the car.

"Friends? More like debtors. Randy owes me a few after all the commissions he's earned off my deals."

"Works either way."

Justin tossed the card to his friend. He mulled it over. Something about it seemed odd. The weight seemed off, even more than you would expect with the heavier cardstock. He'd seen the artwork some place before but could not recall where. There wasn't something else about the card that made him feel uneasy, but he couldn't define it. That's a mystery for another day, he thought.

"I still don't trust Frankie. He could be just setting into motion another attempt to knock you off," Martin said.

"I hear you."

Justin grabbed the card back and dialed the number. After three rings, he could hear the line pick up, but nobody said anything.

"Hello?" Justin said.

No response. Justin could hear a person on the other end, so he kept on talking.

"A friend gave me this card. He said to call when I needed to resolve a problem."

Silence.

"The card says you are Cousin of Babylon."

"Just one moment, sir."

The stoic person put the phone on hold, with an unusual soundtrack of something vibrating slowly in the distance giving way to closer, more rhythmic vibrations. Justin and Martin shared shrugs and waited.

"Who may I say was your friend?" the voice eventually asked.

"Frankie Zimmerman."

"Please hold."

After several more loops of the vibrating phone soundtrack, a fresh voice came on the phone.

"Hello, friend of Frankie."

"Hello," Justin replied.

"How can I be of service?"

"Frankie said I could call this number if something went wrong with his daughter Alicia, I mean, Annie."

Justin stumbled over his words. He felt like he was a teenager talking to the father of his date.

"Well, something went wrong. Not with Annie, but with a close friend of hers. Somebody kidnapped him."

"Who is this person?"

"His name is Dan Vanbeck something I can't pronounce. Sorry, he is more Annie's friend than mine. He is a pastor."

"Oh, he's a man of the cloth?"

"Yeah, I guess you could say that."

"You also say they were close—as in they were a couple close?"

"No. Not that kind of close. He's been kind of a counselor for her. The last few months have been rather hard on her."

"I'm sorry to hear that. I assume that being close to Miss Zimmerman is just your role, Mr. Alexander."

"Yeah, you assume correctly."

"Are you sure you really want me to put this man back into your girlfriend's intimate circle?"

"I don't know what you are trying to suggest."

"I'm not suggesting anything, just asking questions."

"He's a good guy. I owe him a lot."

"But do you really trust him?"

"Yeah, why wouldn't I?"

"I don't know. You tell me, Mr. Alexander."

Anger swelled in Justin. He wanted to protest this line of questioning but could not. It echoed the banter already playing in the back of his mind.

"Can you help or not?" Justin blurted out.

"Tsk, tsk, Mr. Alexander. Let's not lose our heads unnecessarily. I think I can help good old Frankie's daughter. An associate will contact you to get the necessary details."

The phone went dead before Justin could say anything else.

"That was weird," Martin said.

"He's Frankie's friend, so I am not surprised that he's an arrogant jerk, too. Now for the hard part. How do I tell Alicia what we just did without giving up that I think her father is still alive?"

Chapter 76

DOORS WERE ALREADY OPENING when the two black SUVs skidded to a stop by the white tire swing hanging from the old oak tree. Two men exited the lead vehicle and headed for the farmhouse. Two more men jumped out of the other SUV and made their way to the partially opened barn door. The first man to the barn slid the doors farther apart. Its creaking masked the sound of the white van revving its engines. The second man darted across the opening, pulling his partner along with him.

"You idiot!" he yelled.

The van barreled past them and down the driveway. The two men scrambled back to their SUV and raced after the van.

"Jemarr, you think we should follow them?" asked one of the men on the porch.

"No. We need to stay here and ensure the property is clear."

This duo took a more cautious approach. One stayed at the front door while the other circled around the back of the house. After the count of fifteen, Jemarr pushed his way through the front door. The room was empty. His partner came in through the kitchen.

"I'm bettin' they were in the van."

"Probably, but we'd better check this place out anyway," Jemarr said.

They meandered around the house, opening closets and looking under beds. They found nothing but layers of dust. In their wake, however, they left a path of destruction. A similar check of the basement and barn turned up nothing as well. Reluctantly, he pulled out his phone to call Charlie.

"This place is empty," Jemarr said.

"How did they slip away?" Charlie demanded. "There is only one way in and out."

"They hid in the barn and almost ran over Billy when he opened the door. He's chasing the van right now. We stayed back to ensure the house was clear."

"Did you look in the ..."

Before Charlie could finish his question, Jemarr panicked. He could hear multiple police sirens in the distance.

"Gotta go! The locals are coming!"

* * *

Emily strained to hear who was in the house. She had never been in Vic's secret room. Lois had told her about it, but neither of them had been brave enough to cross Aunt Ruth's admonition to stay out. The narrow room, hidden behind a bookcase along the fireplace, was his sanctuary. Lois told her that Aunt Ruth had put her uncle's stuff in here after he died and never opened it again. Lois said there was something behind the mirror that rested on the third shelf, slightly above her eye level, that opened the door. The flaw, she always thought, was the room only opened from the outside, and was the more important reason she and Lana never ventured in here before.

She checked on Lana, who was helping Doctor Callahan keep Jonah quiet. The quirky teen was bound with duct tape and gagged to ensure he did not expose them. Their captor solicited her help after his phone call, which sounded like it was with the same lawyer Clark was working with on his story about all those murders. There was something different now. The doctor seemed genuinely afraid, which convinced her his plea was sincere. He told them Jonah had given up their location, and everyone needed to hide immediately. He pointed to a pair of black SUVs coming down the country road and said the man who orchestrated the bombing scare had sent them. The doctor did not think the goons would know about the secret room, which made him think it should keep them safe until Clark found them.

She hoped it would be soon. In the heat of the moment, she did not question how he knew about the room. As the wait continued, her brain meandered all over the place, even questioning whether sweet Aunt Ruth might have been involved in something nefarious. When she shook off that unwanted train of thought, her brain noticed that the room was smaller than she imagined, not much more than a modest walk-in closet. No windows. A single light bulb hung from the ceiling and only came on when somebody turned on the light in the living room. The limited décor felt austere: a metal cot with a lumpy mattress, a small wooden writing table and uncomfortable chair, and a blue-and-chrome trunk. She tried to stay away from thoughts about hunger, thirst and bodily functions.

Activity in the house interrupted her mind wandering. The first round of sounds seemed chaotic. She could hear doors slam and stuff landing on the hardwood floors. The thought that she would have a big mess to clean up kept running through her mind. After several minutes, there was silence. At first, the lack of sounds was welcoming; the intruders must not know where they were. The comfort soon waned into dread.

"Are you sure Clark is coming?" Emily asked.

"I can't be sure, but he's a smart chap. I can't imagine he wouldn't come," Doctor Callahan said. The word he did not say was hope. He hoped Vernier did not alter the message he left for Clark.

Emily signaled for everyone to be quiet. She heard new footsteps. This time, they were slow and methodical. Whoever they were, she could tell their muffled words sounded commanding, but she did not sense the panic she had heard previously.

* * *

"Okay, here's the sitrep. A couple of thug wannabes were trying to make a getaway when we arrived. We apprehended the perps easily enough. Same goes for their single-digit buddies, who were in hot pursuit of a white van. I don't know what to make of the perps in the van. They eluded my officers pursuing them, yet the rabbits turned up back here. They are all cuffed and stuffed for you. As for your friends, there are no signs of them. The wannabes made such a mess. I can't tell if your friends were ever here," Lieutenant Philpott said.

"Sounds like you had a little fun," Detective Maddox replied.

"Nothing we couldn't handle."

"We are still crawling on I-80. Can your guys sit on the place until we get there?"

"Will do. Maybe next time you can do a better job of keeping the excitement down your way," joked the lieutenant. Maddox also understood the serious undertones of his levity.

"I'll try, but I'm not making any promises."

Chapter 77

A SHOWER OF DUST dancing in a stream of light poking through the painted windows gave Pastor Dan a brief diversion from his unpleasant situation. Charlie had stepped away to answer a phone call that clearly did not make him happy. A second call, however, seemed to change his mood. He walked back toward the pastor, still engaged in his conversation.

"Who is this person?" Charlie asked.

"Oh, he's a man of the cloth?"

"You say there were close—as in they were a couple close?"

"I assume that's just your role, Mr. Alexander."

That name perked the ears of Pastor Dan.

"Are you sure you really want me to put this man back into your girlfriend's intimate circle?"

"I'm not suggesting anything, just asking questions."

Once again, rage boiled inside Pastor Dan. He wanted to push it down, but it kept gaining in strength. All he could hear was this monster toying with Justin, inserting doubts about his relationship with Alicia.

"But do you really trust him?"

"I don't know. You tell me, Mr. Alexander."

"Tsk, tsk, Mr. Alexander. Let's not lose our heads. I think I can help good old Frankie's daughter. An associate will contact you to get the necessary details."

Pastor Dan clanked his cuffs against the metal column.

"Is something bothering you, my dear padre?" Charlie asked.

"My skin crawls when I'm surrounded by lies."

"What lies are you referring to?"

"That's like picking a drop of water out of the ocean."

Charlie chuckled.

"You are such a comedian. But I don't think you are mad because I was lying. I think you are mad because I wasn't."

"I'm not following your riddle."

"You know very well that Mr. Alexander has reason to doubt the true innocence of your relationship with Alicia."

The words stunned Pastor Dan.

"I'm the man you dangled in front of Justin?"

"Who else could it be?"

"Coming from you. It could be anybody or no one at all."

Charlie chuckled again. This time, his laugh was more audible.

"You know. I think I'll take that as a compliment."

"Of course you would. May I ask how you are going to help Frankie's daughter?"

"Oh, I think your funny bone is going to love this. It appears some dastardly person has kidnapped one of her dear friends, and her dutiful boyfriend is using an in-case-of-emergency card left him by her recently departed father."

Pastor Dan stared at his captor in disbelief. He could not imagine how his situation could get worse. He could not imagine how it could get any better, either. He closed his eyes and leaned against the column.

"I don't think your prayers will make any difference, Padre."

Pastor Dan continued his pose.

"You need to be begging me. I'm the one who holds your destiny in his hands."

Pastor Dan opened his eyes and locked eyes with Charlie. After a long few seconds of the intense exchange, he quietly uttered, "I do not pray that small."

"Maybe not," Charlie replied with a wave of his right hand. "But maybe they will."

The portal door opened again. A train of five people stepped through and plotted their way toward them. Two struggled to walk with the leather leg and arm restraints. Pastor Dan blinked his eyes, hoping he did not know who was coming his way.

"Welcome to the party," Charlie said cheerfully as the Gloria-and-Joey parade came to a stop. The three guards stepped back to leave the foursome alone.

"There's no party until we are dancing on your grave," Gloria said.

"Joey, you see why I didn't want to stick around with your mother. She's a mean one."

Joey just stared at Charlie. His confliction brewing. It had not yet steeped enough to overcome the training of Doctor Callahan.

"Well, Joey. You are the man of the hour. Is this the outsider who prevented you from carrying out your mission today?" Charlie asked.

Joey remained silent. He did not want to answer. He feared what might happen.

"Come on, Joey. There was a failure today. And failure must always be punished."

Silence.

"Let's face it, Joey. You know somebody is getting punished today. Did you fail on your own accord, or did this outsider prevent you from completing your mission?"

Joey closed his eyes. He wanted to look at Pastor Dan. He wanted the youth pastor to tell him what to do. He could not. He could not bear to see his face and give in to Charlie.

Pastor Dan could see the tears rolling down Joey's face. The struggle on his face gave away that he was relying on his own grit to figure this out. He could also see it was not working.

"Leave the boy alone," Pastor Dan hollered. "You know I stopped him. You know it was me."

"No coaching from the peanut gallery," Charlie ordered. "Now, Joey, you know confession is good for the soul. Let me hear it from you."

"No!" Gloria inserted. "Joey, you don't have to obey this man. He may have gotten into your head somehow, but he doesn't control you. And despite what he has been telling you, you are not alone. You have a strength to tap that isn't yours."

"Gloria, for your sake, I was trying to give him a way out. I'm surprised you are telling him to take his punishment like a man."

"He knows his actions today will have consequences, but not from you. You have no power over him. Not anymore."

"I don't," Charlie erupted into a full-on belly laugh. "Look around, my dear Gloria. I'm the only one not in restraints."

Joey finally boiled over and let loose an emotionally intense scream as he sprung forward as hard as he could. The commotion surprised Charlie, knocking him backwards toward Pastor Dan. He smacked his head on the column as his body fell to the floor. Joey landed on top of him.

"You don't own me!" Joey screamed. He kept banging his head on Charlie and crying. "You don't own me! You don't own me!"

Chapter 78

BY THE TIME Clark and Detective Maddox made it through traffic from San Francisco to the outskirts of Rio Vista, a mere 65 miles, nearly two hours had passed. All of the sheriff's team had dispersed, except for one patrol car. They took the miscreants to the county jail. The old Victorian farmhouse was once again an eerily quiet place surrounded by open fields grazed by sheep and dotted with giant wind turbines. The deputy rolled down the window as the detective approached.

"We can take it from here," Maddox said as he flashed his badge to the deputy.

"The L-T said to sit tight in case something comes up."

"Philpott covers every base, doesn't he?"

"He sure does, sir."

The detective joined Clark, who had already made his way inside. He was scouring the living room to find something "staring him in the face."

"I see nothing that has a face to stare at me," Clark said. His frustration was already showing.

"I'm not so sure you should take it that literally," Maddox cautioned. "Let's be systematic about this."

"Well, I've eliminated things with obvious faces."

"The entire house?"

"No, just this room."

"I will look over this room myself to see if I see something you didn't. You move on to the kitchen. I'll keep following you from room to room."

Clark sighed. This approach could take hours, and his family is still out there somewhere. The solution was to solve an obscure riddle.

"I know it seems like a slow way to approach this, but it will pay off faster in the long run," the detective assured.

Clark made his way into the kitchen, the pantry, and upstairs through all the bedrooms. Nothing seemed to stare back at him. He stood in the doorway between the living room and the kitchen while waiting for the detective to wrap up his search. It was only a few months earlier when he stood in this spot, taking in the sight of his daughter with her godmother making popcorn in the fireplace. That was when he noticed Emily was more than just Lois's friend. She was somebody important to him as well. He walked closer to the fireplace, just mindlessly staring at the scene.

* * *

Lana took her turn standing and listening intently through the heavy door. Sounds from the outside faded over an hour ago. She never thought of herself as claustrophobic, but the walls of this little room were feeling closer and closer. Her heart jumped for joy when the light came back on but cautioned herself that it could still be the bad guys. First, it was only one person. Then two. She could not hear what they were saying. Then, their voices faded, and all she could hear were distant footsteps.

"We are never getting out of here," Lana decreed.

"We can't give up hope," Doctor Callahan said. "It is all we have."

Another sound came from beyond the door. Lana was not sure what it was, but something told her it was familiar. The sound was distant, then slowly it became louder. Whatever it was, it was getting closer.

"It's a song," Lana whispered. "Somebody is whistling a song."

Without thinking about it, Lana started whistling along. Emily laughed when she recognized the song and joined in. When the person stopped outside, so did they.

* * *

"Clark, what are you doing?" Detective Maddox asked as he was coming down the stairs.

"Just standing here thinking about my family," Clark said. A mournful tone expressed his waning hope.

"But whistling?"

"I was? Didn't notice."

"We'll figure this out and find them. Don't worry," Maddox consoled. Then, he began whistling his own tune. His whistle, however, projected more than Clark's and filled the room.

"Don't worry, be happy. Seriously?" Clark said.

Maddox ignored his friend's gloom and continued whistling. Clark strolled over to the bookcase and leaned against it. He had to admit that he was a little jealous of the deep, rich tone the detective could produce.

"How did you do that?" Clark asked.

"Whistle?"

"No. Whistle two tones at the same time."

"I didn't. I can't."

"I know. I'm telling you, that's what I just heard. Do it again."

"How?"

"Just whistle, will you?"

The detective complied and filled the room with his deep, almost haunting whistle tone. Clark heard the faint sounds of a higher pitch whistle as well.

"There it is!"

Enthusiasm returned to Clark's voice. The detective could not hear it but continued to whistle while Clark moved around the room trying to locate the sound of the extra whistle. He lifted his hand like a conductor, and Maddox stopped. He dropped it, and he resumed. Each time, Clark heard the higher pitch whistle.

"Somebody's here," Clark said.

"Where?"

Clark pointed to the bookcase and noticed his finger pointing back at him. He also saw a smile materialize on his face.

"Look who's staring me in the face!" Clark exclaimed.

He ran to the mirror on the bookcase shelf and started feeling around. The mirror did not move. His hand brushed the left side until he felt a small button. He pushed, and the mirror popped forward. He opened it like a bathroom medicine chest to reveal something like a small boat wheel. Clark spun it until he heard another click. The bookcase slid forward ever so slightly. He ran his fingers along its front until he felt something out of place. He noticed a handle of sorts—something he had always assumed was part of the elaborate carvings on the bookcase.

"Here goes nothing," Clark said as he pulled it forward.

"Daddy!" Lana screamed as Clark came into sight. Emily leaped forward as well, and the family hugged tightly. Doctor Callahan and Jonah remained in the back of the room.

"I'm so glad to see you both." The words struggled to emerge through Clark's happy tears. "When Vernier told us you were with Doctor Callahan, I feared the worst. I literally have boxes of stuff that detail the horrible things that man has done."

Lana turned and pointed at the back of the secret room.

"That Doctor Callahan?"

Detective Maddox rushed past the trio into the room. On the cot sat an old man with gray-streaked red hair and a teenage boy leaning into his side. The boy was bound and gagged.

"Explain yourself, mister," Detective Maddox ordered.

"I'm the terrible man from his boxes, and this is my friend, Jonah."

Chapter 79

DURING HIS DRIVE HOME, Justin noodled his way through a dozen different ways to tell her what just happened. Each came back to the simple fact that he had lied to her. Not that he told her something false exactly, but he intentionally failed to mention certain details that he knew she would find very important. Justin never mentioned that her father had stopped by his house before she got out of jail to say he transferred ownership of a building to him. And not just any building, but a building that makes him the landlord of the art studio where she will be working. Nor did he mention he had been asked to serve on the board of trustees at the art school she will be attending. These little missing facts would undermine her ambition to remake herself by her own merit. "I want to know I can do it on my own," she kept saying about his offers to help. If she doesn't know that, how can she prevent others from thinking that it was just something else Justin and his money bought for her?

Even if he could manage to omit those details from the conversation, he could not figure out how to tell her how he got the Cousin of Babylon business card without revealing that her so-called father was still alive.

"Frankie, how is it you can mess with my life while hiding away on some beach with federal protection?" Justin asked the empty front seat of his car.

As Justin pulled into his garage, he noticed that the living room light was on. He hoped this was a good sign. When he left, she was lying on his bed in a curled ball.

"Thanks for waiting up for me, sweetie!" Justin hollered as he closed the garage entry door.

No response.

"Sweetie. Are you awake?"

No response. Justin walked down the hall into the living room. He was surprised to see an older man sitting on the couch across from Alicia. Her eyes pushed open, the widest he had ever seen them.

"Hi, Justin," Alicia squeaked out.

Something was not right. The balding man in the expensive Italian suit looked like the man who did Frankie's bidding.

"Mr. Taglioni, I presume," Justin said, pronouncing his name in a somewhat pretentious way.

"It has been a long time, Justin," Nikolaus Taglioni said and offered his hand to Justin.

"And it has been a good time." Justin did not accept the gesture and walked over to Alicia.

"Is everything okay, sweetie?" Justin asked, bending down to give Alicia a peck on the cheek. He whispered, "Slap me if you are afraid."

Justin stood up, and Alicia feigned outrage toward her boyfriend. Her slap made Justin think she had spent a little too much time at the gym while she was in jail.

"You think you can come home like nothing happened. Think again. You can't just take off without telling me where you are going," Alicia said with such attitude Justin was not completely sure if she was acting.

"I'm sorry, sweetie. You are right. I shouldn't have done that."

"You bet your sweet bippy, I'm right."

Taglioni sat quietly without interfering in the lovers' spat. Justin sat in the recliner adjacent to Alicia and turned his attention to their guest.

"I guess I should thank you for keeping my girlfriend company while I was out gallivanting."

"No thanks are necessary. I was just following up on an inquiry you made today from one of my clients."

"Clients?" Justin said slowly. "I thought you were exclusively Frankie's boy."

"I try to make all my clients feel like they are exclusive," Taglioni said. His attempt to sound convincing failed.

"So, you represent the Cousin of Babylon?" Justin asked.

"Babylon? As in the Bible?" Alicia asked.

"My firm prides itself on its discretion, so I can't answer that question."

"Okay. What does the cuz want?" Justin asked.

"Just a few details to help find your missing friend," Taglioni said. He ignored the obvious disdain coming from Justin. "Miss Zimmerman was just getting ready to share a recent photo of the gentlemen."

"Oh, yeah," Alicia said. She seemed a little befuddled by the exchange. She showed Taglioni the selfie she took with Pastor Dan in front of the giant colon on stilts outside the Hall of Justice.

"It looks like you two were having a really good time," Taglioni said as he snapped a photo on his phone.

"He's a good friend, that's it. I don't know why you guys keep trying to make a big deal out of it," Justin said. He could not believe the lawyer was making the same inferences as the jerk on the phone.

Alicia placed her hand on Justin's and tossed an inquisitive glance at him. Justin pulled his hand away and kept his eyes on the lawyer.

"When did you lose track of him?" Taglioni said.

"We didn't lose track of him. Somebody took him. In fact, it was one of San Francisco's finest. Can you believe that? They took a man of God, no less," Justin said. His irritation with this man was obvious.

"Oh, so they arrested him."

"No," Alicia said. "No, they didn't. He was escorting the boy who had caused all that havoc downtown with a bomb threat. He apparently knew him."

"Then, he should be at the police station."

"Why didn't we think of that? Alicia, this man's a genius. I bet his buddies at Harvard are so proud of him."

"I went to the Pritzker School of Law at Northwestern, but that's not really germane to our conversation."

"Oh, a wildcat," Justin continued his mockery.

"Justin!" Alicia scolded.

"Thank you, Miss Zimmerman."

"That's Miss Bauer," Justin corrected.

"As you wish. Miss Bauer, I'm assuming then, he is not at the police station."

"Bingo," Justin said.

"No, he's not," Alicia said, not sure why she felt like the adult in the room. "The police officer who was supposed to take Pastor Dan and the boy to the station took them someplace else. The police don't know where or why. That's why we need your help."

Taglioni's phone buzzed, which reverberated louder than expected on the glass top of the coffee table. He responded to the text and then looked cheerfully at Alicia.

"It appears my client may have located your friend already. If you and Justin will come with me, I'll take you to them."

"If you don't mind, I'll drive," Justin said.

Chapter 80

THE THREE GUARDS who brought the human train into the open hangar struggled to restrain Joey. He kept flailing his arms and legs despite the restraints. His bottled-up rage overwhelmed his senses. Joey seemed deaf to the threats and expletives Charlie showered on him. He also could not see the additional guards racing to the scene with taser guns drawn. Pastor Dan could.

"Joey!" he hollered. "That's enough, Joey! That's enough."

Joey slowed his struggle, but kept crying, "You don't own me!"

"He's got the message. He knows it, Joey. He knows he doesn't own you anymore," Pastor Dan continued to soothe him.

Joey slowed some more; enough for the guards to get a grip on his restraints and subdue the teen.

"We'll see who owns whom," Charlie said as he picked himself off the floor. He grabbed the column to steady himself.

"You might be able to constrain our bodies, but you do not own our hearts," Pastor Dan said. "I just realized that's why you killed Tory Avlah. He had something inside him that broke your control over him. Same with Joey."

"You don't know what you are talking about. He did my bidding. The good doctor just hadn't perfected his process yet," Charlie said. He grabbed a guard and with a single tug stripped his shirt from his body and used it to cradle his head. The gash on his forehead from hitting the steel column streamed blood down his face. There were other signs of bruising from his struggle with Joey.

"I'm sure he hadn't perfected his sin, but I know the one who overcame that sin. Once Tory and Joey surrendered to him, they couldn't surrender to you anymore."

"There you go trying to preach your nonsense at me again. Your made-up god has no power over me."

Pastor Dan did not accept his bait. This was not the time for an apologetic debate. He needed a different kind of confession from Charlie.

"That's also why you killed Rebecca. She was just a pawn in your little game of human chess. Their target all along was Tory. She was just a convenient tool to distract, to ensure no curious eyes found their way to your little operation."

Charlie just smiled like a spoiled child who had been caught doing something horrible and had the arrogance to smile that smile that said you cannot do anything about it. Gloria looked dumbfounded at the exchange. Pastor Dan's words sparked her own revelation.

"You ...," she sputtered. "You used that man to kill my mother. That wasn't a stupid, random act by a violent drunk. That was you!"

"Oh, you two are so on the ball, yet still so wrong," Charlie said smugly. "Gloria, I wish I could take credit for her death. The world is a far better place without that sorry excuse of a woman you called Mommy. Even trailer trash looked down on her. As for you, Padre, you were a lot closer. Rebecca was not a pawn. She was just in the right place at the right time to get my mission done. Losing Tory was kind of sad, especially after going to all that effort to get his parole pushed up and everything."

"You truly have sold your soul," Gloria said.

"If so, the devil paid a hell of a price for it."

Charlie motioned for the guards to get rid of the three captives.

"Take the boy to the retraining room and the other two to the cells," Charlie ordered.

Joey squirmed against the tight grip of the two guards holding him and tried to stomp on their feet. He knew what Charlie had planned for him. So did Gloria.

"Miles! No! You can't do that do him," she screamed. "He's only a boy."

"He already knows about it. He already knew that if he failed in his mission, he would have to go back into training."

The matter-of-fact tone disturbed Pastor Dan, as if the rest of his conduct was not enough to burst a confessional into flames.

"I prevented him from doing his mission. He would have carried it out if I hadn't gotten involved," Pastor Dan confessed. "If you are going to punish anyone for today's failure, then I am the one you need to punish."

"Pastor Dan!" Joey yelled.

"You don't know what you are asking for," Gloria said.

The look on Charlie's face betrayed his actions. His eyes sparkled, happy that he had manipulated Pastor Dan into volunteering for his little training room.

"I was hoping you would say that. So be it."

Chapter 81

DOCTOR CALLAHAN SAT across the kitchen table from Detective Maddox. His hands were cuffed comfortably behind him. On the table was the doctor's cell phone on speaker.

"This situation affords you some legal latitude in how you proceed, Detective Maddox. My client wishes to be helpful, but you don't seem to be offering any assurances," Vernier said.

Out of his duty to the court, Vernier sought to secure the best possible outcome for his client. He wanted to tell the detective to crucify the doctor—a likely accomplice in at least a couple dozen murders. Who knows how many other victims existed, but they disappeared into the night, overlooked by acceptable society just like when they were still alive.

"You know I can't promise what the district attorney will do. I can only say I will share how cooperative he was in the investigation. What happens after that, I can't control," Detective Maddox explained.

Maddox sensed the lawyer was simply covering his bases. There was not the typical pushiness, legal arrogance, he often encountered by defense attorneys interfering with his investigations.

"Doctor Callahan, under the circumstances, I think that is the best assurance we can get. Let the detective ask the question, then wait for me to give you instructions on whether or not you can answer. Do you understand?" Vernier said.

"Yes."

"We are ready to proceed," Vernier said.

"Clark, are you set to record this conversation?" Maddox asked.

"All set. Greg, I'll send you a copy," Clark said.

"Thank you, Clark."

"For the record, please state your full name and occupation," the detective officially opened the interview.

"My name is Ambrose Callahan. I am a doctor of emergency medicine with a specialty in psychosomatic medicine."

"I am going to reserve my questions regarding the past murder victims until later. At this time, I need you to tell me if you have information about the whereabouts of Joey Maldoon and Dan Vanbeckhuijsen?"

"Go ahead."

"The direct answer to your question is no. I do not know the whereabouts of Joey Maldoon and Dan Vanbeckhuijsen."

"Doctor, how is this being cooperative?"

"Go ahead."

"That was the answer to your question. I can tell you where Charlie most likely is, which I suspect is where you will find your two missing people," Callahan explained.

"Then where is Charlie?"

Callahan waited silently.

"I guess that's my cue," Vernier injected. "Go ahead."

"He uses a film production company on the old Navy base up in Vallejo as a front for his operations."

"What makes you think they are there?" Maddox asked.

"Go ahead."

"People don't seem to question bizarre things happening on movie sets, so it provides a great cover operation," Callahan said. "He occupies some administrative, warehouse-like buildings around where the old prison is located."

"That's all I need for now," Detective Maddox said and turned to the patrol officer that remained behind, just in case. "For the record, Deputy Tuckett has been observing this interview. Deputy Tuckett, please take Mr. Ambrose and get him a nice, comfy cell."

"Getting around Charlie's operation can be, let's say, tricky. You might find it helpful if I went with you," Doctor Callahan offered.

"He doesn't know that place like I do," Jonah inserted into the conversation from the living room. He was still bound but sitting on the couch with Emily.

"You can't trust that boy," Callahan warned. "I'm afraid my indoctrination process is more thorough than I thought. He will be loyal to Charlie, no matter the personal cost to him."

The events of the day were catching up with Detective Maddox. He rubbed his face in his hands and let out a sigh. Sometimes he hated his line of work.

"I have no desire to take either of you. All my police training tells me it would be a reckless thing to do." He took another sigh and continued. "But this situation is not in the books. Mr. Vernier, do you have any thoughts?"

"Not as a defense attorney," Vernier said.

"Sounds like a typical day in Kandahar," Deputy Tucket said, referring to his recent Army tour in Afghanistan. "We constantly had to decide in whose hands of which bad guy we were going to put our lives today. The guy who helped us in the morning was the same one shooting at us that night."

"Yeah. That's my dilemma," Maddox agreed.

"I think I can better your odds," Callahan said. "Bring Jonah in here."

Detective Maddox motioned for Emily to bring him to the table.

"Jonah. I know Charlie had you tell Joey that he has a brother to get him to follow you to the mansion."

"Yes, Charlie said he would reveal his identity after Joey did his mission," Jonah replied. He seemed excited for Joey.

"I also know that you have really taken to Joey. That you feel a bond that seems stronger than friends, even though Joey doesn't quite share the same bond."

"Yeah, that's true." The excitement waned, and his shoulders slumped.

"I don't suppose Charlie ever told you that you, too, have a brother out there?"

"No, he told me my mother abandoned me when I was about three years old. I know nothing about my father."

"That's not true. Your mom loved you very much. Charlie seduced her with promises to do great things for you; things she couldn't do, given her circumstances."

"You mean because she was a drug-addicted prostitute?"

"Yes, Jonah. That's what I was trying not to say. That doesn't mean she didn't want a better life for you. She didn't abandon you. She gave you to someone she thought could do a better job of providing for you."

"She did?"

"Yes, I was there. I helped facilitate the exchange."

"Oh."

"But you weren't the only child she gave over. She had just given birth to another baby, your little brother."

"What happened to him?"

"Charlie—and so did I at the time—wanted to conduct a rather comprehensive experiment about nurture and environment. Your little brother went to a woman to raise, and you got stuck with Charlie. That little boy was Joey."

"Jonah is Joey's brother?" Lana exclaimed.

"Yes."

Doctor Callahan let the news absorb before he continued.

"Jonah. The detective needs your help to find your brother. You are going to have to decide—are you going to be loyal to your brother or Charlie?"

Chapter 82

IF THERE WAS ONE THING a hard-knocks life had taught Justin, it was to give your trust to a very select group of people. Taglioni had not joined that group. Admittedly, he was guilty by association. Frankie chose his friends because they served his purposes. That automatically put Taglioni on the top of the do not trust list.

The tall, gangly lawyer balked at the idea of squeezing into the theoretical third seat of his chiseled sports car. They hopped into his luxury truck instead. The sexy name for the truck's paint color—red hot—was his enticement to buy. Upon reflection, Justin realized that was a spoiled, rich kid's reason, but he did not care. It impressed Alicia at the time.

She opted to take the back seat, which relieved Justin. There was a part of him that felt uncomfortable having an untrustworthy person in a position where he could easily overcome him. The front passenger seat had its own risks, but it meant Taglioni would have to work harder.

The directions Taglioni shared had them going along a familiar path to the wine country in Napa. However, the next turn took them off the meandering waterfront road to a bridge that crossed the Napa River over to the industrial view that the city dwellers enjoyed.

Justin struggled to figure out why Pastor Dan was here. He had been on the island before but opted to keep his portfolio of investments along the inner circle of the San Francisco Bay. The tired creamy colors of the old Navy buildings, which reminded him of the training base in Chicago, just did not lend themselves to the sleeker, modern buildings he liked to put his name on. What he learned on his tour was that this was not a place where you accidentally find yourself. There are only two ways on and off the island, and they can easily be closed down. Normally, that's a red flag for the criminal element.

Taglioni directed them to a large building—part residence, part warehouse looking—past all the dry docks that were once used to build large ships and submarines. Justin started to get out, but Taglioni told him to wait for their escort. The news made Justin even more nervous. After a few minutes, an older teen came and stood in front of the truck.

"Mr. Taglioni, you and your guests can follow me," the teen said after they all assembled near their escort.

The teen took them into the building through a man-entrance on an enormous roll-up door. They worked their way deeper inside until they reached what looked like another building built inside. A couple of hallways farther and they entered a room with theater curtains on one wall.

"Please wait here," the teen instructed, pointing to two oversized recliners in the center of the room. They looked like someone had used them for medical procedures.

"Something does not feel right," Justin whispered.

"Just wait," Alicia said.

The attorney sat stone-faced on a small, round, rolling stool along the curtained wall until his phone buzzed. He read the text and stood up.

"It's time for me to take my leave," Taglioni said.

Justin bolted past him to block the exit.

"Whoa! You are not going anywhere!"

"My services are no longer required," Taglioni said.

"Something tells me it's more like plausible deniability to me. Sit back down!"

Justin sounded far fiercer than his nearly six-foot stature suggested. His muscular build more than compensated for the extra four inches in height Taglioni had on him. The lawyer had avoided physical confrontations since grammar school. He decided to keep the streak going and returned to his seat. Justin returned to his recliner just as the curtain opened. The large picture window exposed an empty stage surrounded by low-hanging theater lights. It took Justin a second to realize the lights were not pointed toward the stage. Flash. One of the center stage lights illuminated.

"Oh, man!" Justin shouted, lifting his hand to shade his eyes from the intensely bright white light. Alicia did the same.

A man walked to the center of the stage. Justin strained to see, but it appeared whoever it was had recently suffered some kind of head wound.

"Welcome, Mr. Alexander and Miss Zimmerman," they heard the man's voice through the speakers in the corner of the room.

"Turn off the light!" Justin yelled.

"What light, Mr. Alexander?" the man said.

"Stop playing games! Turn off the stupid lights!"

The white light disappeared, and two blue lights illuminated from the outer edges of their view. The blue beam seemed less intense, and they could see the stage a little better. A different man was there. He was sitting on a wooden chair. A rope around his waist strapped him to the chair. More rope anchored his feet to the legs of the chair. His arms looked like they might be bound behind him.

"That's Pastor Dan!" screamed Alicia. "He looks horrible, like someone has beaten him up."

"Very observant, Miss Zimmerman," a bodiless voice announced.

"We are here to pick up our friend," Justin said.

"All in good time," the voice said. "Your friend volunteered for some training first."

Two flashing red lights replaced the blue lights.

"That's annoying," Justin exclaimed.

"Are you comfortable, Miss Zimmerman?" the voice asked.

"Yes, except for these absurd lights flashing in my face."

"We are ready," said a different voice.

"Ready for what?" Justin asked.

Suddenly the stage lights shifted to Pastor Dan. He squirmed under the bright white lights, squeezing his eyes and shifting his head in a feeble attempt to find some relief. A pulsating beat was added to his torture; the deep, thunderous vibrations you feel at a stop sign when someone has turned the bass way up on their stereo. After a few seconds of that commotion, a voice that sounded like Alicia filled the room.

"My little Danny boy. I miss you so much. I yearn to hear you say how much you love me again," the imitation Alicia said.

"I ... he ... we ... never," Alicia sputtered.

The bright light flashed off, and the screen filled with the image of Alicia walking toward them. She wore a flowy white linen dress that scraped the tops of the wildflowers as she made her way through an idyllic meadow. Her long black hair bounced off her shoulders and framed a face that oozed pure happiness, which was echoed by a light and airy melody mirroring the beautiful spring day.

"Danny, you know my love for you. I yearn to have your arms wrap around me and feel your warm breath on my neck. Please, tell me again how much you love me," imitation Alicia on the screen said, pulling her arms into her bosom to punctuate her plea.

Justin could see Pastor Dan's lips moving but could not hear the words. Somebody came on stage, repositioned a microphone and the words started flooding into the room.

"Even though I walk through the valley of the shadow of death, I will fear no evil, for you are with me; your rod and your staff, they comfort me," Pastor Dan said.

"Unless you confess your love, Pastor Dan, they are going to torture Alicia," a voice that sounded like Justin overrode the pastor. The fake Justin sounded agitated and very concerned.

"Surely goodness and mercy shall follow me all the days of my life," Pastor Dan continued.

A flash of lightning changed the imagery on the screen. Fake Alicia screamed. The thunderous vibrations returned. The music turned forceful, penetrating. A pack of three wild dogs ran onto the scene and surrounded a frightened Alicia, each taking its turn to snap, snarl and bark at her.

"Danny, I'm scared! These dogs are crazy. They are going to eat me alive. Don't let them take me away from you. Please say you love me!" she pleaded.

Pastor Dan looked toward the screen, shook his head and continued his recitation. "The Lord is my shepherd; I shall not want. He makes me lie down in green pastures. He leads me beside still waters. He restores my soul. He leads me in paths of righteousness for his name's sake."

"Aren't you going to do something? You see how vicious these dogs are. You know what they are going to do? You know what you must do. You can't let them hurt Alicia like that," fake Justin admonished.

Alicia and Justin stared at the stage in disbelief at what they were hearing. Justin pounded on the glass, commanding whoever was doing this to stop. Alicia's screams denying what was being said never left their side of the glass.

"You prepare a table before me in the presence of my enemies; you anoint my head with oil; my cup overflows," Pastor Dan continued.

The imagery on the screen became more dire. The frequency of the lightning increased, as well as the intensity of the music. A madness seemed to envelop the dogs. Their circling stopped. The image panned back and forth between Alicia's frightened face and the rabid-looking dogs. The camera pulled back just as the dogs lunged onto their prey and an awful blood-curdling scream blasted over the speakers. One last lightning flash filled the sky, and the entire stage went black.

A black light illuminated the room where Justin and Alicia stood. Their bodies felt limp and powerless. While their attention was focused on Pastor Dan, Taglioni slipped out and several beefy orderlies slipped in. The surreal happened next. The orderlies tapped the distraught couple on the shoulder and directed them to the chairs. Alicia and Justin complied, even allowing them to strap them to the odd reclining chairs.

"None of that was real," Justin mumbled. "None of that was real."

"I'm sorry, Justin," Alicia said in her own dazed world. "I'm so, so sorry."

Chapter 83

BACK IN THE SOLITUDE of the brig, the image of Pastor Dan chained to the metal column haunted Joey. His words kept racing through his mind. "... I know the man who overcame sin. Once Tory and Joey surrendered to him, they couldn't surrender to you." He did not feel like he lived up to those words.

"Mom."

"Yes, Joey."

"I've been thinking about what Pastor Dan said."

"Me too."

"He said I couldn't surrender to Charlie. That's not true. I did a lot of things I'm not proud of. I ran away. I stole some stuff. He may not have known about all that stuff, but he was right there when I tried to set off what I thought was a bomb. A bomb that could have hurt or maybe even killed him. He's wrong. I surrendered to the wrong guy."

Gloria sat silently absorbing his confession, trying to decide if she should let the mother in her take the lead or her past life as a special agent.

"Did Charlie threaten to hurt you or somebody you care about?" the agent asked.

"Yes."

"Then I don't think that is surrendering. You may have lacked the courage to trust God, and that has its own set of consequences, but you did not do those things because you idolized Charlie," the mother said.

"No, I hated him from practically the very first time I met him. I just wanted to protect you. I'm only in this mess because of what Candle said about you. He said you would go to prison because I was a stolen baby, and you knew it. Candle told me I had a brother, too. After a few weeks of his pestering me everywhere I went, I started to believe what he was saying. He convinced me that if I were gone, you couldn't get in trouble anymore. He said if I went with him, I would meet my brother. He said this place was so cool, and we could be extras in movies. Some of the guys, he said, got discovered and had starring roles. He talked about Charlie as if he were some kind of rock star. It seemed like the right thing to do."

"Why didn't you tell me about this?"

"How? How was I supposed to ask you if you stole me?"

Silence erupted again. Joey regretted saying that, but it was the truth. There was no way he could ask her about what Candle was saying. He could not talk to anybody else without risking getting her in trouble.

"I am sorry, Mom. I didn't mean to accuse you."

"I understand. So, when did you find out the truth?"

"That you didn't steal me? To be honest, I'm not sure I know what to believe. I could have been stolen."

"I didn't steal you, but I knew you didn't come through normal adoption channels. I thought you were going to be my only chance at having a child, so I ignored that insignificant detail. Even so, I had no inkling back then Miles could do anything like this. But my question was really about when did you learn that this place wasn't what Candle promised?"

"As soon as I got here."

Joey shifted in the bunk so he could get a better view of the door. He did not want to be surprised by a random bed check.

"There are movie sets here, but I saw no real filming going on. Mostly just a bunch of teens, some guys in their 20s, hanging out and bragging about stuff they did for Charlie. I saw a few older people, but they kept to themselves. The only actual adults came when Doctor Callahan did his rounds twice a week. They made you see him every time. Some guys would come back super pumped up, wanting to do something big and cool for Charlie. Others would come back all bummed out and weird like. All he ever did with me was super mundane stuff, but he did it over and over again. Lights would flash, music with tons of heavy bass, and he would keep repeating something stupid, like your shirt is green. My shirt was never green, but there were times I swear it looked green. I don't get it."

"He was trying to see how much it takes to get your mind to capitulate. The idea is that if you tell a lie long enough, people will set aside their truth convictions and believe what they know is false. Let me guess, others would come in and gush about how green your shirt was."

"Yeah, how did you know?"

"That was the kind of stuff we were trying to root out. After a couple of years of getting essentially nowhere in building a case, Miles flipped, or they flipped him. By the time I figured out what had happened, I already had you. If I turned him in, I would lose you. I couldn't do it, so I quit. I guess I didn't have the courage to trust God either."

"I can't imagine you as some kind of spy."

"I wasn't that kind of agent," Gloria laughed and then sighed. "That was a long time ago. I was a different person back then."

Another curtain of silence erupted between mother and son. This time it was from the door opening. Three people walked in.

"Are we going to get out of here alive?" Joey whispered.

The directness of her son's question hurt the mother in Gloria. She wanted to lift him up into her arms and protect him, but two sets of iron bars made that impossible. She could only answer, "I don't know."

Chapter 84

DETECTIVE MADDOX RAILED against his decades of police experience and reluctantly brought Jonah along with him to the former shipyard. He was not sure he could trust Jonah completely, but the news that Joey was his little brother gave him as much of a stake in this rescue as Uncle Bobby.

"They probably have them in the brig, over there in that building," Jonah said, pointing to an old brick building with bars over the windows.

"Brig? As in a jail?" Maddox asked.

"Yeah."

"How many guards?"

"A couple and a cuckoo."

"A what?"

"A cuckoo. It's a newbie who walks through doing a bed check at the top of the hour."

Maddox checked his watch. It was ten minutes to eleven.

"The guards. Are they trained at all?"

"Trained for what? To be bored. I fell asleep every time I pulled duty. The cuckoo's job is to keep an eye out for snitches and wake you up."

"Okay. Getting past them shouldn't be a problem."

"Maybe not, but you must get there first. There are people all over the place, and you kind of stick out here."

"Any suggestions?" Maddox asked, conceding the point to Jonah.

"I take you in. I bring in newbies all the time. Even old-timers like you. Nobody will question you with me."

"You are saying you want to take me in there as your prisoner?"

"Not a prisoner. A newbie. And you are supposed to shadow me for the first week or so. Trust me. Nobody will question why we are there as long as you are with me."

"I guess I'll have to trust you," Maddox said. His trust was backed up by Clark. If Clark hadn't heard from him in thirty minutes, he was to call Lieutenant Philpott. "Lead the way."

Jonah slipped his jester hat back onto his head, brought his phone out to the ready, and jumped out of the sedan. Maddox texted Clark, secured his weapon inside his jacket, and followed him down the street. He had to shorten his stride to make it appear Jonah was in the lead. A couple of teens were sitting on the steps of the building; faces buried in their phones.

"Hey Jonah. Another big fish for Charlie?" one teen heckled.

"Yeah. This is the little one. You should have seen the one that got away," Jonah jested back.

"You've gotta share what you are using for bait."

"For this old fish, cottage cheese and applesauce."

The teens laughed and resumed their phone gazing. Inside, Jonah paraded the detective down the hall and took a left into the west wing. Almost everyone he saw seemed transfixed by their phones. Another hall and another left, and the two were standing in front of a heavy door with a guard on either side. Maddox hid a smile. The drool on one guard's chin revealed the cuckoo had done his job.

"The leash is getting a little old," Jonah said, rolling his eyes toward Maddox. "I'm gonna put my new fish in a tank for a while."

"Did Charlie okay it?" one guard asked. "He kicked everybody out earlier and said nobody could come in unless he said so."

"Is it another old guy in there?"

"No. It's an old lady and your buddy Joey."

"I heard he failed Charlie, so he ain't my buddy anymore. Charlie sent me over with this guy. He is with the old lady. They are part of a school of fish Charlie reeled in."

"She doesn't act like no new fish."

"That's cause she's an old fish," Jonah joked.

The comment spurred a round of hearty laughter among the teens. The cuckoo stepped into the room.

"It's time for my rounds."

"Not until you do it," the guards said in unison.

"Do I still have to do that stupid thing?" the cuckoo whined.

"As long as you are the newbie," Jonah said.

"Fine." He turned to the left, took a step and cuckooed. He did an about-face, took two steps and did another cuckoo. He repeated the movement until his chime matched the hour on the wall clock.

The guard opened the door and stepped inside. The cuckoo followed, and the other guard trailed him. Jonah waited a second for the guards to get into position, and then he entered with Maddox in tow. When everyone was inside, the guard turned to close the door. Maddox grabbed the guard and plowed him into the other teen at his post.

"Hate to tell you this, boys, but this fish bites," Maddox said.

At the same time, Jonah charged forward, hitting the cuckoo behind the knees with his shoulder. The cuckoo let out an "oof" as he plummeted to the ground. A loud snap echoed throughout the brig as Jonah jumped onto the right leg of the cuckoo. This time the cuckoo let out a scream, which Jonah silenced by stuffing a scarf he pulled from up his sleeve into the cuckoo's mouth. He pulled a plastic tie from his pocket and zipped his hands behind his back.

"On your knees, boys," Maddox ordered.

They complied when they saw his weapon staring back at them.

"Give me a hand, Jonah."

Jonah bound the guards while Maddox kept them compliant.

"You lied to us, Jonah," one guard said. He spat at him as Maddox walked him by to the nearest cell. "That's unforgivable."

"There's a lot of that going around lately," Jonah said, wiping his face on his sleeve.

Gloria and Joey watched the events unfold in silence. Joey was more than surprised to see Candle. The person responsible for getting him in this place is now helping him get out?

Maddox grabbed the keys from the guard and slammed the cell door. He lifted the broken cuckoo and put him into a cell, too.

"Don't worry, son," he said. "Help will be here in a few minutes to take care of your injury."

The cuckoo nodded okay as he winced in pain. He did not feel shy about letting the tears stream down his face.

Maddox opened the cell to Gloria. Jonah was already waiting by Joey's cell. Maddox opened the cell door, but instead of letting Joey out, he pushed Jonah inside.

"Boys, you are going to have to wait here," Maddox said. "It will give you too a chance to get reacquainted."

"I don't want to know this guy!" Joey yelled. "Mom!"

"He's right," Gloria said. "You are safer here."

"Joey, you don't really know this kid for who he really is. Joey, I'd like you to meet Jonah. He's your brother," Maddox said.

"That thing is my brother?" Joey said.

"Changes your conversation a bit, doesn't it?" laughed Maddox.

He turned to Gloria and returned to his sober demeanor.

"Do you have any idea where Pastor Dan is?" he asked.

"Some place called the training room. Trust me, it is far more nefarious than the name sounds," Gloria said.

He turned back toward the boys and asked, "Training room?"

"Deep inside the building next door, the long one on Petaluma Avenue," Joey said.

"You're both newbies. You won't make it by going outside," Jonah said.

When Jonah went on this little adventure, he did not want to betray the man who was as close as a father figure he knew. But he knew Charlie treated failure harshly. Joey's failure today meant he would be banished from the group. They did not just kick you out. He had heard stories that some guys would ensure you could tell no tales. Jonah was not exactly sure what that meant, only that it meant something bad. He was feeling rather wild about the rescue so far and was excited about what was about to happen. He never imagined the old cop would flip on him like that and stick him in a cell with Joey. Now he needed Maddox to come back. His old chums could not find him. The guards had made it clear he had violated their trust. They would banish Jonah, too.

"Most people don't know about the tunnel system under this prison," Jonah continued. "Just past the last cell, move the cabinet out of the way. You'll find a trapdoor. It will take you over to Doctor Callahan's office."

As Jonah grabbed some paper to draw a map, Maddox brandished the handgun strapped to his leg.

"Do you know how to use one of these?" Maddox asked.

Joey spoke up first.

"Of course she can. She used to be a spy," he said. "Mom, go kick some butt!"

"Your mom was a spy?" Jonah asked. "So cool."

"Gloria?" Maddox asked.

"Yes, but it was my father who taught me how to shoot," Gloria said. "The Agency just gave me permission to shoot ... at people ... at certain people."

Chapter 85

PASTOR DAN COULD FEEL people tugging on his body in the dark. Somebody lifted his legs, and he fell backwards into the arms of another. His head seemed to rest on the lab coat of a woman whose perfume reminded him of Rebecca. Thoughts of her had been stirred several times in the last few days; each time with a little bit more of a stabbing wound to the heart.

When the lights came on, he was being strapped onto what felt like a padded table. The light was so intense now, he could not see much. The white coats added to the glare, so he used his hand to cover his eyes.

"Daniel," a feminine voice spoke to him.

"What's going on?"

"Daniel, it's me, Rebecca," the voice continued.

"No, you are not. Rebecca is dead."

"I assure you I'm not. You must have had a bad dream."

"No, it was a nightmare, but I was awake for it."

"I'm sure it seemed so. Dreams can seem so real."

"Turn the lights off," Pastor Dan yelled. He was done talking to somebody's cruel joke.

"There are no lights on, Daniel. We are sitting in the dark, like we always do. Can't you see the stars?"

He removed his hand, and the light was gone. He could see a star-studded sky. Slowly, he could make out familiar constellations. He felt like a little kid seeing the stars for the first time: Orion, Sagittarius, the Big Dipper. Then reality set in.

"Where are we? You can't see these stars here. There is too much light pollution," he professed.

"Oh, Daniel!"

This time, it was a male voice. The lights came on, and he could see Charlie again.

"You take all the fun out of this," Charlie said.

"Sorry, you don't find me amusing. I guess it's time for me to go home then."

"Wrong guess, Daniel."

Pastor Dan looked around. He caught the glimpse of a woman lying on a gurney. She looked kind of like Alicia, but he thought that could not be true. Alicia was still in San Francisco. Then the light show began again. White lights. Blue lights. Red lights. White lights.

"Oh Danny! Why did you let the dogs hurt me?" the fake Alicia voice called out.

"I didn't. You are not real. You are not real."

"You keep saying that, but it's not true."

The bright white light started flashing on and off. Between the strobes, he could see Alicia staring down at him. Her ripped dress, soiled and covered in blood. She held a half-eaten arm across her chest.

"Look at my arm. Look what those vicious dogs did to me. Look what you let happen."

Panic enveloped Pastor Dan. He was not sure now if what he saw was real.

"Lord, you are my refuge and my fortress; in you alone I trust," he cried out.

As the lights continued to strobe, the image of Alicia slowly morphed into Rebecca. He saw the same cold, pale stare he had seen before when life faded from her body. He tried to reach out to her, and to his surprise, his arms moved. Just as he was about to touch her, the lights came on and she was gone. Charlie was standing there.

"How could you kill her, Daniel?" Charlie asked.

He stepped away so Pastor Dan could see the woman on the gurney. The sheet was now pulled back to reveal her identity. It was Rebecca. There was no doubt in his mind. There was a lifeless Rebecca lying there. The only doubt he had was whether he had killed her.

"Forgive me, Father!" he cried.

* * *

Alicia had never been the kind of person to sit back and let life happen around her. She learned a long time ago that things turned out better if she set the pieces in motion. Witnessing the torture of Pastor Dan ran contrary to everything she knew what to do. She felt helpless. It made her furious. The sight of the dead woman caused Alicia's anger to burst into tears. Her body could no longer hold back the emotion.

"It's not real, sweetie," Justin comforted. "The woman is not really dead."

"It's real to him," she said, punctuating each syllable with anger through the sobs.

Justin felt helpless too. Watching this madman torture Pastor Dan made his self-loathing even worse. He winced at the constant reminder from his inner voice that he had let Frankie manipulate him, that all this was his fault. Justin had to fix this. Not just for Alicia, but to redeem himself in his own eyes.

Chapter 86

EMILY LOOKED AROUND the house and resisted the urge to clean. She had to keep telling herself that this was still a crime scene. The clutter did not matter, but she had nothing to do. Clark and Lana were rifling through the trunk in the secret room. The deputy sat at the kitchen table with Doctor Callahan, awaiting word from Detective Maddox. She was not comfortable with idle hands; they made her anxious and stirred up feelings of guilt. She could never quite grasp her father's wisdom. "Doing nothing is a planned activity." She was doing something; she was fretting and needed something to distract her.

"Emily," Clark called. "Come here!"

"Hallelujah," she muttered.

"You won't believe what we found," Clark continued, not even checking to see if she had made it into the room yet. "I think I know why Uncle Vic had a little drinking problem."

Clark pushed a journal toward Emily. As she read, her heart wept for Aunt Ruth. She could not possibly have known that her husband was involved in these awful secret mind-control experiments. Yet, she had to know that something horrible had changed the man she married. His journal revealed his regret. Not just about what he did, but about how he let his little brother get involved as well. Tory got involved in the chemical experiments. He touted the company line about how a form of lysergic acid diethylamide would be a game changer in modern warfare. The only game it changed was Tory's. Several times Vic mentioned how a new doctor to the program, a Doctor Callahan, kept pushing Tory to do things Vic found repugnant.

Emily had read enough. She now had something to do. There was a man in the other room who needed to account for his actions. With the journal in hand, she marched through the living room to the kitchen.

"Doctor Callahan, how can you call yourself a doctor? Isn't the core of the Hippocratic oath to do no harm?" Emily chided.

The deputy scooted his chair back to give her a wide berth. Clark and Lana scrambled out of the secret room and observed from the kitchen doorway.

"I make no excuses for what I've done. I'm guilty as you charge," Doctor Callahan said. "In my defense, however, I was convinced that what I was doing was for the betterment of all. In the early days of research, that truly was the case. Others exploited my work and corrupted my thinking so I couldn't see the harm I was doing. By the time I saw things for what they truly were, I was in so deep, I couldn't find a way out."

"I don't buy that," Emily said flatly. "These journal entries are old, somewhere around 35 years ago. Vic talks about how you would not listen then. He begged you to get Tory out of the program, but you wouldn't. You told him Tory hadn't fulfilled your purpose for him yet," Lana said.

"I'm afraid that's true. I guess I wasn't ready to stop believing I was better than God," Callahan said. "I was still arrogant enough to believe I could fix God's mistakes."

The sound of her open hand coming across the doctor's face surprised Emily. It happened without her planning it. It felt good, but she instantly regretted it. As she stood there staring at him, she said a prayer of forgiveness for her actions.

The deputy stood and escorted Emily over to Clark. He walked back to the doctor and tapped him on the shoulder.

"Just for the record, I did not see anything that may or may not have happened in the last five minutes. Is that clear, Doctor?"

"I don't know what you are talking about. Nothing has happened," he replied.

Clark sat on the couch with Emily. Her body was still rigid with anger, and he could feel her heart racing. He knew words were of no use at this point. It was just a time to hold her quietly. Clark's phone disturbed the stillness.

"Speaking of things you didn't see, deputy," Clark said loud enough for him to hear in the kitchen. "Our favorite detective is going in. He calls the place Old 84. Time to report to your boss that a San Francisco police officer is in hot pursuit of a suspect."

Chapter 87

"SO, YOU ARE A SPY," Detective Maddox joked as he and Gloria made their way through a narrow tunnel connecting the old Navy prison to the neighboring building. Kind of ingenious, he thought, to have a secret ingress and egress, as long as it was only the good guys using it.

"I guess that secret is out," Gloria said.

"I wouldn't let anybody know I had worked for them, either."

Gloria reached out and slugged her friend. She knew in some ways it may have hurt his feelings that she had kept something like that from him. At the same time, he probably figured she had her reasons, or more likely, the Agency had its reasons for her silence.

"Ow!! Save that for the bad guys," Maddox said.

"I did."

Maddox raised his hand to signal for Gloria to stop. They came to a bend in the tunnel. He listened for sounds coming from up the tunnel.

He picked up some loose gravel and tossed it forward. It clattered against the far wall. He listened again. He found comfort in the quiet response. With a wave of his hand, they moved forward according to Jonah's map, and he picked up their conversation.

"Ouch! That hurt worse than the smack," Maddox said.

"You are such a baby. I don't know how Gayle puts up with you."

"That makes two of us."

Maddox could see the end of the tunnel, so he started looking up to find an exit hatch.

"Have you noticed everybody seems a little too preoccupied with their phones? I mean, more than regular teens?" Maddox asked.

"Yeah. I'm afraid that has something to do with how they are controlling all these kids. I bet there is something in the games that keeps reinforcing the conditioning from the bad doctor."

"You know Joey is still playing the game he got here. He showed me the game."

"Well, that's an easy fix when we get home. Now, just get me home, please."

"Jonah says it's through that little door up there. It's a little higher than the one we dropped from. Do you want to climb up on my shoulders and take a peek?"

"Why do I have to go first? Do I look like a canary?"

"Okay, I'll jump up on your shoulders."

"No, that's okay. Going first sounds a lot less risky now."

"I think you just insulted me."

"No, I didn't, donut man."

Maddox kneeled slightly and cuffed his hands. Gloria stepped in and climbed up his body while using the wall to keep steady. She pushed the door, and it moved.

"We are in luck; the door is clear."

"Okay, let's go."

Gloria pushed the door open and popped her head into the opening. This side of the room was dark. On the far side of the room, light poured in through a large picture window. She pulled herself into the room and looked around to find something to give Maddox a boost. She grabbed several thick medical books and handed them down. A dozen volumes later, the detective could pull himself up into the room.

They crawled across the room. This time, Maddox popped up. He could see a man in some sort of control room.

"There's one man in there. I should be able to take him," Maddox said. He crawled toward the door.

"Bobby, wait!" whispered Gloria. "Let me see if it is Miles."

Maddox nodded. Gloria popped up and down quickly. It was enough time to identify the man.

"It is. Be careful. He is craftier than any other beast of the field."

They got into position. Gloria pulled the door open and rushed in as quietly as possible. He hoped to get a lot closer to surprise Charlie, but he turned too early. Maddox started to leap forward but held back when he heard Gloria issue a command.

"Stay right there, Miles. I can still shoot the knees of a mosquito at thirty paces," Gloria said.

"Oh, you and your country charm. I suppose you want me to put my hands up," Miles said, feigning his annoyance at the inconvenience.

"Actually, I want you to do something stupid, so I have a reason to shoot you," Gloria said. She took a breath and then said in an even more matter-of-fact tone, "Wait, you've already given me plenty of reasons."

While Gloria was talking, Maddox edged his way closer to Charlie. He was hesitant to get between Gloria and Charlie. He wanted to avoid accidentally taking a bullet for this man.

"Well, detective, I guess this seems like a letdown," Charlie said, outstretching his arms and letting his wrists go limp. "In the movies, there is always some dramatic fight scene at this point."

Maddox grabbed his right hand and pulled it behind Charlie as he slapped on the cuffs. He pulled the left hand in place and finished cuffing him.

"This was too easy," Maddox said. "Why?"

The detective looked out the control room window. He could see into two patient rooms. On the left, he saw a man on a table being tended to by a woman in a white lab coat. On the right, he saw two people in dentist-like chairs. They were prepping them for some sort of injection. It took a second to realize those weren't just any patients.

"What's in those needles?" Detective Maddox said.

"Oh, just a little cocktail I put together. I call it their last best drink," Charlie said.

"Call it off," Maddox demanded.

"Why? Is there something in that request for me?" Charlie said in his typical smug way.

"Because I will shoot you," Gloria said.

"That won't stop them from injecting them," Charlie said.

"Why?" Gloria asked.

"Because I can. Isn't that a good enough reason?"

Charlie let his wit hang in the air awhile so everyone could enjoy it.

"Now seriously, detective, just let me walk out that door, and my little minions will put down their needles."

Maddox looked back into the rooms. Pastor Dan looked drained from whatever happens in these so-called training rooms. He did not know why Alicia and her boyfriend were here. Justin was struggling, but he was getting nowhere. There was no way he could count on them fighting back. He looked at Gloria. She read in his eyes that he had to cave.

"No, Bobby, no. There has to be another way," she cried.

"Not that I can see from here."

Detective Maddox unlocked the cuffs. Charlie turned around and waved his hands as if he were dismissing peasantry. The people in the white lab coats dropped their needles and left.

"Woe to the wicked! Disaster is upon them! They will be paid back for what their hands have done," Charlie said as he laughed and strutted his way out of the control room. "You are not the only one who can quote scripture, my dear Gloria."

"Satan knows the scriptures, too," she said.

Gloria felt defeated even though it appeared everyone was safe. But not the boys. They were still caged up in the brig, and Charlie was not.

"Bobby, the boys!"

Chapter 88

GLORIA PEERED INTO the two rooms. Pastor Dan seemed to be in the worst shape. He would need more than her two hands. She went into the room on the right to help the man and woman she did not know. She spoke softly as she walked into the room.

"My name is Gloria. I am here with Detective Maddox. We are here to rescue you."

Justin was already struggling to get out of his restraints by the time she got to the side of his chair.

"Sir. If you will just hold on a second, I'll get those things off you," Gloria said, setting her hands on his arm. Justin bristled at her touch.

"Why did he let him go?" Justin's anger burst from deep inside.

"He didn't have a choice. If there were another way, he would have taken it. They were going to inject you with some kind of poison cocktail," Gloria said, in as calm a voice as possible.

"The syringes were empty. I kept screaming they were empty."

The exacerbation in Justin's voice only conveyed a small fraction of his frustration. It seemed everything this man did was to emasculate him.

"We couldn't hear you. I promise we didn't hear you," Gloria assured.

She reached down and carefully picked up a syringe. There was no liquid in it, but it was fully retracted.

"It wasn't poison," Gloria exclaimed. The shock in her voice did not share the relief that it should. "It was air, lots of stupid air. If they had injected you with that much air, you would have stroked out."

Justin collapsed into the chair. If he were alone, he might have let the tears fall. A defeated warrior shamed by a dishonorable foe. He was not alone, and he was not about to add more humiliation to this day.

Gloria finished unstrapping Justin and helped him stand up.

"I'll undo Alicia," he offered. "You go take care of him."

Gloria accepted his suggestion. As she walked back through the control room, her heart sank a little. Bobby had not returned with the boys yet.

"Lord, please bring them all back to me safe and sound. Evil has had enough triumph for today," she prayed.

Pastor Dan mumbled something as she entered the room. She could not quite hear it.

"Pastor Dan. It's all over. Whatever that monster did, it's all over," she said. Her heart ached to see him so broken.

"Not if I'm the monster," he sputtered.

This time Gloria could hear his lament. She did not know that his mind was stuck on the horrific image of Rebecca lying on the gurney. Everything inside him screamed that her death was his fault. He had killed her. Not seven years ago, but just a few minutes ago.

"You are no monster. You are the kindest, sweetest, most gentle man that has ever existed," Alicia said.

Gloria turned around to see who had said those generous words. The woman in the other chair was standing in the control room doorway. Tears were streaming down her face.

"What he put you through was not true. He made us watch it all, and it was all a lie. Don't let his whispers of evil tell you otherwise," she continued walking toward him.

Gloria just watched as Alicia plodded forward. When she finally arrived, she collapsed at his feet. Alicia sat there crying and hugging him across his legs. Justin saw this too for a moment, then disappeared.

Gloria finished unstrapping Pastor Dan. He let his hand fall, landing on Alicia's head. Slowly, his hand moved back and forth, stroking her hair.

Chapter 89

JUSTIN DID NOT KNOW where he was going, but he knew Charlie could not have gone very far. He was too cocky just to run off. The control room emptied into a long corridor, with several small rooms spilling off from there. At this time of night, the corridor was empty. His footsteps echoed on the checkerboard tile flooring. Justin stopped. He could hear a faint echo ahead and plunged forward toward his target. Around the corner stood Charlie.

"Are you looking for me, Mr. Alexander?"

Justin did not slow his stride and plowed into Charlie, pushing his body through the open door behind him. Justin could feel the smirk slide from Charlie's face as they landed hard on the cold floor with an audible thud.

"Tell me where Frankie is!" Justin puffed out as he struggled to keep Charlie subdued.

The charging bull tactics, however, were not a match for the training of the former CIA agent. Charlie was soon free and strategically positioned across the room.

"Frankie?" a winded Charlie asked.

"Yeah, Frankie. I know he put you up to all of this to torment me. One last shot to settle a score."

Charlie tried to laugh, but the stabbing pain in his ribs ended his moment of gaiety.

"How self-centered you are! You really think all of this is about you, you and some petty playground beef with Frankie?"

He edged his way to the right toward Justin, who mirrored his movements, going left to keep the distance between them the same.

"Why else would he send us to you? All that hoopla about getting into the witness protection program and trusting me to take care of his daughter. What a crock! He clearly does not want me anywhere near his daughter. He created all of this disaster today just to force my hand to call you."

"I never thought of Frankie as that imaginative."

"Oh, he's devious. He probably plans to double-cross you as well."

"I doubt it."

"Why are you so confident?"

"Didn't you hear? Frankie had a little accident."

The two did the little dance move again. Charlie shifted right, Justin left.

"He couldn't have been shanked in prison. He was already out because he rolled on several of his acquaintances. That's how I got that strange business card of yours. I assume you weren't one of his pals that he squealed on."

"Oh, that story. It was mostly true. Frankie didn't squeal on me, but he seemed less trustworthy. A risk that I couldn't afford to take."

"Did you ..."

"Let's just say he has taken up gardening."

"Then why?"

"Why what?"

"Why all this?"

"Because I can."

A calmness overcame Justin. He knew this arrogant killer was telling the truth. He also knew we would continue to haunt all the little loose ends and get rid of them, just like Frankie. On the wall behind Charlie, he could see an intricate bronze sculpture of a ship's anchor resting on a wooden pedestal. The tips of the anchor protruded outward like sharp arrows.

"Then this is for Frankie."

Justin charged forward. His shoulder plunged into Charlie's chest. Justin could feel the anchor tear into his arm as the pedestal careened to the ground. Justin pulled himself off Charlie and watched his body go limp.

Chapter 90

DETECTIVE MADDOX RACED BACK through the tunnel to the brig. This time, he did not cautiously peek his head up through the trapdoor. He plunged his body through as if he were mastering an insane obstacle course.

"Hold it right there, mister!" a deep voice commanded.

Maddox held his position halfway through the open tunnel. He struggled to cock his head to see the owner of that voice. He could not. More black boots came into view, pulling him up onto the floor. They kept his face pushed to the floor and maneuvered his hands behind his back. Once bound, they rolled him over, pushing his shoulders to the floor with a boot.

"Yeah, that's the guy. He's the one who locked me up in the cage."

Maddox recognized the voice. Making his way past a couple of guys dressed in SWAT gear was a silly-looking teen in a court jester costume.

"I think you should throw the book at him," Jonah proclaimed.

"That sounds good to me. I could use a few days off," Maddox said with a smile.

"I thought we talked about keeping your excitement down there in the city," said Lieutenant Philpott as he walked to the front of the crowd.

"I tried, but you have such nice digs up here."

Maddox rolled to the right to expose the plastic cord binding his hands. The lieutenant nodded to the officer, and he cut them. The detective rubbed his wrists before pulling himself up off the ground.

"You got here pretty fast," Detective Maddox announced.

"No thanks to you. It took quite a hustle to get here from Fairfield while coordinating with the local SWAT team. That's a lot to do in only 45 minutes," the lieutenant explained.

The detective looked at his watch. Clark should have called only fifteen minutes ago. He was glad he hadn't followed orders.

"I assume a bunch of kids scattered when you arrived," Maddox said.

"Like cockroaches when the light comes on."

"Don't suppose you nabbed an older cockroach, someone they call Charlie."

"Didn't have to. Somebody else had already squished him. His name sounds familiar—a Justin Alexander."

"Yeah, you know him. He did a good thing today. A really good thing."

Detective Maddox looked around for Joey. He was still sitting in the cell. The detective walked over and sat down on the bunk beside him.

"It's all over, Joey. Your mom is taking care of Pastor Dan," Uncle Bobby said. "Why are you still sitting in this cell?"

"It's where I belong."

"No, you do not. You belong in your mom's custody," Uncle Bobby said, putting his arm around his godson. "There are some formalities that will happen over the next few days, but this is all over."

"What's going to happen to Jonah?"

"I don't know. He's got a long road ahead of him, and he's going to need all the support he can get."

"Like a brother?"

"Yeah, like a brother."

"He could use some parents, too."

"He sure will. I don't know if they will find anyone willing to take on a kid with that kind of past."

"I do."

Uncle Bobby leaned back to read Joey's face. The corners of his lips turned until a full smile beamed from ear to ear. Something swelled in his chest until it ached so much that tears swelled in his eyes. He gave Joey another squeeze.

"Me too."

Chapter 91

CLARK STOOD IN THE DOORWAY between the kitchen and the living room, just taking in the sight of his daughter making popcorn with his girlfriend. Lana and Emily were laughing. He had seen this scene before. It was when he let his guard down long enough to realize he had feelings for Emily. He did not rush to act on those feelings then. Mostly because Rudy Johnson intruded on the moment and propelled their lives into a made-for-TV movie. The drama of the last few days mirrored that weekend, but it appeared it was over. The police were gone; the house was theirs again, and his family was safe again. His family. That phrase stirred up emotions he once thought lay buried in the casket with Lois. Her cancer had stolen that from him, too. His family. He could not wait to act anymore.

"We need to have a family meeting," Clark announced.

"Oh, we do?" Emily liked the sound of the word family.

"Yes, we do."

Clark sat on the ottoman facing Emily and Lana on the couch. He rubbed his hands on his pant legs, trying to dry the shower of perspiration that emerged in the few steps from the doorway.

"What's wrong, Dad? I thought this was all over," Lana asked.

Clark smiled and patted his daughter's hand.

"I hope not. I actually hope it has just begun," he said. Emily caught the tremble in his voice. Lana did not.

"What? You have got to be kidding!" Lana exclaimed.

Emily laughed and nudged Lana with her shoulder.

"I don't think he means all the nightmare stuff," Emily whispered playfully. She felt like a schoolgirl, hanging on to every word her beau was about to say. Emily reached out and grasped Clark's hands in hers. He pulled one hand away and placed Lana's hands onto the pile.

"What I need to say affects all of us. I've been thinking about it for a while now. It will mean a lot of changes for us and possibly some sacrifices," Clark rambled.

He paused to gather his thoughts. Lana seemed to gather them faster.

"Just ask her, Dad."

"Ask her what?"

"Come on, Dad. I know the two of you belong together. I miss Mom, and I know Auntie Em will never replace her, but Mom would have wanted us to move on."

A tear made its way down Lana's cheek.

"That's not what this meeting was about, sweetie," Clark said. He winked at Emily and mouthed the word "later." "I meant I was thinking about leaving the newspaper and moving into this place."

"You mean you don't want to marry Emily?" Lana asked.

"I didn't say that," Clark said. He turned to read Emily's eyes. Had the news of leaving San Francisco tempered their sparkle? It was still there. "I would really love for Emily to be part of that new career change. It wouldn't be instant. There are still a few things I would have to wrap up at the paper. Of course, we would have to sell the house and wait for you to finish the school year."

Clark paused for a response.

"I guess I could stay at my folks' place for a while until I found a place in town. The commute shouldn't be too bad," Emily said. Her voice was timid, unsure of her answer. She thought Clark meant more, but did not want to assume anything.

"That's not exactly what I had in mind," Clark said.

"Oh?" Her voice perked up with a coyness that sounded playful.

"I thought you might want to stay here with us?" Clark could tell she was going to make this difficult for him.

"As an honest woman?" Emily asked.

"I've never known you to lie," Clark said. This time it was Clark's turn to be playful.

"I think you are supposed to get down on one knee," Lana chimed in.

"Why?" Clark smiled. "I might not be able to get back up."

"I'll help you, old man. Just don't blow it. They don't make them like Auntie Em anymore," Lana said.

"I agree." Clark stood and pushed the ottoman back with one foot and made his way to one knee. He wobbled on the way down, but Emily and Lana righted him until he was firmly on his left knee.

"Emily, to say our lives have been a whirlwind over the last few months would be an understatement. One thing I know for sure is that I don't think either of us would have made it if it weren't for you."

"Thank you," Emily said.

"He's right, Auntie Em. I was a mess and made sure everyone knew it," Lana confessed.

Clark cleared his throat.

"Sorry!" Lana giggled and twisted an imaginary key signifying the locking of her lips.

"Emily Geoffrey, will you consent to being my wife, to making us a happy family again?" Clark finally popped the question.

Emily looked at Clark and then at Lana. She studied their eyes for a moment, then looked into her lap. Lana saw she was praying. Clark did not.

"Yes! I'll consent."

Epilogue

HIS LAPTOP CAST a gloomy glow across his face, making it seem wearier than he expected. The last couple of months had been a difficult time for him. The agent he knew as Miles Maldoon had left a lot of loose ends for him to clean up. He was watching the icons on the screen to tell him when everyone had entered the meeting.

"Good evening, ladies and gentlemen," he said when the last of the seven avatars displayed.

A murmur of good evenings responded.

"Tomorrow's newspapers will report that a private investigator named Tim Martin was found dead in his car. They will report that something went wrong during a surveillance activity he was conducting. Their reports will say it is not clear at this time if the person he was observing was involved in his death."

"What about the red card?" barked the altered voice of Avatar3.

"Our team recovered the card, all of his notes and anything else that they thought might be linked to it. Mr. Martin is the only person to discover its true function, and it only took him two months. Too bad our recruitment efforts failed. He would have been an effective addition."

"And Callahan?" Avatar2 asked.

"He is now in our custody at our alternate training site. Technically, he is in CIA custody. He tried to push for his trial to be held in local jurisdictions, but the local lawyers were not all that interested in taking on such a complex case. Neither were the district attorneys. The freezing of his assets was an excellent suggestion from this group."

"Is he still useful?" Avatar2 asked.

"Not at the moment. We will reassess his utility after he spends some time in the training room."

"Have they busted Buster yet?" Avatar 6 asked.

"Surprisingly, the good senator seems to be weathering the political storm with no direct accusations, despite the way Mr. Solo painted him in the newspaper."

"Governorship?" Avatar 3 asked.

"It was never likely that the governor's mansion was his, and his chances are slimmer now that you've pulled his funding."

"Did all those teens get returned to their homes according to the plan?" Avatar 4 asked.

"Yes. I think this group's strategy of using local law enforcement to close Mr. Maldoon's operation worked successfully. We didn't anticipate his personal outcome, but he knew the risks."

"And they kept their devices?" Avatar 4 asked.

"Yes."

"Are we confident that Maldoon launched the next phase before his demise?" Avatar7 asked.

"All indications show we have several successful implementations. We are currently tracking biometrics. Over the next few months, we will slowly activate and test functions in real-world engagements."

"That's nice, but when will we get a return on our investment in this project?" Avatar1 asked.

"You know I can't speak in terms of guarantees, but we are on track with our agreed-upon timeline."

"I didn't agree to those timelines, Mr. Taglioni," an adamant Avatar1 pointed out.

"I am aware, but we are making good progress. Unless there are other questions, that concludes tonight's update."

Another murmur of voices concluded his conclave. He closed his laptop and unlocked the bottom left-hand drawer. He pulled out the basket containing various office supplies to reveal a built-in lockbox. The lawyer leaned over for the lockbox to scan the retina of his left eye. The drawer opened, and he slipped the laptop inside. He reversed the process and was finally ready to call it an evening.

As he walked out of the office, Nikolaus Taglioni stopped at his wall mirror to examine his face. It was more aged than his actual years would suggest. He decided the laptop was right; he needed some time off.

About the Author...

For nearly three decades, Stephen Pierce either reported on the newsmakers or served as a spokesman for them. When the opportunity arose that allowed him to trade all that in to pursue a simpler life, he grabbed it with both hands. He now lives in a quaint rural setting in East Texas with his wife and two dogs, and not too far from children and grandchildren. When he's not busy writing, he attempts to be creative in the kitchen, garden, and woodworking shop.

Stephen began his writing career as a journalist in the United States Air Force, which allowed him to pen stories about military life in Louisiana, Spain, Saudi Arabia, and California. He succumbed to the enticement of a traditional newspaper gig and landed at a daily newspaper in Northern California. He worked his way up from the copy desk to associate business editor. The lure of journalism eventually gave way to the necessities of life, so Stephen switched gears to marketing and public relations. Bookends to this career focused on communications were jobs stuffing hams, selling carpets and kitchen cabinets, managing a restaurant, and running a county fair. Along the way, he earned degrees in public affairs, industrial technology, and public administration.

All this eclectic experience means Stephen has plenty of real-life experiences to draw upon to build the characters for his writing. His book titles include *Invisible Defense* and *Expunged*.

www.stephen-pierce.com

www.ingramcontent.com/pod-product-compliance
Lightning Source LLC
Chambersburg PA
CBHW020356260626
47156CB00007B/2128